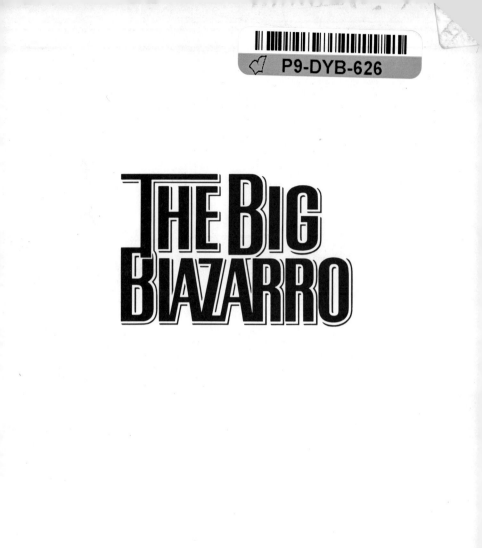

# THE BIG BIAZARRO

# THE BIG BLAZARRO

## LEONARD WISE

A DRUM BOOK
1986

Dedicated to My Father
He taught me to be happy, to respect other people,
to stack a deck, and to never give a sucker an
even break—but not necessarily in that order.

# 1

Ace White and I weren't always friends and partners. What I'm saying is there was a point and a place, several places actually, that had to do with our meeting. Places such as Manhattan, Paris, Harlem, the South of France, and Ferno, New York.

I was born the only child of hard-working parents and raised liberally and independent in the small river city of Ferno. As a child I was a loner, an avid reader, and a constant card player. If I couldn't talk my neighborhood kids into a game, or any other neighborhood's kids into a card game, then you could find me sitting above the river on Parade Hill Park with my nose stuck in a book. I read everything from love stories to psychology books.

Cooncan Bill once told me, "The best poker players in the world are the ones who know people as good as they know cards." I believed old Cooncan, and since I intended to become the world's best poker player, I read whenever I wasn't playing cards, just to learn about people.

Ferno, New York, at that time was a happy little hamlet that was a haven for the good life, gamblers, and "johns" until

Governor Rockefeller, seeking re-election, decided to clean up the town and turn it into one of those boring, dull, industrial river cities—and that's the way it is today.

I would love to hear some politician with balls make a speech that says, "I am running for mayor of our fair city and my platform is to keep things exactly as they are. The backbone of our flourishing economy is gambling and prostitution, and I'll be damned if I'm going to change it."

And then to have the townspeople be cool enough and smart enough to elect him with an overwhelming vote of approval.

Anyway, while my hometown of Ferno was alive and well and thriving with excitement, I was growing up and learning how to gamble, play cards, shoot dice, and hustle.

Ferno at that time had a population of about five thousand with only two hundred of us, but the entire town was more or less on the same economic scale. When I was a child, it was completely integrated, but dominated by Irish culture, and that's probably the reason I knew all the words to "Danny Boy" and "Irish Lullaby" even before I heard "Night Train."

Ferno was known as an "open city" in those days, and was constantly flooded with tourists and transients. Most of the transients were nonprofessional and professional hustlers, and sooner or later the very best of the country's gamblers would stop and try their luck. Needless to say, I had some of the greatest teachers in the world. Poker sharks, skin gamers, dice men, rummy players, blackjackers, roulette players, and so on.

The most beautiful thing was that there weren't any narcotics around and hardly any crimes were being committed in the entire city. Everyone was making money, staying happy, and living good. Even the churches and the Holy Joes had little or nothing to say about what was going on because they were getting their cut right along with everyone else.

Politics, complete and simple, goofed it up. And when it happened, I knew I had to get the hell out of there.

But while I was growing up and learning my craft, there was a poker player everyone always talked about but he never came to town. They said he was an old, gray dude by the name of Ace White. He was known as a poker player's poker player. Even the coolest, most confident sharks spoke in awe of the great Ace White. I had no idea at the time that one day he and I would be partners.

By age twenty-two, I had been told by almost every hustler who passed through Ferno that I had the makings of a player, a champion, a mechanic, a shark. Some even stated that I should play in "the Big Biazarro"—the world's most lucrative and exclusive poker game. Not to be confused with the Las Vegas Championship that is played each year, the Big Biazarro is The Game. Held every five years with a million dollar buy-in per man and five markers worth no less than ten thousand dollars each from five internationally known Poker Masters (of which there are only twenty-seven in the entire world), the Big Biazarro is for "Gentlemen Only."

The reigning champion is the sponsor and chooses the location (and the date sometime within the fifth year) where the game will be played. It is his choice alone, and it can be sanctioned anywhere in the world. It is up to the other players to get there. In 1972 the reigning champion was George Palmer Deeds, a cattle and cotton man from Dallas, Texas. Deeds chose the living room of the mammoth, Spanish-style ranch house of his 400,000-acre cattlespread for the game. Six men played for nine days, twenty-two million dollars was won and lost, and Telemachus Andreas Sporados, from the Greek island of the same last name, became the new champion by beating Deeds' three deuces with his three treys in the final hand. Now Sporados, an oil and shipping billionaire, would be the reigning champion and would choose the place for the next Big Biazarro to be played in 1977.

Needless to say, no small-town hustler like myself ever dared to dream of getting into that game. But not only was I daring to dream in 1974 about playing in the next Big Biazarro, it became an obsession. My preoccupation for the next three years would be: one, to leave Ferno, find Ace White,

3

and study with him; two, play in as many big poker games as possible; three, win five master markers; four, save a million-plus; and five, play in the 1977 Big Biazarro and win.

Meanwhile, I was learning the critical art of playing serious poker from the shark, Jimmy Palusso, dealing seconds from Big Nig Beechum, stacking from Lawdy Roberts, and blackjack from No-bet Harris. Benny Canada had taught me the simple game of skin and I had learned the "sequence system" of roulette from a huge, gray-eyed woman named Ju Ju Parker.

But they all agreed on one thing—before I could even think about the Big Biazarro, I would have to study with Ace White. So, at the ripe old age of twenty-two I skipped off down the river and planted my claim on Manhattan. Within a week, I had played in my first game on West Forty-sixth Street with a group of Broadway actors. They were nice guys, but it was like taking eucalyptus leaves from a stuffed koala. Unfortunately, none of them knew Ace White, so I gave them half of their money back, my number at the Park Sheraton, and told them to let me know if they heard of him.

In the following weeks, I played in poker games in Chelsea, Greenwich Village, Newark, Queens, Chinatown, Little Italy, Brooklyn, and the Bronx. It finally dawned on me that I was the only one who *didn't* know the whereabouts of Ace White. I knew goddamn well I had met and played with at least a hundred gamblers or more, and every one of them denied knowing him. And yet every hustler who came to Ferno couldn't wait to talk about Ace's great skill with a deck of cards. Not being a complete idiot, I figured Ace must have done something shady and was hiding out from "the Man."

Jimmy Palusso's hustle was sailing the luxury boats first class back and forth to Europe and ripping off the rich tourists, a business which has dropped off considerably in the last two or three decades mainly due to air travel. I figured I could catch him sooner or later booking passage—I was right. We had coffee for an hour before he boarded his liner and he told

4

me that I was asking too many questions around town. Giving me a name and an address up in Harlem, he suggested I stop playing in penny-ante games until I talked to Ace.

"Don't waste your talent, kid," said Jimmy. "Roses always grow above the thorns. Aim high. You can kill a man a lot quicker by hitting him in the head than you can in the ass. Heaven is up, hell is down. You lay down with dogs, you get up with fleas, and all that other shit. You know what I'm talking about, kid. Eagles fly high, worms wallow in the dirt. Aim high. Aim high."

He boarded the boat then, and I waited for him to wave to me from the top deck . . . but he didn't.

# 2

Harlem is black. The people are black, the streets seem darker, the music coming out of the record shops, churches, department stores, and restaurants is Black Soul, and the mood is shady. In Harlem, you can have the greatest time of your life, or the worst, depending on your luck.

The address Jimmy Palusso had given me was on the corner of 118th Street and Lenox Avenue, right where the rats eat the cats. I lived there for three weeks and was robbed only once, and by a little, dusty dude who stood five-foot-two with a nine-inch Magnum. He said just three things to me as he stopped me in the lobby of the building. "Give me everything you got, I'm in a hurry, and I'm sorry."

I gave him my watch, wallet, and Ferno High School ring and said just three things to him. "Don't be sorry, be careful, and don't let me catch you without that Magnum."

Bessie Poindexter, an obvious dancer, stood five-foot-ten in her pretty bare feet. She was a large woman who weighed close to 150 pounds, but she was sound, sturdy, and solid. She had one of the prettiest ebony faces you'd ever want to see, with sparkling brown eyes and a medium-high Afro hairdo.

She also had a beautiful pair of watermelon tits with round protruding nipples that could give a breast-man delirium tremens. Plus, her rear end was as round and full as a Georgia moon and could cause an ass-man to have cardiac arrest. And stems—this woman had stems that were so long and shapely they could make a leg-man kick his bowlegged wife in the shins.

"How did you get my address?" were Bessie's first words to me.

"Jimmy Palusso gave it to me. Said you could help me find Ace White."

"What you want with Sweet Daddy?"

"Obviously not the same thing you want. I'm a card player. I came to study with him."

"To study what?"

I looked at her and said, "The atmospheric pressure of a frog's fart on a lily-pad stalk."

She laughed then and a beautiful, sensitive woman emerged from under that tough exterior.

"How much money you got?"

"Very little," I said, while hoping the $800 I had in my left-front pocket wasn't bulging too much.

"You got enough to buy me dinner at Frank's?"

"What's Frank's, a hot-dog joint?"

Bessie laughed, and said, "Frank's is the best damn restaurant on one hundred and twenty-fifth, bar none."

She was right. While we were stuffing ourselves on rare steaks, baked potatoes, fresh greens, and sweet potato pie, every gangster, pimp, gambler, and businessman was eying the hell out of us. Being as young and naïve as I was, I didn't realize it at first, and then this long, lanky, obvious pimp diddy-bopped over to our table and hissed to Bessie, "You makin' an adoption, baby?"

I didn't like what he said or the way he said it and was about to defend Bessie's honor, but when I opened my mouth all I did was burp. That's what I get for eating so fast.

7

I learned something that night I had never seen before. It's a silent weapon known as "the mean stare-down." And Bessie Poindexter could stare someone down like you couldn't believe. She just sat there and glared at that pimp with cold frigid eyes without saying a word. The pressure became so much for him that he just finally turned and disappeared.

"Goddamn pimps," she said. "I can't stand 'um."

While walking home, Bessie told me that the pimps were constantly after her to go to work for them. The gangsters, gamblers, and businessmen were just after *her*.

"I likes my freedom, baby. I want to do what I want to do, when I want to do it, and with whoever *I* want to do it with."

"That's the way I feel too," I said.

Bessie smiled at me then, and shook her head. "This world is going to eat you alive, boy."

"You think so?"

"Oh, yeh, baby. The old men will abuse ya, the young men will try to use ya, the cops will peruse ya, the young girls will amuse ya, the rich womin will blues ya, the pretty girls will confuse ya, and womin like me will . . . choose ya. But the world will probably tear your heart out before it leaves you be."

"You really think so, huh?"

"Yes, I do."

"I'm not as square as I look, act, and talk."

"If you're not, then why do you do it?"

I thought for a moment, and said, "I'm from a small town. I'll get rid of this squareness."

"Ain't you never heard the saying 'You can take the boy out of the country, but you can't get the country out of the boy'?"

"I heard it, and it might be true, for a boy, but I'm a man!"

"You are, huh?" said Bessie. "Well, you gonna have to prove that to me."

She took my hand then as we continued to walk, and told me she liked me. I said I liked her too, but I have to admit,

8

since she was at least four inches taller than me in her heels, I was a bit inhibited at first. But as the evening funned on, I soon got over it.

It was a foregone conclusion, I suppose, that we would make love at the end of the night, but being dedicated to my obsession, I was more interested in finding Ace than I was in balling Bessie. However, soon after we started, I completely forgot about Ace White and every other kind of white. I just lay there and let Bessie's blackness enfold me. She laid down and pulled me on top of her and I disappeared into a valley of huge, soft, clean, sweet arms, legs, and breasts. Have you ever taken a ride on a Pullman car? You know how you sort of lie there while the train clickety-clacks along and the melodic vibrations lull you to sleep while relaxing your entire body. Well, let me tell you, Bessie, with me sort of wombed-up inside of her, moved and vibrated and hummed and humped and lulled me into a state of unbelievable ecstasy. I lay there all tight and snug while she held me and gave me a ride and a screwing as smooth as the flight of a 747 and as sweet and warm as hot morning biscuits.

Not that I wanted to leave or anything as asinine as that, but I was being held so firmly that even if I had got the idea to stop, I couldn't have.

"Whip it to me, Bessie honey," I cried.

But she wasn't a "whipper." She was a "groover." She sort of lay there just grooving and grooving and grooving.

I began to tear. Honest to God I did, but just a little. When my entire body cramped and knotted and perspired and let loose with a flood, I actually cried.

"Let it out, baby," she said. "Come on, give it all to me."

I did.

For the next three weeks, I lived in Bessie's fancy Harlem apartment, read books at night when she went to work at the Apollo Theatre, got robbed once, and kept right on grooving with Bessie. Finally, it grew a little tiresome, wailing every night like that, so I asked her when she was going to tell me about Ace.

"What's the matter, pretty boy, you getting tired of the same old soup warmed over?"

"No, that's not it," I said.

"It's the action, ain't it, baby? You need the action, the ruffle of the cards, the smell of the smoke and the green? There ain't nothing Momma can give you to take its place, is there?"

I shook my head.

"God, I wish I could," she said sadly. "You been good to me, baby. You been good to me. I'm thirty-six years old and I know I ain't never gonna have nothing nearly as sweet again as long as I live."

"You can get any man you want, Bessie."

"A good man is hard to find, baby. And a good, young man is impossible to find. You and Ace are the two best men I've ever had, and it seems I've lost you both to smoke-filled rooms."

"Please, Bessie. Tell me where he is."

She stared forlornly at me, then shook her head and said, "All right. He's in a place called Kannis."

"Where's that?"

"I don't know. Someplace over in France. The night he left he said he had to get away in a hurry, and that he was going to Kannis."

I started to say something—maybe that I was sorry, or something equally mundane, but she placed her hand over my mouth and asked me to please be gone when she got home from the theater that night.

I was.

## 3

A week later I arrived in Paris late in the evening, grabbed a room at a small hotel on the Rue Bertrand, and immediately hopped a cab for the Enghien Casino that sits just outside the city. It was there I was informed, while trying my luck at roulette, that the place I was looking for wasn't "Kannis" but Cannes, and it was way down south on the Riviera.

Being a Moon Child and a romantic at heart, I would ordinarily let nothing drag me away from a city as gorgeous as Paris is in early April, but I had been literally screwing around enough back in Harlem. So that very same night, I took a late plane for Cannes, rented a room at the beach-front Majestic Hotel, and finally got a full day's sleep. The next evening I went straight to the beautiful summer casino, which sits out on a peninsula overlooking the blue-green harbor. I didn't want to make the same mistake twice, so I refrained from asking about Ace. I just kept looking for him. Bessie had showed me several photos and I couldn't miss him if he was a mile away—that's how bad I wanted to find him.

A week passed, and then one bright, fantastically sunny day while I was sitting on the wall that overlooks the white sand

11

and the dozens of multicolored beach umbrellas lining the shore, a girl, with an awesome Brooklyn accent, came up behind me.

"Hey, ain't you Lefty from New York?"

"No, I'm not," I said, in an effort to brush her off.

"Oh, come on, I ain't gonna try and hustle you. You took my boy friend Tony for over two hundred bucks in Brooklyn Heights one night."

"What are you looking for, baby, a refund? Get lost. I'm busy."

"Busy? You're just sitting here," she said, climbing up on the wall next to me. When I asked her what she thought she was doing, she ignored my question and asked, "How long you been in France?"

"You want to see my passport, too?"

"Aww, don't be nasty. We're both Americans. The least you can do is be friendly. You were so nice the night I saw you play. Are you pissed about something?"

"Look, I don't want to be rude, I just want to be alone."

She was silent for a moment, then said softly, "Is it because I'm white?"

"Use any excuse you want, but just get away from me, will you . . . please?"

"Why don't you look at me?" she persisted. "You might like what you see."

"I wouldn't give a damn if you turned out to be the most gorgeous thing on this beach. I don't want to know you right now!"

"How do you know you don't?" she shouted as if she had the right to.

"Take my word for it."

She grabbed my face and turned it, forcing me to look at her—and, believe it or not, she had one of the cutest, pixie-type faces I had ever seen, and a body wrapped in a tiny bikini under an open terry-cloth robe that could make a bulldog break his chain.

12

"Now, do you see what I'm up against?" she asked and the question perplexed me.

"What the hell are you talking about?"

"Everybody just takes a look at me and they want to lay me."

"Well, I don't. I'm all layed-out, and I'm very, very busy."

"Good. I'm glad you're all layed-out, but don't give me that busy bullshit, because I don't buy it."

"Look, Naked Nelly, did it ever occur to you there might be two or three million guys in this world who don't really care about how pretty you are, or how many guys have tried to screw you?"

"Everybody wants to screw me."

"I don't," I said simply.

"Ah ha!" she exclaimed. "That's why I like you."

"Do me a favor, don't like me. Hate me. Please, hate me. I want to screw you right along with everybody else, so hate me!"

"Nope. It's too late."

"What in the hell do you mean it's too late? You ought to have . . ."

I didn't finish the sentence only because my long, desperate search had come to an instant conclusion. Standing across the Boulevard Croisette on the steps of the famous Carlton Hotel was the man himself—Ace White.

"What do you see, a ghost?" the girl asked.

"Wait here. Don't follow me. I'll be right back," I said, climbing down from the wall and dodging the traffic to get across the boulevard. Reaching the other side, I stopped to size him up. Even though there were aging lines around his gray eyes and his brown hair had long since turned to silvery white, he was taller and straighter than I'd imagined him to be. I pictured him a frail little man, wrinkled with time. Instead, he was young for his age, which I had learned was approximately sixty, and good-looking for an old gray dude. Dapper, too, in his beige suit tailored to perfection, which spoke vividly

13

of his wealth and good breeding. In other words, he was "clean"—*clean* as a cleansing machine.

"Hi," I said, walking up to him nonchalantly.

He looked me up and down, then turned and gazed back at the boulevard while smiling at the beautiful sunny day.

"I've been looking all over the world for you."

"Busy hands are happy hands, kid."

"They call me Lefty. I'm from Ferno. Ferno, New York."

"Congratulations," he said, starting to walk away.

"Hey, wait a minute. I came ten million miles to see you."

"Nothing ventured, nothing gained, kid."

"I want to study with you."

"Study what?"

I looked at him. "The rising cost of camel shit on the Arab open market. Cards, what else?"

"You wasted your time. I don't play cards anymore."

"You don't have to play. I'll play. You just tell me what I'm doing wrong."

"You're bothering me, for one thing."

"I've played with Jimmy Palusso, No-bet Harris, and all the best."

"Did you beat them?"

"I beat them all . . . except you."

"Then you don't need me, kid, and I sure don't need you."

"They told me you were an all-right guy. They told me you knew where it was at. That you'd be willing to take on a talented kid like me and mold me. They told me you weren't a jive turkey . . . they told me a lot of lies."

"How do I know you're who you say you are?" he asked.

"I can prove who I am . . . can you?"

"You can prove it, huh? Well, if you can, what's the password?"

"The password?"

"Yes. If you played with Jimmy and No-bet, they would have given you the password."

"Password? What password? I don't know no stinking password. What is this you're giving me about some damn password?"

"You came ten million miles and you forgot the password.
Shame on you, kid. Well, if you remember it, look me up."

He walked away, leaving me standing there with egg on my
face and my hand on my head. "Password . . . ?"

"He's putting you on," said the girl. "I heard the whole conversation and he's putting you on. It was his way of getting rid
of you."

"Get lost, will you, lady? I've got to remember that password."

She chuckled and took my arm. "Come on," she said, "I'll
buy you lunch."

Without thinking, I let her guide me to a sidewalk cafe,
while I was racking my brain trying to remember if anyone
had given me a password.

"My name is Angel. Angel DuPont," the girl was saying.
"I'm really glad I met you. I figure we can be friends and hang
out together. You know, like buddies. If you see something
you like, or I do, we split, okay?"

"I don't remember any friggin' password."

The waiter came and she ordered spinach salads for us and
a bottle of rosé. I didn't remember eating the salad, or drinking the wine, or even talking to Angel—which I don't think I
did.

"I used to live in Delaware," she continued rambling on,
"but I ran away from home with Tony when he was a sailor to
live with him and his family up in Brooklyn. That's where I
got the accent, I guess. It ain't bad, is it?"

"Password. Password? Nobody gave me a password."

"I loved Tony, but he was still in love with some fat-ass
broad named Rosemary Baglio. I caught them getting it on in
our bed one afternoon and I split the very same day. I'm still
hurting from it because it only happened last month."

"Nobody told me nothing," I mumbled.

15

"Oh, will you knock off the shit!" Angel snapped at me. "Forget the fucking password, will you?"

"How can I forget it, if I don't remember it?"

"Well, you just sit here and worry about it," said Angel. "Worry about it as long as you want to, but pick me up in the lobby of the Carlton Hotel at ten-thirty. I want you to teach me how to play roulette."

# 4

Ace had put me off, put me off good with that password bit. I
didn't know what else to do, so I picked up Angel and we went
to the casino.

As we stepped up to the roulette wheel, there was a weird
thing taking place. Every player was using the same color
chips. There were different colors, sizes, and shapes for the
different denominations of money, but not different colors for
each player. Roulette, as played in the States, is a limited par-
ticipation game in that only so many players can play because
each person uses a different color chip—brown, blue, white, or
whatever. But in Cannes there was a mob around the table, everyone placing chips wherever they wanted and everyone remembering the bets they made. When the wheel stopped, the
croupiers piled up the winners' chips and waited for each to
say which pile was theirs.

I couldn't believe my eyes. And the most amazing thing was
that everyone was honest about it.

When I told Angel I wanted a drink, she was perplexed and
asked why I didn't want to start playing.

"It's a different game over here," I said. "Let's have a drink and think about it for a few minutes."

"What's to think about?" she asked. "You put your moola down and you wait for the little ball to drop. That's all there is to playing."

"That's all there is to *losing*—but we're not going to lose. Let me think about it for a minute."

As we walked over and took stools at the bar, I noticed how sharp Angel looked in her tight-fitting yellow dress, which had ruffled sleeves and hit her just above the knees.

"You look great tonight," I offered.

"Don't get any funny ideas, buster!"

"I'm sorry. You look like hell."

"I want to play roulette," she said. "I don't want to sit here and drink."

"Then go ahead. The croupiers will gladly teach you."

"All right, I will." She sashayed back over to the mob that surrounded the table and was reaching over each other to place their bets.

Sitting there, nursing a delightful glass of Piper-Heidsieck, I indulged in one of my favorite pastimes—people-watching. And I can tell you the people who frequent the Cannes casino are beautiful. The men are sophisticated, clean-shaven, worldly-looking. They are quiet, poised, conservative in dress and manner. The women, yes, the women are fantastic. They come there, these lucky ladies who look as if they've never washed a dish in their lives, and parade around in thousand dollar dresses with large diamonds sparkling on their ears, fingers, and necks. Cool, smooth, witty, fast, intellectual women who are so damned pretty they could make a devoted, life-long monk jump the wall. Sexy, sultry belles with long stems, pretty arms, full lips, and simple hairdos. Women from Sweden, England, Nigeria, Bombay, New York, Tokyo, Paris. All sizes, shapes, and colors. All dignified. Women who don't have the slightest idea where Ferno is and couldn't care less.

At that age, I thought the English women were the best.

Not because they looked any better than all the rest, but I really dug that English accent. It was so . . . proper-sounding.

One dainty young bird came up to me and asked in her British best, "Are you an American?"

"I'll be anything you want me to be."

She laughed and said, "I thought for sure you weren't. My friend, Sybil, bet that you were."

"Whatever amount of money you lost to Sybil I'll make it up to you."

"Get lost, you limey!" said Angel, charging over and shoving the woman away.

"Hey, Angel," I began firmly but softly, "I thought you said we were going to be just friends? That if we saw something we liked, we could split?"

"I don't like her!"

"I know . . . but *I* do!"

"Look, if you want that pasty-faced nothing, you can have her—but I just dropped a hundred francs and I want you to show me how to get it back. Once I have it, you can go screw anybody you want to—I don't care."

I took a deep breath, gulped my champagne, and walked over to the table. Taking out a pen and piece of paper, I told Angel to come and stand by me.

"Now, what you have to do is watch the table carefully and keep track of the numbers as they fall," I began to explain. "If the table is running in sequence, we can win. If it isn't, then you're out a hundred francs. *C'est la vie.*"

When Angel asked what I meant by a sequence, I told her that there are several hundred combinations a table can run in. One of the simplest being similar numbers.

"Some nights, I don't know why but I've seen it, the numbers seven, seventeen, and twenty-seven will come up more often than any others."

I explained to her that was one of the simplest combinations a table will run in. There are many others, and you have to at least be excellent in mathematics to be able to figure out even the simplest sequences. Of course, the sequence can stop with any turn of the wheel and not fall in line the rest of the evening.

"One thing you've got to remember," I warned her, "this casino isn't built with French pastry. It takes a lot of francs, and this table is designed for one thing and one thing only—to take and not give!"

"But we're going to take it, right?" Angel said, grinning broadly into my face.

I smiled, shrugged, and said, "I hope so."

Angel, like all new players, was impatient to see me place a bet. But patience is the name of the game. I wanted to wait until I was positive the table had a sequence running on it before I began to play. The wheel had spun around forty-eight times before I caught a sequence forming. The number five and touching numbers two, four, six, and eight were coming up about every third time. Which also meant the first twelve on the roulette board was coming up regularly. There was also another number popping that night and it was one of my favorites—twenty-seven.

I placed fifty francs each on five and the surrounding numbers. Fifty francs on the first twelve. Fifty francs on twenty-seven and the line twenty-five, twenty-six, and twenty-seven. Finally, another fifty francs on the center line. The wheel turned fifteen times, and Angel and I won over two thousand francs.

"Why are we quitting?" Angel shouted as I cashed in our chips.

"Because we're ahead and I want to stay that way."

"But the way our luck is running, we might break the bank!"

"Oh, sure we could," I said, "and the earth is flat, there are no cows in Texas, and Willie Mays won't make the Hall of Fame."

As we left the casino, I told Angel to remember, ". . . it won't always be this easy. We were lucky. That wheel could have changed at any time. We probably quit at exactly the right moment."

Angel and I left the casino and decided to walk the half mile back to the Boulevard Croisette. As we strolled, she took my hand and said that the gambling had been fun. She leaned her head against my shoulder and giggled, saying she was glad I made her quit when we did.

"Hey, look there," she shouted, and pointed to a motor boat tied in at the dock. "Let's take it for a ride."

"It's probably someone's private property. Do you want to go to jail?"

"They ain't gonna put us in jail for one little ol' stinkin' ride," she said and pulled me out on the small wooden pier. Untying the boat, she yelled for me to hop in. I did as she told me and then she stepped in and shoved us away from the dock. We were no more than ten feet from shore when a guard, wielding a night stick, came rushing out onto the pier screaming at us in French, which neither one of us understood.

"*Venez ici! Venez ici!*"

I lifted the oar and paddled us back to shore. When I stepped out of the boat, the guard grabbed me by the arm and slung me up against the boathouse. He then put his night stick at my throat and called me a "*voleur*" over and over again. Suddenly, Angel DuPont shoved her way in between us, pushing the guard away from me. When the guard pulled back his stick to hit her, she whacked him across the face so hard it staggered and stunned him. Then she let out a scream that could be heard as far as Lyon. The guard, completely befuddled by the actions of this insane American, began to back away. And when the nineteen-year-old tiger charged after him, he took off like a shot.

"And he's the guard?" I said to myself.

Angel walked back to me and placed her arms around my waist and asked if I was okay. I said, "Sure, I'm okay."

To tell you the truth I was more shocked by Angel's affection toward me than I was hurt by the guard's shoving.

"You're quite a fighter, aren't you?"

Continuing to hold me, Angel said, "Nobody messes with my partner. Anybody ever bothers you, you just tell me about it, and I'll kick their ass all over the lot."

"You're rather small for that, aren't you?"

"Small's got nothing to do with it. It's nerve. I ain't afraid of nobody, especially if they're gonna bother you."

Looking down into her eyes, I could feel her warm breath against my lips. Neither one of us made the move to kiss, and I finally said, "It's getting late."

She agreed, and we walked silently back to the Carlton Hotel steps where I split the money with her. She kissed me on the cheek and insisted on buying breakfast in the morning.

"It's a date," I said, and turned and started to walk along the nearly deserted Boulevard Croisette back toward the Majestic Hotel. Everyone, it seemed, was behind closed doors, or sleeping on the beach, or lying about the many luxury boats that cluttered the harbor, or were still playing in the casino.

It was a quiet, warm, moonlit night. The kind of night when young lovers take the time to stroll, touch, kiss, and say nice things. As I walked I heard someone whisper, and turned to see a devoted young couple who appeared almost as one person as they stood caressing in the privacy of a doorway. I watched them for a minute, envied their love, but approved of their act.

Walking on, I took a full, deep breath of the clean night air and snapped a photo with my eyelids of where I was and what I was doing. Pleased with my life at that moment—I smiled.

# 5

As I entered my room, instinct told me I wasn't alone. Ace White was playing solitaire on the coffee table.

"What's the password?" he asked, without looking up.

"Screw off!"

"So you remembered," he said nonchalantly, as if that was really it. "How much money did you win tonight?"

"Enough."

"How much?"

"You know, Ace, you were right, I don't need you."

Ace put down the deck, saying, "Yes, you do, Lefty. You're young, you're square, you're stupid in some ways, you're silly, you're uncouth, you're inexperienced, and you're from a jerk-water town. But . . . in all honesty, you're probably the best damn hustler to come along in years. You've got looks, charm, talent, style, nerve, and great possibilities. You need just one thing, kid."

"What's that?"

"Me."

"I got along without you before I met you, and I can get along without you now."

"Don't look a gift horse in the mouth, kid. You've got a choice right now of eating steaks or baloney for the rest of your life, don't flub it."

"I've eaten steaks before."

"For breakfast, lunch, dinner . . . and midnight snacks on solid gold plates?" he asked.

I hadn't.

"Have you ever slept on silk sheets, kid, on a sixteenth-century canopied bed? Or sailed on a ninety-foot yacht through the Mediterranean? Or danced at 6:00 A.M. in a small cafe in Le du Marche in Paris? Have you, Lefty? Have you done any of those things, or anything like them? Well, I have, and I'm going to keep doing them, with or without you. But you won't ever, ever do them without me."

"I'm young, old man, but I'm not hungry. I've made it this far. I can go all the way. I think you're almost through cutting the mustard, Ace, and you need me to steady your knife. So, if, and that's a big IF, if we're going to be partners, we're going to be exactly that—partners. Doing equally, sharing equally, working equally, or not at all."

Ace smiled and shrugged. "The thought of not eating steak for the rest of your life doesn't bother you, does it, kid?"

"Not if I have to eat crap, too."

Ace got up, walked over to the window, and gazed quietly down at the water. "Tell me," he said without turning, "is it true you hustled some Broadway actors out of a lot of money and then gave it back to them?"

"Half of it, yes."

"Why in the hell did you do that?"

"I wanted them to help me find you."

"Did they?"

"No."

"A penny saved is a penny earned, kid."

"I'll remember that . . . old man!"

"Tell me, did you like Bessie?" Ace asked.

"Yes, very much."

"Did you make love to her?"

"That's our business."

"Wasn't she fantastic?" he asked, not expecting an answer. Turning to me then, he said, "Now, I know who you are. You're the kid they've been talking about; the one they've warned me about. You didn't come ten million miles to study with me. You came here to play me, to beat me, and get a ten thousand dollar marker on your way to the Big Biazarro. Well, well, well, Lefty, you're twenty-one—"

"I'm twenty-two."

"Okay . . . you're twenty-two, and you beat Palusso and Harris and the rest, and you think you can take me, too, and get instant stardom, right?"

The thought of playing against Ace was always in the back of my mind and maybe in the front of it, but I had honestly told myself that I came to Cannes to study with him. But now that he mentioned it, Ace White was a Poker Master and a marker from him would start me on my way.

"Do you know what it takes to play in the Big Biazarro?" Ace asked.

"A million dollars in cash and five master markers."

"That's right. Now how do you propose to get all that?"

"I've got three years; I'll get it."

"How much of the million do you have right now?"

"Not much."

"Well, you've got *less* than three years, don't you think you should get started?"

"I'm starting."

"Let's see," said Ace. "You've got eight months left in this year, plus twenty-four gives you thirty-two months. You'll need a million in cash as your buy-in and you've got to figure another half million at least to live off."

"Five hundred thousand dollars to live on for two and a half years?"

"Lefty, don't be an ass. If you're going to live this kind of life, you live it in style. You eat the best foods, stay at the best hotels, travel first class, and date only ladies. You've got to establish yourself as a gentleman, or they won't allow you in the Biazarro no matter what you've got."

For the first time since deciding I would go for the big game I felt a little depressed, but I snapped out of it and said, "I've got to do it, and I'm going to do it!"

"I'm not saying you can't," said Ace, "but with only thirty-two months to go, you're going to have to be averaging fifty thousand a month."

"Have *you* ever averaged fifty thousand a month?" I asked.

"I always average fifty thousand. If the twenty-ninth of any month comes and I don't have it, I don't sleep until I get it. It's not as hard as it sounds . . . when you've got talent. Now what you have to decide is whether you want to play with me or against me."

Ace looked at me, and I was getting a little bored and tired of his patronizing attitude. I had made it this far without him, and, if I was forced to, I could go all the way on my own.

"All right, Ace," I said to break the silence, "do you want to play me and get it over with?"

"Oh, yes, I want to get it over with, but not right this minute. I'm not the fool Palusso, Harris, and the rest of them are. You're going to pay some tribute to my rep. To my talent. To my class."

"Don't count on it."

"Oh, but I am. As you put it, I need you to steady my knife so I can cut the mustard. Yes, I'm old, but I'm not dead. If you want to play me and take my crown, then we're going to work together for a while as partners—doing equally, sharing equally, working equally, or not at all. But there has to be a leader in every gang of bandits. I think my age and experience gives me that privilege."

I watched him skeptically for a minute, then said, "I guess it's my move, isn't it?"

"Yes," he said, and his voice cracked as if he was a tiny bit afraid of what I might say.

I hesitated a moment more and said, "Okay, leader, what do we do?"

"Can you deal placement poker, kid?"

"I can put the ace of diamonds anywhere you want it, old man."

"Top or bottom?"

"In your ear, if you want it there."

Ace smiled. A full, broad grin of relief. A sign of good times and good things to come. "We're going to get them, kid. We're going to get them good. We're going to live good, eat good, and everything else good. We're going to get them."

"Before we get them, can I ask you a question?"

"Of course, partner. What is it?"

"Why are you here?"

"Bessie didn't tell you—bless her heart," he said. "Okay, I'll tell you. Do you know those little hot-dog pushcarts they have around New York?"

"Yes."

"My brother, who was my only living relative, loooooved those hot dogs. I always thought they tasted like pure-dee shit. He ate at least one every day for years while standing around on Broadway figuring the horses. One day he was over on Second Avenue, bought one of those dogs, and died right on the spot. So, I found the guy who sold it to him, made him eat fifteen of them . . . and while he was gobbling them down he got indigestion and a coronary and died right there, all slumped over his hot-dog wagon. The word was beginning to get around that I had something to do with it, so I figured I'd better split for a while."

"Are the cops after you?"

"I don't know. But why wait around for them to get the idea. I figured I'd spend some time here and then drift back into town nonchalantly like. Is that all right with you?"

"Yes, it's all right with me, but is that all?"

"That's all," said Ace, staring skeptically at me.

27

"No, Ace, that's not all, and you know it. The man you killed happen—"

"I didn't kill anybody! His hot dogs killed him!"

"Yeh, but you made him eat them."

"You can lead a horse to water . . ."

"Oh, come on, Ace. What I'm trying to tell you is your problem isn't with the cops but with a very dangerous macaroni named Stanislaus Kondorwicz."

"What in the hell is a Stanislaus Kondorwicz?"

"A bad-ass hood who is after you with revenge in his heart and a .38 in his armpit. You killed his father for killing your brother. Now, I know it sounds like a silly soap opera, but he's serious, Ace, and he means to put you away!"

"Lefty, if I sat around and worried about every two-bit hood who threatened me for one reason or another, I wouldn't be able to sleep at night—and I love to sleep. But thanks anyway for telling me about it."

I couldn't tell whether Ace was bluffing or not. If he was afraid of Kondorwicz, it was impossible to see.

"Are you satisfied?" he asked.

"I guess so."

"I'm always going to be straight with you, kid—and I know you'll be the same with me, right?"

"Right."

"Okay, partner," he said, "there's a private club here in Cannes called La Mer where I've been picking up some spending change. I figure we can throw a couple of card tricks at them, with me betting against you, and clean up—if you're good at placement."

"I'm good," I said.

"And modest as well," said Ace, chuckling. "It's okay, I admire confidence. Do you need some extra poke?"

"No, I'm fine, but thanks anyway."

"All right then, I'll see you in the morning."

"Ace," I called to him as he opened the door to leave,

"there's just one last question. Why haven't you played in the Big Biazarro?"

The question hurt him.

He tried to hide it, but a line in his aging cheek gave him away.

"You don't have to answer unless you want to," I said, wishing I hadn't asked.

"Thanks," he said. "I'll tell you someday."

"Okay, partner, I'll see you tomorrow."

"Right," Ace said and closed the door as he left.

# 6

The next morning the telephone rang at 10:15 A.M. It was
Angel. She was waiting for me in the Carlton dining room. I
told her I would be right down. After shaving, showering, and
dressing, I left the room, went downstairs, and was crossing
the lobby when I saw Ace coming in the front door.

"Good morning, partner," he said, "are you ready to meet
'em, greet 'em, jam 'em, and beat 'em?"

"I didn't know we were starting so early."

"The early bird gets the worm."

"I could have won a bet you were going to say that," I said.
"I've made a breakfast date over at the Carlton."

"We have to make hay while the sun shines, kid. You can
eat breakfast over at the club."

I took a moment to consider the consequences, decided
Angel would be so peeved that she wouldn't speak to me ever
again, and said to myself, "Oh, what the hell."

"Okay, let's go."

We grabbed a cab in front of the hotel and went to La Mer,
which turned out to be a huge villa hidden in the hills back of
town behind a grove of cypress trees.

The only feasible entrance was a white brick path running under a solid shade of shrubbery. As we walked toward the house, Ace asked me who the girl was I was talking to on the boardwalk.

"Some young nymph from Brooklyn, who thinks the whole world wants to screw her."

"Did you?"

"It's none of your business, but no, I didn't."

"Why not, don't you like white girls?"

"I have no preference, I love them all."

"I don't dig white women," said Ace.

"So I heard. Why?"

"They've had it too damn easy. They expect too much. Black women are the best if you can cope with their bitterness. They'll take care of everything, including you. I like a strong woman. Strong emotionally, physically, and every other way."

"In other words," I said, "if we come across a fine black sister, it's every man for himself?"

"No, Lefty. Don't waste your time. I can't lose with the stuff I use. Your best bet is to grab off one of those powder-puff broads, or go sit in a corner and beat your meat."

We were both laughing as we came up to the door of the gray stone mansion that would have cost no less than ten million dollars had it been built in the States.

"Just let me know whether the card is top or bottom," said Ace, as we walked inside.

The house had large rooms with high, beamed ceilings. The decor was white on silver gray carpeting with black walnut walls. The people walking around, sitting, and drinking were the super elite of the ones I saw the previous night at the casino.

"You like it, huh?" Ace asked, as he saw the gleam in my eyes.

"It's nice. Real nice. Where's the action?"

"Upstairs. Come on."

Walking up the spiral staircase, I couldn't help being

31

impressed by the collection along the wall. There was a Van Gogh, a Cézanne, a Toulouse-Lautrec, and a Michelangelo sketch.

"Are these real?"

"You bet your ass they're real."

"What does this guy do?"

"No one knows, but whatever it is, he's doing it right."

"You bet your ass he is."

We moved along the balcony and went in through a large, Spanish-style door. In the room was a mini-casino, and almost immediately I noticed a lucrative poker game blazing away in the corner. As Ace and I approached the bar, I asked why we couldn't get into the game. He ignored me and asked the bartender to give us a couple of scotches and milk.

Bitterly, I said, "I don't drink scotch."

Ace said, "It's a good time to learn," and handed me a glass.

"Come on, quit stalling. Why can't we play? I bet it's worth thousands."

"Probably a hell of a lot more than that," said Ace.

"So, what's the problem?"

"I told you, I don't play cards anymore."

"I don't want you to go into shock or anything, but *I* play cards—and pretty damn good, if I must say so myself. Now, how about it?"

"I say no."

"Ace, are you crazy? Look at those guys—they're so old they can barely lift those cards. Let's play!"

"I don't care about poker anymore. I've switched to dice."

"Dice?"

"That's right—dice," he said. "You're not going to believe this, kid, but I've got a built-in thermostat right here in my heart that tells me when the old bones are going to heat up . . . and then I bet like crazy."

"Do you really expect me to believe that crap!"

"You mean you don't?"

32

"Not if God himself stripped me naked, sat me in a corner, and told me so."

"I'll prove it to you when we get to London."

"Why wait until we get to London?"

"Because there aren't any dice tables between here and London."

"Right," I said. "No dice tables. But there is a poker table. Please, Ace, for God's sake, get me into that game."

"We came here to do card tricks and win some money."

"Tricks? Monkeys do tricks on grapevines for peanuts. Ace, I'm a card player. I was born and raised to play poker. I come from several generations of careful breeding just to evolve into the greatest poker player of all time. You can't stand in the way of my great destiny."

"You sure can talk some shit, kid. I got a headache," said Ace. "I don't know what you're talking about—grapevines, peanuts, monkeys, destiny. Look, all I'm saying is if we do this thing my way, we can pick up a couple thousand dollars. But if you get stuck in that game, it could cost us more than all the money we've got in the world, or could borrow or steal for the next ten years."

"I'm not going to lose, Ace. Please, let me play," I pleaded.

"No," he said too simply and it pissed me off.

"Can I get into that game without your help?"

"No."

"Ace, do you want me to get on my knees in front of all these people?"

Ace sipped his scotch and looked over at the table. He eyed each man, then looked at me and shook his head.

"Please?" I begged.

"How much money you got on you?"

"About seven hundred," I said anxiously.

"Seven hundred?"

"Seven hundred to invest," I explained.

"How much you got altogether?"

"About fifteen hundred."

33

"Do you have it on you?"

"Yes. Why?"

"Because, my little chickadee, that game happens to be a twenty-five hundred dollar buy-in."

Needless to say, I was shocked. I was twenty-two years old and the highest stakes I had ever played for was a five hundred dollar buy-in, and I'd almost shit when I sat down to play then.

Ace reached into his wallet, handing me a thousand dollar bill. "Take this with your fifteen hundred, walk over there and tell the man in the blue suit that Mr. Horace Bartlow Whiting sent you. Ask for a one thousand dollar blue chip, a five hundred dollar red chip and ten one hundred dollar white chips."

"That's only twelve chips," I said, almost whimpering.

"That's all there is," said Ace. "What's the name of that jerkwater town you're from?"

"Ferno."

"It looks like the people of Ferno can't lose today."

"What do you mean by that?"

"Well, if you win in that game you can go home a hero. If you lose, you can just go home. Either way, Ferno gets its star back."

"That's not very funny," I said.

"My thousand bucks says I'm not laughing either."

I gulped down the scotch, coughed, and started across the room. I spoke to the man in blue, told him who sent me, and got my measly dozen chips.

Jimmy Palusso once told me if I was ever nervous in a game, I shouldn't attempt to hide it because they would know anyway.

The game was five-card stud. My down card was the ace of hearts. The second card was the queen of hearts. The first bet was a white chip—a hundred dollars. I called.

My next card was the eight of hearts. Someone caught a pair of jacks and bet two hundred. Four of the seven players folded. I called. So did the blue-suit man.

My fourth card was the ten of hearts—one more heart for a flush. The man with the jacks bet another two hundred. I raised him two hundred. The blue-suit man raised us both five hundred. The man with the pair of jacks raised him back two hundred. We had to figure him for three jacks because the blue-suit man had a pair of kings up. It was my turn to bet or fold. I had counted the other hearts that had fallen. There were three others besides my four. I had a pretty good chance of catching another heart, but I had a better chance of not being dealt one.

I decided to drive one of them out, so I held my breath and threw in the blue chip. Silence fell over the room. The blue-suit man looked closely at my cards, then smiled. I had the queen, ten, and eight of hearts up, and the ace of hearts in the hole.

When I heard another blue chip hit the pot, I almost fainted. Then the third blue chip dropped in right on top of it.

The dealer dealt very carefully and my last card was the nine of hearts. I'm sure you'll believe me when I say I almost leaned across the table and kissed him.

The man with the jacks folded. The blue-suit man caught a pair of sixes to go with his pair of kings. I looked at the blue-suit man, saying, "I check."

He stared dead into my eyes, trying to figure out what I had. It was definite now that he had two pair, but I had the flush.

He looked around the room and asked, "Partisan?"

Ace stepped up close to the table and nodded to him.

The blue-suit man looked at me again, decided not to bet, and nodded for me to flip over my cards to reveal my flush. I did, and then he nonchalantly flipped over his cards, showing me his full house.

I'd lost the entire twenty-five hundred in one hand.

The blue-suit man said he thought I had a straight flush. That's why he didn't bet.

I sat stunned in my chair, watching him pull in the money.

Just as I was about to rise from the table, a gift of five blue chips was placed in front of me. I turned and saw Ace smiling at me.

"I like your style, kid. Meet 'em, greet 'em, jam 'em, and beat 'em, partner."

An hour later, I had won back the original twenty-five hundred plus another twenty-seven thousand dollars. Sitting there, calm and cool as a cucumber, I rested back, counting all the chips in front of the other players. I estimated there to be more than a hundred thousand dollars, and I, little Lefty Wilson, from the jerkwater town of Ferno, New York, was going to win it all.

As a new hand was being dealt, my fabulous luck continued. I caught three tens in the first three cards. I bet two hundred dollars on each ten, and as the chips hit the table, I heard these words in an awesome Brooklyn accent: "I don't like being stood up, Lefty! I mean a simple phone call woulda taken care of the whole damn thing, ya know. I ain't had nothing to eat all day, so what do ya say ya get your ass up from that table and take me to lunch!"

I didn't know what else to do, so I put my hands over my eyes, praying that when I looked up again, Angel would be gone. Meanwhile, Ace reached over, shoved my chips to the houseman, and cashed us in.

"You've lost your concentration, kid," said Ace. "We'll try it again sometime."

# 7

The three of us returned to the Carlton Hotel to grab a quick, farewell lunch. Quick—for obvious reasons. It was time for Ace and me to "get our hats." He had been hiding out in France for over a year and he was getting homesick for the States. Also, he wanted to leave Europe before those thousands of asinine American tourists arrived.

"Why in the hell can't I go with you?" Angel asked.

I looked at Ace, and he sat staring impatiently out across the dining room, as if to say, "It's all yours, kid, let's see how you get out of it."

"Angel," I began, "Ace and me are partners."

"Partners, my ass. You're just a couple of drifting hustlers, and I want to go with you. I won't interfere."

"You already did."

"When?"

"At La Mer. I had a streak going and we could have won a lot of money, baby."

"Well, I was hungry."

Ace exhaled a sign of impatience.

"I know you were, but when we're winning like that, hunger and everything else has to wait."

"I'm sorry. I won't do it again."

"Sorry doesn't pay the rent, Angel. We can't afford to be sorry. We've got to be sure . . . all the time."

"You're just going to dump me here, right?" she asked as tears came to her eyes.

"You don't have to put it like that," I said. "After all, we just met yesterday and you were doing fine before that."

"Well, thanks a lot. Thanks a hell of a lot. I thought we were going to be buddies."

"We *are* buddies, and if we ever run into each other again, we'll probably have a great time."

"Miss Angel," Ace said with his most patient tone.

"Don't give me that miss-shit, mister. I'm hip to you old fags. You just want him all to yourself."

Ace took a deep sigh, and stared back out across the room.

"Come on, Angel, knock it off," I said.

"What do you need with this old fart? We did okay at the casino. We could travel the rest of the world just hitting the casinos together. We'll get rich!"

"Don't you understand . . . I *want* to go with him. And we've got to go alone."

"You must be a *fag,* too."

"Think anything you want, but you can't go with us."

"I'll follow you."

"You don't know where we're going."

"You're going to New York."

"New York is pretty big."

"I'll haunt every poker game until I find you."

"And then what?"

"I'll tell whoever you're playing against that you're cheating."

"Okay," I said, finalizing.

Tears were running down her cheeks now, and she sniffed and wiped at them. "It ain't fair, Lefty. It just ain't fair. We

38

formed a partnership, and now you're dropping me to go with him. You're fucked, you know that? I really think you and me could have helped each other. You're just a fucked person, Lefty, and I'm going to tell everybody wherever I go that the great Lefty Wilson is a fucked person."

Ace and I sat looking at her. Staring at her, feeling sorry for her, and disliking ourselves for having to hurt her the way we were.

"Well," she said, finally calming herself. "I'm not going to let it bother me. It's your loss as much as it is mine. But, you'll be sorry. This isn't the end, I promise you that. You'll be sorry."

Angel stood then, leaned heavily against the table, sniffed once more, and then turned and left us.

I looked at Ace and waited for him to say something. He didn't disappoint me. "Life, kid, is not always what you would have it be."

"Knock it off, Ace. You couldn't care less about her and you know it."

"Lefty, my boy," he began, "the heart that beats beneath this tattered, worn, and fragile bag of bones is a cold one, but if anything can thaw it out . . . it's the warmth of a woman's tears. . . ."

We killed off the remainder of the afternoon and a bottle of Montrachet while remaining silent and just watching the beautiful half-naked girls walk by.

That evening we went back to our respective hotel rooms, packed, and caught a late evening flight for London.

On the plane, I told Ace that I was certain I could have broken the game if Angel hadn't shown up. Ace merely chuckled and said, "If. If wishes were horses, beggars would ride, kid. Beggars would ride."

# 8

I don't have the slightest idea what time it was when we arrived in London, but during an incoherent haze I was taken off the plane to a hotel, forced to shave, shower, and dress in a tuxedo—and all by Ace White, who kept yelling, "Come on, kid, come on."

I swear I don't know where that man got his energy.

We went to the old, private, and now extinct Allanbee Casino in the West End. The sound of the dice, the rattle of the roulette wheel, and the fact Ace was going to demonstrate his "thermostat" in action brought me more to life.

The casino was small compared to others, and consisted of a room about forty feet by fifty with one large dice table, three roulette wheels, two blackjack tables, and an alcove for baccarat. We walked directly to the dice table, where there were three blue-clad croupiers and a dozen players. Ace whispered for me to buy two hundred pounds in chips and to wait until he gave me the high sign to start betting the numbers.

I did what he told me, and tried to remain patient. And patience, of course, is the secret word again, and again, and Ace had enough for both of us. He lay around the table concentrating on every roll, mumbling to himself, making mental notes, frowning at the ridiculous betters (which most of them were), and occasionally dropping a chip to test the bones. Then, functioning like a million dollar thermostat, he automatically began to smile with the heat of the dice. And when Ace White smiled, *he smiled!*

His entire face became a mass of sunshine and glowing laughter. His pointed chin quivered, his steel-gray eyes teared profusely, and his perfect teeth gleamed in his wide mouth.

"Amen," he uttered aloud, and I started to bet—ten pounds each on the numbers four, five, six, eight, nine, ten; five pounds each on the "hard ways," double deuces, treys, etc., and five pounds each on the "come line" on each roll.

"Make numbers, make numbers," Ace shouted at the shooters, and "Let it ride, let it ride," he said on the side to me.

One large, hairy, but beautiful Italian woman from Salerno, a fast shooter, kept the dice for twenty-seven minutes, and Ace, *phenomenally*, yelled, "Take it off!" just before the woman threw a seven and said, "Ah, *merde!*"

Ace walked over, kissed her on the cheek, and we cashed in our chips.

"That's it?" I asked.

"That's all there is to it."

"How often can you do that?"

"Not too," said Ace. "You limit how much you take out of a casino and you're always welcomed back. Remember that."

"We won over four thousand pounds," I said. "Are you sure they don't mind?"

"Well, they're not exactly ecstatic, but they know we can afford to lose much more than that any time we play."

While Ace ordered us two scotches and milks, I told him that if we kept winning at the pace we were going, we'd end up with our fifty thousand per month in less than a week.

"We're going to get it, kid, don't worry," he assured me, as if I bothered him with such trivia.

41

When our drinks came, I tasted mine and decided I would rather have sleep than booze.

"Why are we hanging around here now?" I asked.

Ace didn't bother to answer me. He kept staring across the room. I turned to see what or who it was, but there were only gamblers and on-lookers.

"Who are you looking at?" I asked.

When Ace refused to answer me again, I looked right at him and shouted, "Who are you looking at?"

He continued to ignore me, and it really got on my nerves. I finally gave up and turned and tried to find something or someone who would fill my interest. Sitting at the baccarat table and fingering a stack of five pound notes was this gorgeous Nigerian-looking princess, dressed to love, and gazing right at me. I looked at Ace out of the corner of my eye and said to myself, "This will fix his ass if I score with her." But as I started to slip quietly off the seat, he grabbed my arm and said, "Forget it, kid, she's been staring at me all night."

I looked back at the princess, and sure enough, her eyes were focused on a spot just to the right of me—Ace.

"I'm tired," I said, sounding as frustrated, angry, and bored as I was. "What do you say we go back to the hotel?"

He ignored me again and I took a big gulp of the scotch and milk and choked on it. When I finally got control of myself, Ace leaned over and whispered, "Do you want to play in the Big Biazarro, kid?"

"Huh?"

"I said, do you—"

"I heard you. I heard you," I said, suddenly wide awake, bright-eyed and bushy-tailed. "What are you saying?"

"Over there . . . in the blue tux."

"I see him."

"His name is Duxbury. He's a Poker Master."

He was a distinguished-looking man who looked more like a London psychiatrist (who ate crumpets in the morning, enjoyed afternoon teas, and went to bed every night by nine)

42

than he did a poker player. His appearance was very misleading—except for his eyes. Lawdy Roberts told me that the eyes don't lie. Duxbury had sharp, clear, piercing, intelligent eyes that had seen more than their share of straight flushes. He was a poker player, no doubt about it. Probably one of the best.

"Think he'll play me?" I asked.

"I don't know," said Ace. "Why don't we go see?"

Crossing the elegant rose-colored room, I walked a half step behind Ace while straightening my jacket and trying to compose myself.

"Albert," Ace said and nodded to Duxbury. "May we sit?"

"Good evening, Horace; how goes it?" the suave Duxbury asked while keeping his dissecting eyes fixed on me.

"I'm sure you've heard of my associate, Mr. Wilson," said Ace.

"Are you the one they call Lefty?"

Needless to say, I was impressed he had heard of me.

"Some call me that."

"I don't particularly like nicknames," said Duxbury. "I have always preferred proper ones, so I'm certain you won't mind if I call you Lester."

"How did you know *my* proper name?"

Ace and Duxbury looked at each other and laughed at my ignorance.

"You're being watched, Lester," Duxbury informed me. "Whenever there are millions at stake, people watch people."

There was a long pause then where a great deal of realization came to me, and the three of us sort of smiled at each other. Then I stopped smiling, looked directly at Duxbury, and said, as firmly as I could, "Do you want to play five-card stud with me?"

"With you . . . or against you?" the man asked.

"Call it anyway you want to, mister, but I would love to sit down at the table with you tonight."

"What do you think will happen?"

43

"I don't know," I said honestly, "but I know what I would like to happen."

I hadn't noticed, but all of the other people in the casino, including the croupiers, had stopped what they were doing and had begun to maneuver for seats around a small poker table in the opposite corner.

Duxbury stared coldly at me for a few more moments and then rose without a word and walked directly across the casino.

"What's the name of that little jerkwater town you're from?" Ace asked.

"Not now, Ace, not now," I said, and got up to follow Duxbury across the room.

"Lefty," Ace called, and I stopped after a few steps.

He rose from the table and came over close to me and said softly, "There's no sweat here, you know. Just psych him out."

"What do you mean?"

"You know exactly what I mean. Play with his head, unnerve him. He's a snob, a perfectionist, a disciplinarian. He thinks of poker as an extreme art that should be played with manners and dignity. Shake him up a little. Do it to make sure, but in my opinion you've already got him beat psychologically."

"I have?"

"Of course you do. That's why he's been checking on you. You can beat him with ease, and when you do you've automatically got yourself a European backer."

"But I don't want a backer, Ace. I want a marker!"

"Don't be an ass, Lefty. This man's got an inexhaustible supply of money. He doesn't give out markers."

"So what in the hell am I playing him for?"

"Because he's a Poker Master, and if you beat all twenty-seven Poker Masters and don't get one single marker, you're the best in the world, stupid."

"But that won't get me into the Big Biazarro, will it?"

44

"Holy shit." Ace sighed. "Only Poker Masters have been allowed in the Big Biazarro."

"I didn't know that."

Ace frowned at me, and then smiled and said, "Well, you just stick with me, baby, and I'll teach you a few things."

I smiled and said, "I'm going to hold you to that."

"All right," he said. "Let's meet 'em, greet 'em, jam 'em, and beat 'em."

**9**

Before sitting down, I took a few seconds to stand there and capture that moment in my mind. I wanted to remember clearly and be completely aware of that initial and important step toward the Big Biazarro—my first Poker Master game.

"You can deal," Duxbury said as I took a seat. I pressed my fingers to the sealed deck he had tossed across the table, trying to receive any vibrations, negative or otherwise. There were none.

"What are the stakes?" I asked.

"One hundred thousand dollars!" Duxbury announced and waited for me to flinch—I didn't.

"Can you afford it?" he asked.

"Does a bear poo-poo in the woods?" I answered, and more than half of our audience laughed. Duxbury didn't find it very funny. As a matter of fact, he looked at me as if I had said something very distasteful.

You know you've arrived when a casino croupier hands you a healthy stack of chips without first asking for some sort of collateral. They were in the usual colors: blue, red, and white. Sixteen blue chips worth five thousand dollars each; eighteen red chips worth one thousand each; and twenty white chips priced at one hundred dollars each, coming to a flat total of one hundred thousand dollars.

I sat there in my smooth black tux, white ruffled shirt, black bow tie, and one hundred big ones sitting in front of me, and I said to myself, "Boy, I sure wish the people in Ferno could see me now."

I broke the deck, shuffled it, and placed it down in front of Duxbury. He continued to stare at me with those penetrating eyes of his. He didn't know I was hip to the "mean stare-down." I had seen Bessie Poindexter use it to perfection on that pimp back in Harlem. So, when he continued to stare at me, I looked right back at him, cocked my eyes while tilting my head, and gave him a silly grin. This unnerved him. He snatched the deck from me and shuffled it. I could feel Ace, who was standing directly behind me, throwing off all kinds of good vibrations in my direction.

When Duxbury was finished shuffling, he tossed the deck back at me and remarked, "Now *that's* the way you shuffle cards, ingrate!"

"That's cute, Duxy. Would you like for *me* to show *you* a trick?"

He slammed his fist on the table, upsetting our stacks of chips, and screamed at the top of his voice, "NO!"

"All right," I said calmly, "in that case, I will proceed to deal a game of five-card stud. A game in which I shall win, and you, Duxy, shall lose."

I began to deal. "You have a down card. I have a down card. You have a king of diamonds, I have a trey of spades. It's your bet, Duxy."

"You're not going to make it in this world, kid," Duxbury prophesied.

I smiled at him, shook my head, and said simply, "But I'm already here, Duxy. Can't you see me? I'm here. I'm dealing the cards and it's your bet."

He threw in a five thousand dollar blue chip.

47

I called the bet.

I dealt him a six of clubs, and me a jack of hearts.

He bet ten thousand and I scratched my head, stretched my back, giggled, yawned, and finally called his ten thousand and raised twenty.

The casino was so silent you could feel the pressure.

He had to figure me for a pair of jacks. He just called the bet.

I dealt. "You now have a wonderful eight of diamonds to go with your impressive king of diamonds and your less than impressive six of clubs. I now have a ten of diamonds to go with my impressive jack of hearts and my also less than impressive trey of spades. It is still your bet, Duxy."

He was fuming. His nostrils were enlarged and his face was a blood red.

"Well, it looks as if we're right down to the wire," I said, "let's see, it looks like your kings against my—"

"Shut up!" he yelled at me.

"Aww," I said. "Someone lied to me. They told me you were a gentleman."

"If you don't shut your mouth this instant, I will withdraw from the game."

"Are you going to forfeit the game?"

He just sat there staring at me, and then finally he looked down at our cards, and, realizing he had me beat, he shoved all of his chips into the pot.

"How much is there?" I asked.

"It's exactly the same as you have in front of you."

"Are you tapping me on the fourth card?"

"What does it look like?"

I put on a kid's sad face and, talking baby talk, I said, "That's not very nice. Are you sure you don't want to wait until the fifth card?"

"I'm sure."

"Are you certain?"

"It's your bet!"

"Hmmmm, so it is, so it is. Let's see, you've got a king, an eight, and a six. I have a trey, a jack, and a ten." Breaking out into a loud laugh, I threw my head back. "Oh, I see, I see. You've got a pair of kings, and you think I've got a pair of jacks, so you win, right? But what you don't know is that I do not have a pair of jacks, so . . ." I put on a very sad face. "You win anyway."

"It's your bet . . . idiot!" said Duxbury.

"Oh, well, you win some, lose some," I said and pushed my sixty-five thousand dollars into the pot—which, of course, brought all sorts of "oohs" and "ahhs" from the audience.

Duxbury was stunned. He looked at me as if I was completely insane.

"It's only money," I said simply.

"Put the deck down on the table!" he ordered.

"Oh, of course," I said, and placed the deck on the table to my left. "Anything else?"

"Deal."

"Deal, yes, of course. But don't get so excited, Duxy, it's only a game."

"Deal!"

"Yes, sir." With the tips of my fingers, very meticulously I lifted the top card off the deck and flipped it over to his hand. It was a deuce of hearts. And then, very slowly and carefully, I lifted the next card and flipped it over on my cards. It was an ace of diamonds. I smiled and asked Duxbury if he wanted to bet.

"We're tapped," he said, realizing at that instant what our hands were. He had kings back to back, and I had an ace in the hole all the way and hit one on the last card.

I turned my hole card over and he quickly buried his hand into the deck. He raised his eyes to me then, and they were filled with hate and pain, and skepticism. I felt sorry for him. And I also felt like an ass for having acted like an ass. It wasn't necessary, and I wished Ace hadn't told me to do so.

Softly, I said to Duxbury, "I'm sorry. Would you like to keep playing? I promise to keep my mouth shut."

"I don't think you can."

I rested back in my chair and waited for Duxbury to make a decision. He kept staring at me as he had done all night, and then he finally calmed down, shook his head, and said, "We'll meet again. Next time, try to play like a gentleman."

"I give you my word, I will."

As quickly as they had gathered, the on-lookers moved away from the table with the exception of one glossy-looking hooker, who took Duxbury's seat. She was a tall girl with frosted blond hair and a not so pretty face but who spoke with that soft English accent that I liked so much.

"What are you going to do with all that money?" she asked.

I smiled and shrugged at her.

"Given the chance, I could make you feel quite good."

"I'm sure you could, but I really need to be alone right now."

She stood, smiled, and said, "That's really a shame. But if you change your mind, just call here and ask for Katherine."

"Thank you. I will."

As she walked away, a croupier began to stack up my chips and said that Ace White was waiting for me in the men's room. I nodded, pushed my chair back, walked out into the lobby and into the john. Ace was leaning against a sink, and when I entered, he politely asked the attendant to leave us alone. Once he was gone, Ace turned to me and I saw a fury in his eyes I didn't know he was capable of.

"We're through," he announced bitterly. "You know that, don't you?"

"What?"

"Don't try to con me, Lefty. I started playing this game the day after the Persians invented it."

Kidding, I said, "I knew you were old, Ace, but this is ridiculous."

50

"Well, you don't have to worry about it, because you'll never see me get a day older."

"Wait a minute, Ace. What's eating you?"

"What's eating me? I'm out there laying my life on the line for you and you pull some jerkwater shit like that!"

"Like what, Ace?"

He looked directly into my eyes and said, "You're amazing, you know that? You're really amazing! Do you really think I'm that stupid? Do you think I've got bells in my head or something? And you said you were going to be straight with me."

I lowered my eyes and said, "All right, all right. What do you want to know?"

"All of it. Why you did it. How you did it. And when you did it. But mostly, why?"

"Which do you want to know first?"

"When?"

"When he threw me the deck face-up. Remember, he tossed me the sealed deck, I shuffled it, he took it from me and threw it back at face-up?"

"And you picked up the deck, stacked him kings and yourself aces."

"Well . . . yes, I guess I did."

"Why?"

"Why what?"

"Why in the hell did you do it?" Ace yelled at me.

"Shhh, Ace, do you want the whole world to know about it?"

"Why did you do it?" he asked again, but quietly and through clenched teeth.

"I wasn't planning on doing it. Honest to God, Ace, but when he threw that deck at me and those aces and kings were just lying there so pretty and inviting, well, I just automatically picked them up and while kibitzing with him—he wasn't paying any attention to me—I shuffled in the stack. I swear to you, Ace, I don't usually cheat. I don't have to."

51

"Bullshit!"

"I play great poker. I beat Palusso, Roberts, and all those guys without ever touching a deck. We had dealers."

"I can't believe it," Ace said, while loosening his tie. "A Poker Masters game, your *first* Poker Masters game and *you stack the deck!*"

"Nobody knows I did it."

"*I* know you did it!"

"That's true, but you just guessed. But, tell the truth, did you see me do it?"

"I didn't have to see you do it, Lefty. But I know goddamn well that even a country idiot like you isn't going to bet sixty-five thousand dollars on an ace-high hand when he knows he's facing kings!"

"You already said I've got nerve."

Ace took a long, deep breath, and then finally stopped grimacing.

"I swear to God, I'll never cheat again. Please!" I pleaded. "Let's stay partners. There's only twenty-six Masters left."

Ace walked across the room, slapped his thigh, and exhaled noisily, "Lefty, Lefty, Lefty." He spun around and looked at me and finally smiled. "You sonofabitch, if you ever—"

"I swear to God," I said, and raised my right hand.

"I'll have you killed if you do," said Ace.

I shrugged my shoulders, relaxed, and said, "No, you wouldn't."

"I wouldn't, huh?"

"No."

"Why?"

"Because . . . who's going to steady your knife so you can cut the mustard? And who's going to listen to all those stupid clichés you throw at me all the time? And who's—"

"Shut up," said Ace, "before I change my mind."

# 10

The flight from London to New York took nine and one half hours—something to do with a headwind, or heavy cumulus, or some damn thing. It was a horrible flight, boring, lonely, and long, long, long.

Ace, the lucky flake, had decided to stay on in London for a few days with that Nigerian princess. He put me on the plane with a list of things I was supposed to do once I got to New York. He even gave me a list of restaurants and clothing shops to visit. Sort of a way of getting known around town in the right circles. One thing I wasn't to do before he got back was play poker. He also told me that someone would pick me up at the airport.

But, meanwhile, there I was on that airplane flying at a stork's pace in the dead of night with some country-talking pilot who kept coming on the PA every fifteen minutes to apologize for what was happening. "Ahh, ladies and gentle-men, I would like to keep you informed of our progress. Ahh, things have not changed. The weather in New York is cloudy and rainy, but, ahh, we should have no problem landing. As stated earlier, ahh, we will be arriving at Kennedy International Airport at approximately four-thirteen in the morning New York City time. And, once again, I would like to convey my apologies for the delay, but thank you for flying TWA," or some damn thing.

As luck would have it, it turned out to be one of those "ugly flights." I'm sure you've seen them. Not only are the stewardesses late-shift Sallies with zits on their cheeks and runs in their pantyhose, but the only two pretty girls on the flight were sitting in the last seat of the plane, next to the john, and before take-off they cuddled up in each other's arms and fell fast asleep.

Being a night person, I was wide awake and, as fate would have it, sitting next to me was a loquacious pediatrician from Newark who was writing a book on child abuses and decided to tell me all eight hundred pages of the manuscript.

"Are you aware that none of the women who have been found guilty of child abuse have been able to explain why it happened?"

No shit, Ben Casey.

After about forty-seven maudlin minutes of little broken arms, and lacerated tu-tus, I excused myself and walked back into the economy section of the 707. On both sides of the darkened aisle, people were sleeping soundly, except one young black mother who sat openly nursing her infant. I thought about some of the things the pediatrician had told me, and, as she and I smiled at each other, I was relieved that there would be no such abuse with this mother and child.

Continuing, I came upon a student who had his head buried deep into several psychology books, which were scattered all over the seat. He didn't bother to look up, so I didn't bother.

In the last seat were the two girls, both in their twenties and cuddled up in each other's arms. One had her head covered, but the other's angelic face, with a lock of her shiny auburn hair lying sensually over it, was exposed. I stopped and looked at her and she opened her eyes. She stared at me for a moment, and then cleared her throat and whispered, "What's the matter, can't you sleep?"

"I'm a night person."

She smiled and said, "You should try and become a day person, you get a lot more done. Probably make a lot more money."

Just then, her partner stirred, so she cuddled her closer, winked at me, and went back to sleep.

As I stood up in the back of the plane, afraid to return to my seat, one of the late-shift Sallies came back and asked me if I needed anything.

"Can I get a drink?"

"Sure," she said with her midwestern accent. "What would you like?"

"Scotch and milk."

"Coming right up."

As she bent down, her knee widened the run in her pantyhose, but she didn't notice it, or maybe she had already thrown a fit about it, or perhaps she just didn't give a damn. And, why should she; only a chauvinist snob like me would make a big thing of it anyway. I told myself I would have to stop that.

Handing me the drink, she asked, "Why do you mix them?"

I gave her a ten dollar bill and said, "My partner Ace White says the scotch is to make you feel good and the milk is to make you be good."

"That's good reasoning?"

I watched her as she began to straighten up the area. She was a plain-looking Irish girl with stringy, coarse hair that refused to stay in place. Her body was well-rounded, healthy, and could easily be turned into a baby factory should she marry an old-fashioned devout Catholic. She would keep a messy house, but her five children, three sturdy boys and two girls, one plain, one pretty, would grow up smart and healthy like she was. The boys would all be athletic, and one or two of them would probably go on to be a doctor, or a lawyer, or, at the least, a cop. The girls would grow up strong, sensuous, and

55

maybe even smarter than their mother. They would be "good" girls, virtuous until the first time, and then they would turn into ardent lovers who knew how to make a man feel good—in and out of bed.

"Would you like something else?" she asked.

"Why do they have you on the late shift?"

"I asked for it," she answered simply.

"Really? Isn't it a drag?"

"No. I'm really kind of lazy. You have a lot less people on this flight, and I get all of the benefits the day girls get."

"You're a hustler." I smiled.

"So are you," she said, certain of what she spoke.

"No, not me. I'm a pediatrician from Newark."

She looked me right in the eye and said, "You want to bet?"

I almost said, "How much?" but caught myself and laughed.

"You win the change," I said and turned and walked back to my seat.

The pediatrician was asleep when I got there, thank God, so I nestled back and tried to catch a few winks. I shut my eyes, but less than five minutes later I opened them again as the stewardess passed me going up the aisle to the first-class kitchen.

A minute or so passed and she came back down the aisle, smiled, winked at me, and caused my heart to double-time. I waited. Thought about it. Decided to do it. Changed my mind. Considered it again, and followed her to the back of the plane.

When I came to the alcove, I caught her in a private moment as she reached inside her blouse and was attempting to adjust or repair her bra strap. Watching her, I became even more excited over her nonchalance.

Feeling my eyes, she looked up, a bit angry, and said, "Well . . . ?"

I couldn't find a word to explain my presence there.

She placed her hands on her hips and glared bitterly at me.

"I'm sorry," I said finally.

"Do you expect it right here?" she asked. "Or do you want

56

me to step into one of the johns and prop my ass up on the sink?"

"No, no, I . . . I don't know what I expected. I must be crazy."

"You sure are. This is my work, my job!" she said as if she hated it, especially at that moment.

"I'll . . . I'll just go sit down. Try to get some sleep, I guess. I'm really sorry. Really."

I dared to look at her then, and there was a sudden softness in her eyes.

"What's your name?" she asked, maternally now.

"They call me Lefty. Lefty Wilson. What's yours?"

"Maggie. Maggie O'Donnell."

"I love the name Maggie."

"What's your game, Lefty?"

"Poker's my *home game* and five hundred rummy is my *road game.*"

"What does all that mean?"

"I guess it means I can get rich playing poker, but if I had to I could make a living playing five hundred rummy."

"What game do you like the best?"

"Poker."

"I thought so," she said and smiled. "My dad's a poker player. Not nearly as good as you are, but pretty good for our neighborhood."

"Depending on your neighborhood, that could be great."

Maggie stared at me, and then leaned forward and peered down the dark and empty aisle. Then, surprisingly, she pulled the lapels of my jacket, causing me to move into the alcove with her.

I was so nervous I was visibly shaking.

"Put your arms around me," she commanded, and I immediately obeyed. "Now kiss me. One long, good, full, fast kiss. Kiss me so I'll remember you. So I'll never be able to forget Lefty Wilson, poker player. Kiss me as if I was your one and only dream girl. As if I was really honest-to-God as beautiful as you are."

57

"I'm not beautiful," I said.

"Oh, Christ, yes you are. Don't you even know that? Kiss me, kiss me as if you really wanted to love me. As if I meant more to you than just some chick to . . . Please kiss me."

I pressed my lips softly and slowly against hers—then stopped and pulled a short distance away. Turning my head in the opposite direction, I pressed my lips lightly again, then let my tongue slip between my lips and run all over hers. My hands slid down over the large, round firmness of her ass and I squeezed it as hard as I could and pulled her into me, and kissed her fully.

Stopping suddenly, I pulled away again to look at her. I would never be able to explain it, but in that alcove, in the dim light, that plain, straggly-haired, pale-faced, late-shift Sally became a queen. For one brief, glittering moment she was a queen! A beautiful, adorable, desirable queen.

And when she leaned up and kissed me—I became a king—with weak, jittery knees. We held the kiss for a long, lovely moment, and then parted.

"Here's my phone number," she said, handing me a scrap of paper. "Put it away somewhere, and in three or four days, take it out, think about me, be honest with yourself, and then either tear it up or call me. And, Lefty Wilson, poker player . . . please be fair."

"You're not bad at all, you know," I said honestly.

"Here, at this moment, I'm magnificent. But would you spend money and time with me somewhere else?"

"Of course, I would."

"Then you'll call, won't you?"

"I will," I said, trying desperately to sound sincere. "I'll call, you'll see."

Turning then, I walked back up the aisle and, without realizing it until I sat down, I was crumpling the paper. Sitting there, completely perplexed by the entire incident, I straightened out the piece of paper and was shocked to see there was nothing written on it.

It never ceases to amaze me . . . the games people play.

# 11

As it turned out, the pilot was wrong. We didn't arrive at approximately 4:13, but exactly at 5:02 A.M.

My luggage has never been the first to come down the airport chute. It seems I always have to wait while the more privileged snap up theirs and are on their way long before my bags appear.

While waiting, Maggie O'Donnell, with two other stewardesses, passed through the area, and, even though I was all but directly in her path, she didn't notice me, dare to glance at me, or even take a tiny peek at me. I felt sad, mostly for her. Because what the hell is life all about if two ships that pass in the night can't rub bows. Or wave flags, or at least blink lanterns.

Turning back to the luggage chute, I was bitter when I didn't see my bags. Just then, a tall, handsome black man wearing a gray chauffeur's uniform came up and asked me if I was Lefty Wilson. When I told him I was, he said he had come to meet me. I had always thought of chauffeurs as being really cool guys who knew where it was at. Well-mannered dudes with deep voices and an air of being able to handle anything from a flat tire to a donnybrook all by themselves. Well, this guy was tall, broad, and strong-looking, but a cranky old bastard who looked at me as if I was about to cramp his life-style.

"I didn't expect this!" he grumbled under his breath while we waited.

"You didn't expect what?" I asked.

"You . . . if you must know."

I knew right then he was one of those Uncle Toms who believed that any black person above his station in life was someone to avoid at all costs. Looking at him I told myself that I would con, cajole, and hustle this man until I won him over. Alas, while looking at him with his jaws tight and his mouth pouting, I knew it would be one hell of a task, but I would do it. Somehow, someway, I would do it. Patience, of course, would be the key to success.

When my two bags slid down the ramp, I pointed to them and he took them off, turned, and walked outside without a word. He didn't bother to open the door for me, so I did it myself and stepped into the back seat of the long, sleek, white Continental limousine.

"Did Ace call you?" I asked as we drove onto the Van Wyck Expressway.

"Do you mean Mr. White?" he snorted.

"No, as a matter of fact, I mean just what I said—Ace."

"I think me and you is gonna have some trouble."

"You want to stop the car and walk up into one of those fields?" I asked.

He turned and looked at me, and he was furious.

"Well, answer me," I said. "Do you want to stop and go into a field?"

"I might just do that!" he said.

"Well, if you do, you'll be walking in that grass by yourself," I said and laughed.

He looked at me again, but without the fury.

"You crazy, you know that?"

"*I'm* crazy because I don't want to go up into some damn field with a big dude like you? You're crazy for thinking I'm

60

crazy. You must weigh at least, let's see, two hundred and forty pounds, right?"

"I weigh two fifteen."

"With or without your ass upon your back?"

"My ass ain't up on my back."

"Then you must come from a family of hunchbacks."

"Don't start no shit, boy!"

"How can you hate me and you don't even know me?"

He was silent, but I could hear him huffing.

"I asked you a question."

"I don't have to answer you."

"How can you hate me so much and you don't even know me?"

"I just can't stand you young, brown-skinned, half-educated niggers who think you're better than everybody else, that's all."

"What's your name?" I asked.

"John," he answered gruffly.

"Well, John, I am about to half-educate you. I don't think I'm better than anyone else and that's the God's truth, but I do know, as sure as you and I are sitting here at this moment, that I am as good as anybody, anywhere and anytime, and so are you. And if you're going to go around thinking you're not, then you're an oof-goof, a grau-frau, your feet stink, and you don't love your Jesus."

"You crazy," said John. "You know that? You talk crazy, you act crazy, and you is crazy. You the craziest damn fool I ever saw in my life."

"If you're looking for an argument, John, you'd better get a different subject."

"You crazy."

"I love you, John," I announced, and then rested back and closed my eyes.

Regardless of what anyone tells you, there is no city more exciting, more tantalizing, more entertaining than New York.

Crossing the Fifty-ninth Street bridge, I opened my eyes to

look at the towering and magnificent island of Manhattan from this, the best of all low vantage points. Entering the city, I asked John if we could take a ride, and he nodded his approval. We streaked down the FDR Drive, around the Battery, slanted through Chinatown, Greenwich Village, cruised over on the rich East Side, across Germantown, and up into Harlem.

Driving along 125th Street, I thought about Bessie and made a mental note to call her later.

I was really enjoying the tour, but just as we reached 112th Street and Lenox Avenue, I saw something that ruined the entire ride. Standing there on the corner, leaning and depending on each other, were two young Puerto Rican teen-agers. Their eyes were drooping shut and their bodies, frail and almost lifeless, were draped over each other like worn burlap bags. The girl's tiny, beige fingers, dangling purposelessly down at her side, quivered as if the nerve endings were trying to summon more dope to their tips.

Both kids were obviously heroin addicts.

The boy, who was slightly stronger than the girl, peered directly at me and tried desperately, but in vain, to smile.

It was the longest red light I have ever suffered through.

As the light finally changed, I said, "Please, John, take me home."

# 12

Ace White remained a constant mystery to me in many ways. It was difficult to know what he was thinking at times, and quite often I would be fooled and made to look like a fool (as with the Nigerian princess) because he was so wise in the ways of women, gambling, but especially in the ways of life. But, I've got to tell you, more than anything else, Ace White knew how to live. John drove the limousine up to the garage of this three-story brownstone that was tucked away on Sutton Place and merely honked his horn, and the garage door opened. I assumed that the distinct sound of the horn triggered the opening mechanism, because John just honked once and the door began to open. He just honked once. And when we were inside, the door automatically closed and fluorescent lights, hidden behind the beams in the corners of the ceiling, sprinkled and spreckled and came on to light up the entire garage. Ace White really knew how to live.

This time John opened the car door for me and pointed to the house door that led to the stairway that went up into the living room. I stopped at the head of the stairs and looked around the house, which was much larger than it looked from the outside.

I don't know enough about furnishing to tell you whether the decor was mostly French provincial or whatever, but I can tell you that each piece of furniture was an expensive antique, and everything was polished, clean, and in its proper place.

The main thing that caught my eye was the huge red-brick fireplace covering a large portion of the west wall. I knew that I would lie there when winter came and read before the fires. I would probably have as many meals as possible there, and even sleep there some nights.

"Mr. Wilson?" an elderly, rotund, silver-haired Swedish woman spoke as she came down the black wrought-iron staircase.

"Yes?"

"My name is Hilda. Mr. White telephoned you would be here for breakfast. What would you like?"

"Ahh, just some coffee and toast, please."

"Will that be all?"

"Yes, thank you."

"How would you like your coffee?"

"Cream and honey, please."

"Your toast?"

"Ahh, medium brown."

"I was asking what type of bread would you like, sir?"

"Ahmmmm, egg bread will be fine."

"Where would you like it?"

I looked at her, smiled, and said, "I think I would like it in bed."

"Fine, sir." She didn't blink an eye.

"Just a minute, Hilda," I said, deciding it was time for me to exert myself. "First, I am going to soak in a hot tub for a half hour; run it for me, will you, please? Then I will have the coffee and toast in bed. After that I will sleep until noon at which time you will awake me and have John waiting down at the front door with the limousine . . . *and in gear.* Can you remember all that?"

"I think so, sir," she answered without an inkling of a flinch.

"Good," I said. "Now if you will be so kind as to show me my room, we'll get started."

Needless to say, at twelve noon on the dot, Hilda spoke over the intercom and woke me. "Mr. Wilson, it is twelve noon, sir."

I woke up completely unaware of where I was.

"Mr. Wilson, it is twelve noon."

"Yes, yes, okay, okay."

"Would you like something to eat before you depart, sir?"

"No, no, ahh, Ace, Mr. White suggested a place. Thank you very much."

"Fine, sir."

"Hey. Hey, Hilda," I called, not knowing whether or not she was still listening.

After a pause, she said calmly, "Yes, sir?"

"Is John ready with the car?"

Another long pause and she said, ". . . and in gear, sir."

Schiffron's East is much classier than Schiffron's West because the latter is so Broadwayish. I ate there one time with one of those actors I hustled when I first got into town. I liked Schiffron's East better—I thought.

Sitting at a table directly across the room from me was one of the biggest and ugliest men I had ever seen. He had a red, bulldog face, a hog's nose, beady eyes, and a weird porcupine hairdo. But worst of all he was staring directly at me as if I had shot his dog, burned his house, hung his father, bungholed his brother, and married his daughter. I wasn't positive, but I had a feeling it was Stanislaus Kondorwicz, the man who was after Ace. "Screw him," I said to myself. That's their business.

I won't deny it, my heart skipped time when he rose up and started across the room toward me. I decided to pull a trick I saw Gregory Peck use in the movie *The Gunfighter*. Old Greg put his hands under the table in front of him and bluffed a young gunny into thinking there was a gun pointing at his pecker.

"Is your name Lefty Wilson?" he said, leaning with his burly knuckles on the front edge of my table.

"That's right."

"Well, my name is Stan Kondor," he said proudly and waited for me to show some sign of recognition.

"So what?" I said. "What am I supposed to do now, faint dead away in awe, or do a back flip off the table?"

"I think you should know you're hanging out with the wrong man."

"Who's that?"

"Ace White."

"Don't tell me he's got a contagious disease."

"No, but he may as well have an incurable one, because they're already writing his epitaph."

"Really. What does it say?"

"Here lies Horace Bartlow Whiting, who was killed by Stan Kondor."

"Sounds tough," I said. "You better tell whoever's writing it to start writing another when he's finished."

"I hope it's not going to say what I think you're going to say."

"I don't know. That depends on how optimistic, pessimistic, and realistic you are, Stan."

"I can't wait to hear."

"It's going to say: Here Lies Stanislaus Kondorwicz, who was killed by Ace White's best friend—Lefty Wilson."

"You love that bastard that much?"

"No . . . I need him that much. When I'm through with him, then maybe I'll let you have him. But for the time being, Ace and me are going to be plowing some very rich ground and I don't want no big ugly piles of shit standing in our way."

Stan straightened up and huffed and puffed his chest out.

"Listen, little Lefty, I stand six-foot-four, weigh two hundred and eighty-four pounds, got a thirty-inch waist, and I kick ass with a size thirteen shoe. Now, what have you got to match that?"

"Nothing except for a forty-five under this table to erase all those numbers plus your two-inch pecker."

It scared him. He looked dead into my eyes and said, "You're bluffing."

"I could be, but if you're wrong it'll be too late when you find out, won't it?"

"You'd do this for Ace White?"

"Does Carter have a little liver pill?"

He looked down at the table, then back up at me and said, "Congratulations. You have just received the distinct honor of becoming the number two man on Stan Kondor's shit list."

"That's a coincidence, because Stanislaus Kondorwicz is number two on my shit list, and numbers one, three, and four as well."

Stan took a breath and snickered. "My old man ate fifteen hot dogs and died. But right now I wouldn't bet fifteen hot dogs against a million dollars for Ace White's life . . . or yours, Lefty Wilson."

"Stan, you might find this hard to believe, but I'm no longer amused with you. You've worn out your welcome, you're ugly, and you've got very bad breath."

"Oh, boy," said Stan. "And someone said you were a nice kid, Lefty. They said I should come and talk to you and see if I could save you some trouble. But you've already been taken in by that old bastard and he's going to drag you right down with him. Just remember, Lefty, *I* came to you."

He turned then and walked back past his table and his two henchmen followed him outside. I kept my eyes on the door as they disappeared, and, after a few seconds, John rushed inside and was relieved to see me sitting at the table. It suddenly dawned on me that this entire thing was planned. Ace had sent me there perhaps knowing Stan would be there. And he had told John to watch out for me. Beyond that, I couldn't figure out what the hell was going on.

# 13

Isadore "Some Say" Rodriguez, the half-Puerto Rican, half-Jewish, all-hip Broadway computer, who knew everything about everybody on an hour-to-hour basis, caught me at Thursday's one Wednesday afternoon. Or was it at Friday's one Thursday afternoon? To tell you the truth, I don't really know for sure, because I was so damn busy completing Ace's list and not playing in any card games that I was about to go out of my mind. His "weekend" with the princess over in London had now turned into a ten-day marathon, and I had spent the time being "good" while buying clothes at Meladandri's, having lunch at "21," dinner at the Four Seasons, etc., and so on. The food was sensational, I was dressing as sharp as anyone in town, and I loved New York City more than any other place in the entire world, including Ferno—but here I was playing the rich boy in the jet-set circles, while anxiously waiting for Ace to fly back so we could get into some action.

On the fourth day, Ace called and told me to relax. ". . . you made forty-one thousand dollars last night."

"What are you talking about?" I asked.

"I talked your friend Duxbury and a few other gentlemen

into a friendly game of baccarat last night and they dropped eighty-two thousand. Your share is forty-one."

"Great," I said. "That takes care of my finances, but what about my nerves? Ace, I need some action."

"You can't wait until I get there?"

"Why should I?"

"No special reason except that I'm asking you to. You're my partner, and we agreed that because of my age, I would be the leader of this gang of bandits. But most importantly, we're working our way toward something big, Lefty, and you getting mixed up with the wrong elements could ruin everything."

"What are you talking about, the wrong elements? I grew up playing in penny-ante games, remember?"

"That's right, and if you blow this, you're going to be playing in them the rest of your life. Just keep saying to yourself, 'the Big Biazarro. The Big Biazarro.'"

"What am I supposed to do, Ace, sit here and die of boredom while you're over in London living it up for the sake of the Big Biazarro?"

"What about the list I gave you?"

"I'll be finished with that list tomorrow. Will you be here tomorrow?"

"I might be."

"*I* doubt it."

"What we're talking about is a lot more important than your doubts, Lefty."

"What I'm talking about is you getting back here so we can start doing something important."

"Trust me. I'll be back."

"You'd better make it soon."

"I will, I will," he said. "Oh, by the way, you've been handling yourself pretty good around town. I'm proud of you."

"Don't hustle me, Ace. Just get back here, or I'm dealing myself a lone hand."

"Don't be stupid, kid."

"I'm not stupid. I've made it this far, and—"

"I know, I know," said Ace. "All right, I'll wind things up here and grab the next plane."

On the sixth day, Ace was still in London, and I had completed the list and was sitting around reading and practicing dealing in front of a mirror. For obvious reasons, I decided to give Bessie Mae Poindexter a call.

"Hello."

"Hi. You'll never guess who this is," I said.

"I don't even give a damn. How does that grab you?" she answered.

"This is your lover man."

"Who the hell is this?"

"It's Lefty, baby."

CLICK! Brrrrrrrrrrrrrr . . .

"Bessie. Bessie! Bessie?"

I dialed the number again and she let it ring a half-dozen times without answering it. I finally hung up and went reluctantly back to the book I was reading.

Returning home that night from a late dinner at O'Henry's, I found a fantastic surprise lying asleep in my bed. It was Bessie, and when I crawled in beside her, she turned and enveloped me into that huge, clean, warm valley of arms, legs, and breasts and I went for another joyous ride on the Pullman car.

"Oh, Bessie," I cried softly, and she just lay there and held me so tightly and kept right on grooving and humping, and humming into my ear.

There was something exclusive and original about the way Bessie moved. She had a rhythm all her own. And I don't mean that same old cliché about Black Soul rhythm. I'm talking about that special Poindexter rhythm. It was sort of a syncopated blues movement. Not the "St. Louis Blues," or even a down-home blues. It was more like a "Don't bother me now, blues, cause I'm trying to get it on."

Bessie was strong. Stronger than me. Strong as an Amazon,

but what a warm, sensitive lover. She flip-flopped me. Turned us over without letting me go or missing a beat.

"Oh, shit, Bessie," I cried. "Where am I now?"

"You're on the bottom, baby. Just relax and let me do it all."

"Yes, ma'am."

I can't tell you how long we made love, but I remember the ecstasy of it all, and I don't recall how long we did it before I fell fast asleep.

When I awoke the next morning, Bessie was gone.

I swear, if God made a better lover than Bessie Mae Poindexter he must have kept her for himself.

That was the sixth day, so naturally I rested on the seventh.

On the tenth day, Ace White was still in London, and that is when I ran into Izzie Rodriguez. Izzie's information was always exact, so depending upon how badly you wanted to know something, and how thoroughly, would depend on how large a bill you handed him when he walked up. I always gave Izzie a C-note.

"What's happening, Lefty?" he asked.

"Not bad, Izz. How goes it with you?"

"Oh, just slipping and sliding, creeping and hiding. Some say you won enough money over in foggy town to buy up the crown jewels."

"Not quite."

While we were talking, the extremely thin, fuzzy-haired smiler was meticulously creasing and bending the hundred dollar bill into a tiny square fold, which, when completed, he deposited into a secret pocket somewhere inside his suede jacket.

Clapping his hands together, he asked, "What can I help you with?"

"Tell me about Ace White."

"He was born 1914 in London, England. His father was killed in the Great World War One. Some say he was shot down by Richtofen in a Sopwith Camel. Others say it was in a

Nieuport by some second lieutenant named Heppole, who was killed the same day. I guess it depends on how romantic you are, which version you prefer. His mother was supposed to be a fabulous beauty turned alcoholic because she couldn't handle the loss. She died in 1923. Ace was eight years old at the time, and his brother was seven, and they went to live with his uncle in South Africa. Uncle Randolph Tillotson, his mother's brother. Some say he was the meanest man to ever own and run a diamond mine. They say he killed at least a thousand blacks during his reign. And from all reports, he wasn't much better to Ace. Used to lock the little dude up in a closet for being bad. Ace would sit there with a deck of cards and play games to keep from cracking up. He obviously made good use of the time. Probably sat there hating his uncle and dealing seconds from the deck."

"Has he ever been married?"

"Yes. To a fantastic, beautiful American woman named Elizabeth Smith Collins. That's how he got his citizenship. She died of pneumonia in 1958. Some say they had been walking in the rain in Central Park. She hadn't told Ace she had had a history of pneumonia. She wanted the moment. That twenty minutes or so of walking hand in hand in the rain. It broke Ace's heart. Especially when he found out she was three months pregnant."

"How rich is he?"

"His uncle left him that diamond mine for starters. He owns Schiffron's East and West."

"I didn't know that."

"Now you do. And who knows what else he's got."

"Would you like something to eat?" I asked.

"Just a quick cup of coffee."

"Waitress," I called.

After giving the waitress an order of coffee for Izzie and a chef's salad for myself, I asked the Computer, "Why does he like me?"

"I don't know, but he paid me five thousand dollars six

months ago to send him all the information I could learn about you. It seems people have been talking about you for a few years now. About how you never lose in a poker game, and about how nice you are. And comical. Then there is the old bullshit line about every man wanting a son, but I don't think Ace would want you for a son. You're a little bit too square for him. He'd probably want a son who had at least a Ph.D. from Harvard."

"You're not calling me an idiot, are you?"

"Of course not. But let's face it, Lefty, there are a lot of guys who are sharper than you, and definitely hipper. I mean, coming out of Ferno! That town is filled with apple-knockers and migrant workers and—"

"Come on, Izzie, quit beating around the bush. What is it?"

Izzie took a breath, sipped his coffee, and said soberly, "I can only guess, Lefty, and I hate guessing at anything."

"Go on."

"Well, Ace has never played in the Big Biazarro. He's been invited, of course, but he hasn't played."

"What's the reason?" I asked anxiously.

Izzie stared at me, reached into his secret pocket, took out the C-note, and handed it back.

"What's this?"

"I don't want to say any more."

"Are you trying to hustle me, Izzie?"

"I'm not a hustler, Lefty, and you know it."

"Then why won't you tell me?"

After a pause, Izzie said, "Because I'm not sure and I don't want to say something like that unless I'm sure."

"Say something like what?"

"Have you ever asked Ace?"

Lowering my head, and remembering what happened when I had asked, I said, "Yes, I asked him and then withdrew the question."

"Why don't you try to figure it out yourself?"

"I started to one day, and when certain thoughts came to my mind, I chickened out."

"I wouldn't want to tell you anything unless I was sure, you understand?" said Izzie.

"Yes," I said, and handed him the C-note with another one folded around it. "What else you got?"

"There's a chick running around town bad-mouthing you. Do you know about it?" he asked.

"I've been expecting it."

"No one's paying her any attention, but she says you're a fucked person."

"She's right," I said, and smiled thinking of Angel DuPont.

"What did you do, leave her stranded somewhere?"

"No. I made her an offer I couldn't deliver."

"Well, anyway, there's a game tonight over at Cadillac Gene's on West Fifty-sixth Street and she'll be there. She's been doing a number with Saint Laureate."

"Who's he?"

"He's a writer. Unpublished, but he's working on it. He's doing his father's autobiography," said Izzie, and waited for a question. "Aren't you interested in who his father is?"

"Should I be?"

"Yeh, I think so . . . seeing that he's a Poker Master."

"Will he be there tonight?" I asked, barely able to wait for an answer.

"No chance," said Izzie. "At best this is going to be a fifty dollar buy-in. Besides, he lives down in the Virgin Islands. Some say he's got a castle down there."

"I wouldn't mind owning a castle," I said and looked at Izzie for a reaction.

Izzie laughed and nodded. "I wouldn't bet against you getting it. That's for sure."

"Tell me, what's with Stan Kondor?"

"He's a mean sonofabitch. Saw him kick a girl's brains out last week on Ninth Avenue. He's into a lot of shit. Pushes; got

74

a few Eighth Avenue whores, and buys and sells anything he can get his hands on."

"Is he really after Ace?"

"He says he is, but everybody knows that if he wanted to get Ace as bad as he says he does, he would have at least tried by now."

"What do you think?"

"My guess is, he's building his reputation selling wolf tickets about what he's going to do to Ace, but from what I hear, old Ace White can take care of himself in a fight."

"But do you think Stan's going to wake up some morning and come after him?"

"No. I don't think he's that crazy."

"What do you think then?"

Izzie sipped his coffee and looked at me over the cup.

"My guess is," said Izzie, "that he's going to get you."

"Me?" I said, and looked at Izzie and saw that he wasn't kidding. There was honesty in his eyes and a bit of concern, as if he had already heard something to that effect.

"When is it coming?" I asked.

Izzie looked around and in back of him for the first time since sitting down. Then he leaned forward and whispered, "He knows how Ace feels about you. He figures you're the easier target. Be careful, Lefty."

Izzie got up then and walked away.

# 14

Cadillac Gene had a "mean machine" and everyone who had spent any time at all along Broadway had seen it. It was a violet and gold "LD" (Cadillac Eldorado) that had everything in it. Everything from a small color television set below the dash to a vibrating back seat.

His full name was Gene Van Mean. He had dropped the final "s" on his last name because no one had bothered to use it in years.

I had first met the infamous black pimp one summer when he came up to Ferno with four of his most gorgeous girls. During the months of July and August, Gene had dropped over ten grand at the tables, but his girls had picked up over twenty grand in the houses.

Need I say, those chicks could *turrrrn* some tricks!

Cadillac Gene loved his automobile. I had no idea how deeply involved he was with it until I won it playing deuces-wild poker at his apartment on West Fifty-sixth Street.

Izzie had guessed right. It was a minimum fifty dollar buy-in, and I had arrived ahead of everyone else, so Gene and I started to play a game of head-up five hundred rummy.

Before leaving the brownstone and going to the game, John and I had an argument. He called me all kinds of funny and vicious names and said he didn't understand why Mr. White wanted to be bothered with me for anyway.

"You don't have to drive me around," I said. "There's cabs all over this city waiting for fares like me."

"I do what I'm told," said John.

"All right, then I'm telling you to take the night off. Take the week off! I don't want you anymore. I don't need you anymore. I'll rent a car and drive it myself."

"You know Mr. White don't want you goin' to them places."

"I go where I want to go!"

"Mr. White told me—"

"I don't give a damn what Mr. White told you! I don't want you with me anymore."

"Mr. White don't want you goin' to no damn poka game. You know this! Why you want to do it?"

"Because I'm tired of sitting around this house, sitting around coffee shops and restaurants and waiting for Mr. White to get tired of balling and come back here. And I'm tired of you looking at me as if I'm screwing your wife behind your back. I don't need Ace White. I've made it this far without him. I can go all the way. And I sure don't need *you,* so just get off my back!"

I slammed the door as I left the brownstone, went over to First Avenue, and caught a cab to Cadillac Gene's building.

Gene's apartment was decorated in bright red and white, richly furnished, and professionally designed. The money he didn't lose at gambling was obviously put to some good use. But he was a loser when it came to cards. By the time the other players arrived, Gene had already lost sixty-eight hundred dollars to me in our rummy game.

"You sure are lucky at cards, Lefty," said Gene.

"Come on, Gene, quit kidding yourself. It's not luck, it's

skill and stupidity. My skill, and your stupidity for playing against me at a dollar a point."

"Shit, if you hadn't been catching all those fifteen point aces, it would have been different."

"Probably. I would have won sixty-five instead of sixty-eight hundred."

"Lefty, come on, man, cards have a lot to do with it. The cards were against me tonight. I bet I get you in the poker game."

"How much?" I asked.

"What do you mean?"

"Do you want to make a side bet you don't win more than I do in the poker game?"

Gene thought about it for a moment, probably looking for a way out, and finally said, "Well, if it was just you and me in a head-up game, I'd take the bet, but seeing that there's going to be other dudes playing, I don't have any control."

"Gene, you just gave me sixty-eight hundred dollars in a game where you *had* control. What happened?"

"I told you, man, the aces were killing me!"

"Don't blame it all on the poor little aces," I said. "All the cards were killing you?"

Gene stared at me skeptically and said, "Why you being so hard, Lefty. Lightin' up."

"I'm not being hard, Gene. I just want you to see the trees and the forest."

"You're bursting my bubbles, Lefty. You're turning my dreams into harsh realities, baby. Let me dream. If I want to delude myself into believing that I can someday beat the great Lefty Wilson, let me dream. It don't hurt nobody, does it?"

I lowered my eyes and shook my head in agreement. Just then the doorbell rang as the other players arrived.

The first person I saw was Angel, pretty as ever, hugged up tight to the tall, blond, blue-eyed, quiet Saint Laureate. Angel refused to look at me.

The third person to come in the door was Gatsby Brown, a

78

foul-mouthed, super-fly, second-story man from Brooklyn. Following him was Fast Eddy Youngblade, a freckled-faced, tow-head boy who had left the skin games of Georgia and arrived in the big city to make his fortune. A year before, Fast Eddy had a serious problem. He was so excited about playing in the New York games that every time he had a good hand, full house, four of a kind, etc., his nose would turn a blood red. Needless to say, Fast Eddy didn't do too well when he first got to the big city. Somehow, he had learned to control it, and was a good enough card player to recoup most of what he had lost during his Rudolph phase.

Big Manny Robertson was our sixth player. Manny's claim to fame, besides being a good, nervy poker player, was that he had played fullback for Grambling College back in 1969 and was the tenth or eleventh leading ground-gainer in the country —so he said.

"My main man, Lefty!" shouted Gatsby "Gats" Brown as he came over to the table and slapped my outstretched palm. "Baby, I heard you won enough money over in London to stick it to the Queen."

"Not quite," I said, and shook hands with Big Manny, who tried to make pulp of my fingers.

"Wow," said Fast Eddy. "If I had known the champ was going to be here, I could have gotten some big rollers to come."

"Never mind," said Gene bitterly. "This is my game. I invite who *I* want, not who *you* want."

"How many mothafuckas you got comin' to this game?" asked Gats.

"Watch your language, man, there's a lady present," said Manny, nodding and smiling toward Angel, who ignored him while she leaned heavily on Saint Laureate's shoulder.

"What you talkin' 'bout?" Gats asked.

Manny nodded toward Angel again.

"Oh," said Gats. "But shit, she looks like she knows where it's at. Don't you, baby?"

"Say what you want," said Saint Laureate.

"See what I mean," said Gats. And then turning to Cadillac Gene, he asked, "How many persons dos' thou have appearin' in your abode tonight . . . Sir Gene Van Mean?"

"This is it," said Gene simply.

"What?" Fast Eddy exclaimed. "This does not make sense. Suppose somebody drops out?"

"Can't you count?" asked Gene. "Somebody drops out, we got five. The way I figure it, it's ten o'clock now, by twelve it's gonna be just me and Lefty anyway."

"The day I can't outplay you, Gene, I'll kiss your black ass in Times Square on New Year's Eve," said Gats, "and you *know* how many cats are there on New Year's Eve."

"Let us play," said Fast Eddy, and Gene began to sell the chips.

The game was a fifty dollar buy-in and the deuces were wild. No table stakes—which meant you had to cover every bet or you're out of the hand. It was dealer's choice, and five-card stud, five-card draw, and seven-card stud were the hands being dealt.

It is my opinion that wild cards have no place in poker. It is *not* real poker. As opposed to other games, there are only two things exciting in a deuces-wild game: a tremendous amount of bluffing goes on; and if you get a couple of deuces with something like a high pair for four of a kind, or three to a suit for a straight flush, you can bet your ass off, because eight out of ten times, you've got the best hand at the table.

We were two hours into the game and I was thoroughly enjoying the fact that I was playing again, even though it was a low-grade game in every way. To this point, Saint Laureate was the only big loser. While he was shuffling the cards for a new game, I looked at Angel, who was leaning on his shoulder, and said to Saint, "Who's the broad?"

"Watch your mouth, Lefty," Angel snapped at me. "I ain't no broad!"

Saint told her to cool it and she obeyed, but stared daggers at me.

"Have I had the pleasure of your acquaintance, miss?" I asked.

"You're going to have the displeasure of my foot in your teeth if you don't lay off."

Once again, Saint told her to cool it, more firmly this time. Losing badly, he didn't need this aggravation.

Saint dealt a hand of seven-card stud and I had nothing in the hole, so I folded. Fast Eddy Youngblade ended up head and head with Saint, and Fast Eddy beat his full house with a straight flush. Saint had dropped the nine hundred he had brought with him. He sat silently with his head down, trying to guess who to make the hit on. He chose Cadillac Gene.

"What you got on you, baby?" Gene asked.

Saint unstrapped his watch, an expensive Omega, and handed it to him.

"How much you expect for this?" Cadillac asked, examining the timepiece.

"It cost me a grand," said Saint.

"A grand what?" Gene asked, and the other players laughed.

"A grand four dollars and ninety-five cents," said Manny Robertson, and everyone laughed, including Saint.

"I'll give you a break," said Gene to Saint. "I'll give you a hundred."

"A hundred!" Saint complained.

"Look, man, you ain't selling it to me, right? You're just hocking it. Take it or leave it."

Saint looked around the table and asked, "Anybody want to up the offer?"

"I'll lower it," said Gene, "if you don't hurry up and take it."

Saint took the hundred dollars, and Fast Eddy placed the deck in front of him to cut.

I continued to look at Angel and asked, "Are you sure we

81

haven't met somewhere? You look awfully familiar. Same sweet face. Same shapely, slender body. Was it Paris? Tangiers, maybe? Casablanca perhaps?"

"Why don't you try the Belgian Congo?" Angel snapped and it made the racially mixed group a bit uneasy. There were three whites there, Saint, Angel, and Fast Eddy, and even though we weren't an overly sensitive, up-tight group, quite often a losing player, black or white, will use a statement like that to start an argument as a way of relieving the frustrations of losing.

But this was a friendly group, and I believe almost anything could have been said without starting a hassle.

"Hey, Angel," Saint shouted bitterly, "knock it off, will you?"

"Why doesn't he lay off me?"

"He'd probably rather lay on you," said Gats.

"Not on my table," Gene chuckled.

Saint looked at me in a weird way for a moment, and then went back to his hand.

"I met a girl like you in the South of France," I said to Angel. "Nice girl. Had a lot of fun with her. Said she wanted to be my buddy. I wish I could meet that girl again. She was beautiful, but not quite as thin as you are."

"Hey, Lefty, what in the fuck are you talking about?" Gene asked.

"Nothing. I'm just going through one of *my* dreams."

"Well, save it for later, will you? We're trying to play poker."

It took just four hands for Saint to lose the hundred dollars he got for the watch. And once again he was looking around the table for another loan.

"Manny . . . ?" Saint said.

"I don't have anything, Saint. My rent's due."

Gats Brown threw up his hands and said, "My goddamn car payments are overdue."

"Saint," said Fast Eddy, "if I had it, you know you could

get it, but my old lady gave me just enough to play with. Besides, I must split soon."

"Me, too," said Gats.

Saint then turned to me.

"I don't even know you," I said.

"Don't ask him for anything," Angel snapped bitterly.

"Shut up, Angel," he yelled at her.

Angel leaned up off his shoulder for the first time since he sat.

"I need money, Lefty. My luck will change," said Saint.

"I told you, I don't know you. We just met tonight. For all I know, your bags could be packed and waiting for you at the airport."

"I'm not asking for something for nothing. I've got something you want."

"I doubt it."

"For a hundred bucks, I'll let you take Angel in the bedroom there."

The room fell so quiet at that moment you could hear a flea tap-dancing on cotton. Everyone had their eyes on Angel, and then to Saint, and then back to Angel.

"Damn, Saint," Gene uttered to break the silence. "If you wanted to do something like that, baby, you and me could have talked one hell of a good deal."

"I was going to, but since I'm broke, I've got to make a deal with Lefty."

Staring at Angel, I asked, "What's the deal?"

"A hundred bucks. Take her in the room."

"Shit, Saint," said Gats. "I didn't know you were going back into the pimping business."

"You didn't say you were in it before," Angel said, surprised at this revelation.

"It doesn't matter what I did before. You said you would do it if you had to. Well, right now, you have to. Now either you do it, or get out of my life."

"Do not sugar-coat it, Saint," said Fast Eddy. "Hit her with it hard. Let her know who is boss."

"You guys mind your own business," Saint said, and then, without looking at Angel, he asked, "Well, baby, what's it going to be . . . a trick or me?"

Angel and I were staring at each other all this time, and I finally lowered my eyes. When I looked back at her, she had gotten up and was starting into the bedroom.

"I hope you keep losing," said Gats to Saint, "'cause I'd like to tear up some of that pussy myself."

I hesitated a moment, and then looked at Saint.

"It doesn't bother you, does it?"

"Why should it?" he answered honestly in his constant soft voice.

"Don't you care about her at all?"

"Evidently not the way you do," said Saint. "I wouldn't pay a nickel to fuck her."

I felt a sudden rage swell up in me, almost as if I wanted to tear his head off at the shoulders. Trying to calm myself, I lifted two blue fifty dollar chips and threw them over in front of him.

"Thanks," he said, and then turning to Gene, "Let's play cards."

# 15

Walking into the bedroom and closing the door, I saw Angel stepping from her dress and leaving her gorgeous, shapely body clad only in her yellow bikini panties. As she stuck her thumbs under the elastic band to pull them down, I said, "Don't bother," and walked over to the window.

"Why not?" Angel asked, as if a bit insulted.

I smiled and said, "I'm all layed-out . . . remember?"

She shrugged and propped a pillow up against the wood-carved headboard and sat there with one foot on the carpet and one on the bed, with her legs spread. Brushing her long, auburn-colored hair back from her forehead, she stared directly at the bedroom door.

"It doesn't have to be this way, you know," I said softly.

Angel ignored me, got up, and clicked off the lights, leaving the room in complete darkness except for a dull beam coming in the window from a streetlamp. Returning to the bed, she took up her original position.

After a silent moment, I repeated, "It doesn't have to be this way, you know."

"What have you got against whores?"

"Nothing, but you just aren't cut out for it."

"You don't think I can hack it, huh?"

"Frankly, no."

"You got any better ideas?"

"Anything but this."

"Well, how about us being gambler partners?" she asked.

"You know we can't do that."

"You don't want me and you don't want anybody else to have me, right, Lefty?"

I took a moment before answering, and in that moment a loud roar of thunder echoed across the Manhattan sky, giving fair warning of what was to come.

"I thought we were buddies," I said, aware of the kind of answer I would receive.

"Buddies, my ass! You killed any friendship we had when you dropped me for that old fart, remember?"

"You know what Saint's going to do for you, Angel—use you, take your money, and kick you out!"

"So, what makes you think you're so goddamn righteous? Who in the hell are you to tell me what I should or shouldn't do?"

"I don't know. I guess by some ridiculous stretch of my imagination I thought we were friends."

"I told you about our friendship. It's dead!"

"Is that the way you really want it?"

"Yes," she snapped and turned away.

"I don't think so," I said just as another rumble of thunder ran across the sky and large, heavy drops of rain began to tap, tap, tap on the window pane next to my face.

I walked over to the bed then, and when I attempted to touch her, Angel scooted over and shouted, "Come on, let's get it over with so you can get back to your damn poker game. That's all you care about, anyway."

As I sat on the edge of the bed, tears broke and ran down Angel's cheeks. And when I touched the soft velvetness of her thighs, she immediately brushed my hand away.

"It isn't that I want you, Lefty. It's just that I don't have anybody. I just drift around from man to man. I'm beautiful, I'm sexy, and I'm unhappy."

"You've got to try and get your head straight, Angel. Why don't you take some classes, or something?"

"I hate school," she snapped at me. "I've always hated school."

"Then why don't you go home for a while and think things out?"

"Fuck home! Fuck the whole state of Delaware," Angel said, and began to cry aloud.

When I handed her my handkerchief, she took it, dried her eyes, and blew her nose. She was trying, but all in vain, to calm herself, because all too soon the tears came again, and she cried out, "I love him! I must love him, or why else? Why else . . . ?"

"It's all right, baby," I said, and patted her leg.

She was trying, once again, to gain control. Trying desperately this time, and I felt she would succeed. Reaching down, she placed her hand on mine, closed her eyes, and then grimaced while gripping my hand as hard as she could.

Finally, Angel was there—in control of herself. Turning to me, she forced a smile, said, "I'm all right now," and slid down on the bed, stretching out. Pulling me over, she whispered, "Let's do it. If I don't, he'll kick me out."

She kissed me then. A long, full, passionate kiss, and it was good. As we parted, she placed her hands on my face and said, "You're so sweet, Lefty."

Frowning in despair, I held Angel close to me and said, "What kind of a practical joke is God playing on us—throwing us together like this without giving us the love we need to really dig each other? What number is he doing?" Burying my lips into Angel's silky auburn hair, I whispered that I was sorry. We kissed then—just as a loud roar of thunder echoed overhead. I kissed her cheek, her ear, and slid down to her neck—just as a bright streak of lightning zigzagged across the midnight sky and lit up the room and the entire island of Manhattan.

Pressing my lips against her young, satiny shoulder and moving, I arrived at one of her breasts and tasted the tiny pink nipple. The flavor was utterly delicious. The warmth and softness of Angel's body was divine, and her fragrance was childlike.

Angel cried out with pleasure as I attempted to suck her entire breast up into my mouth.

Suddenly, she held me away and snatched off her panties. She then reached up and began to unbutton my shirt. I grabbed her hands to stop her.

"What's wrong?" she asked anxiously.

"I can't do it—if it's for him."

Angel stared at me, directly into my eyes as if she couldn't comprehend what I had said. And then, frowning sadly, she lowered her eyes, and dropped her hands.

"Leave him."

"What for?" she asked.

"For yourself."

Angel was sad now. "Why don't you stop trying to be a savior, Lefty. Even God can't save this world. It's too late, don't you know that? It seems the only thing left for me is a little pleasure every now and then, but a hell of a lot of pain."

"It doesn't have to be that way."

"Maybe not for you."

"For you either."

"Bullshit!"

"You know, Angel, you bring a lot of this on yourself."

"You don't make it any easier. You broke my heart in Cannes, and now you've put me in a position where I've got to be a whore."

"I didn't put you in this room; *he* did!"

"Didn't you just hand him a hundred dollars?"

"Yes, but . . ."

"You're a loser, Lefty. No matter how much money you

88

win, you're going to come up on the shitty end of the stick tonight, I guarantee it."

I grimaced at that moment, not knowing how I had put myself into that position, or whether I was right or wrong. I
hadn't paid Saint the C-note to make love to Angel, I just
wanted to be alone with her. To talk to her.

"God, I hope I never, ever see you again," Angel said and
turned her back on me. "Please leave me alone. I want to take
a nap now."

Hesitating, I tried desperately to summon up something
constructive to say. Nothing came—so I dried my eyes,
straightened my clothes, and started for the door.

# 16

With a pain in my heart, bitterness in my soul, and larceny on my mind, I entered the smoke-filled room where the poker game was still in progress and I stared directly at Saint Laureate.

"How was she?" he asked.

I ignored him and looked around the table. Gats Brown and Fast Eddy were gone. Sitting there with Saint was Manny Robertson, and Cadillac Gene with one of his tainted painted whores leaning on his shoulder.

Taking a seat, I noticed that Saint Laureate's luck had changed. He now had approximately three thousand dollars in front of him. Gene was also sitting heavy. My eyes darted from one pimp to the other. Both Gene and Saint stared at me, wondering why I was so angry. Turning to Manny, I said, "How you doing?"

"I'm down about two hundred."

"Cash out."

Without hesitating, and knowing exactly what I had in mind, Manny counted up his chips and pushed them over to Gene, who accepted them but kept a wary eye on me.

As Cadillac handed him the money for his chips, I tossed Manny three C-notes. He said thanks, and asked if I would mind if he stayed around.

"Suit yourself. Whose deal is it?"

"It's mine," said Saint, and shuffled the cards.

Cadillac Gene wanted to know what I had my ass up on my back about.

"I can't stand the rain," I said coldly, and cut the deck Saint placed down in front of me. I peered at Saint, and then again at Cadillac, and then at the white hooker who leaned on his shoulder. She *was* a whore. Born to be a whore. She had thin, chalky white skin with a few useless freckles dotting her wide nose that some roughish pimp had decided to flatten one night. She had slivers for lips with an excess of tomato-red lipstick trying to make them look larger and sensual. She also had white eye shadow above and below her eyes, and it made her look even more like a sick ghost.

Becoming uneasy at the way I was staring at her, she sort of hid her face behind Cadillac Gene's large Afro.

"Seven-card stud," said Saint as he began to deal the cards. I had caught three bad cards, so I folded. Saint also folded and, while tossing the deck to Gene, said, "I heard you were a square, Lefty, but broads like Angel are a dime a dozen. You ever been out in the Midwest? They breed them out there like they do cattle. Every farmhouse has at least two."

Gene laughed, and told Saint to cut the cards.

He cut the deck and continued, "They raise them square just like you. Square and pretty and ripe and dumb, so that men like me and Cadillac won't have to work so hard when they come here. We just tell them how fucking stupid they are, and how badly they need us, and the next thing you know they're out there turning tricks with suckers like you and bringing the money home to us."

"Every penny of it," Gene said, and patted the girl's hand on his shoulder.

"Angel's no different," Saint explained in that soft, malicious voice of his. "All she needed to feel was that I needed her."

"That's all they need," Gene concurred.

"I know about you and Angel over in France. She said there wasn't anything to it. Said you were just a down-town, small-town chump who was lucky enough to be picked up by Ace White, otherwise you'd still be playing penny-ante games up in that pigsty called Ferno."

Gene and the whore laughed. I looked up at her and she kept smiling, but once again hid her face behind Gene's head.

"If it's any consolation to you," Saint said, "you were the first john. But you can bet your sweet Jesus you won't be the last. I'm going to work that little bitch's ass off. She's going to be turning tricks day and night, weekends and holidays. And then when she gets a little older, maybe I'll give her to you. Since you love her so much, you won't mind if she's a little . . . tired."

"Saint," Manny Robertson said and leaned down across the table directly into his face, "would you like a good ass-whipping?"

Saint looked up at the massive Manny, saw the fury in his eyes, and shook his head.

"Then shut your goddamn mouth and play cards."

Cadillac was laughing as he tossed the deck to me. I lifted the deck and began to shuffle.

"Come on, Manny," said Gene. "You know Saint's just trying to shake the champ up. Rile him to see if he can stand the pressure. Ain't that right, Saint?"

Saint and I looked at each other without a word.

"Besides," said Gene, "he ain't doing nothing but telling the truth. These bitches come here thinking they've got the world between their sweet legs, and they're right, but they don't know what to do with it until we show them."

For the next two hours, Saint kept dropping an occasional snide remark at me. He and Gene were angling with their betting, refusing to bet much against each other while sandbagging me in between the two of them every chance they got.

"She didn't know a damn thing when I got her," Saint continued. "Had to teach her how to say 'tu-tu twain,' that's how young and stupid she was."

The cards were really running bad for me, so I was dropping out almost every hand. Only occasionally would Gene and Saint go against each other, and when they did, it wasn't all out. They were waiting to catch me in a big hand, not knowing I was waiting for exactly the same thing.

It was nearing two-thirty when Saint Laureate decided to buy his Omega back from Cadillac Gene. I was about twelve hundred dollars down, and Saint and Gene were snickering, sipping scotch, and bragging about being pimps.

"Any chick who won't work to keep her man looking good and feeling good ain't worth her salt," Saint declared.

"She ain't worth shit," said Cadillac Gene as he tossed me the deck and kissed the ugly hooker.

"I think we're going to break you tonight, Lefty," Saint announced, and chuckled. "Me and Cadillac here are going to stop you tonight and then *we'll* go to the Big Biazarro."

Cadillac Gene laughed aloud and threw his head. The girl took this moment to kiss his cheek.

"Wouldn't that be something," Gene shouted, "if Ace White's little machine went broke?"

As Saint and Gene continued to laugh, I looked directly at Gene and said coldly, "Why don't you get your rotten teeth fixed?"

Gene, whose teeth were crooked and discolored, reached instantly inside his coat. He stopped, took a quick peek at Manny, and then chuckled, pulling out his empty hand.

"Don't you talk to my man like that!" the girl screamed across the table.

"You need iron tablets, baby," I said, and placed the deck down for Gene to cut.

"Seven-card," I said, and began to deal. I caught two wild-card deuces in the hole and decided instantly that this would be the hand.

The first bet was fifty dollars and we all called.

Peeling off the cards, I caught a fourth-card ace.

"Your bet, champ," said Saint.

I bet a hundred. Saint raised five hundred, and Gene topped the bet off with a thousand raise.

It was on the fifth card, I learned later, that they had both caught straight flushes. I caught a four of spades to go with my seven and ace up. The two pimps began to snicker aloud now, like jackals circling a baby gazelle and waiting for night to come.

"Your bet, big ace," Saint said, while counting up his chips to make a large raise.

"I'll check," I said, and they laughed again.

"You get your checks at the bank, Lefty," said Saint, and dropped two thousand dollars into the pot.

"I'm going all in," said Gene. He counted his chips, which came to a total of two thousand, seven hundred and fifty dollars, and then shoved them all into the pot. I called the bet.

Saint now turned from me and was staring skeptically at Gene and his cards. He felt Gene was his only stiff competition in this hand.

Saint counted what he had left and it came to one thousand, four hundred. He dropped it into the pot. Gene wrote an IOU for the six hundred and fifty dollar raise. I called and dealt the sixth card. They already had their hands, and both were easy straight flushes with a wild card in the hole. Gene's was diamonds and to the queen; Saint was in clubs and to the jack. I caught a seven, which gave me a pair up.

Cadillac Gene and Saint were eying each other cautiously now, while both were keeping one eye not on me but on the deck. We all checked the sixth card, and I dealt the seventh.

"It's my bet," I announced, and they looked down at my cards, and then frowned as if I was interfering and wasting time.

Using cash, I threw ten one-thousand dollar bills into the pot. In unison, the two pimps turned slowly and looked at me as if I had gone completely crazy.

Calmly I said, "Do you call or pass?"

Saint stared at me, looked down at my sevens, and then, turning to Gene, he asked, "Did you cut those cards?"

"Of course, I cut the cards."

"Either bet or fold," I said.

Saint took a piece of paper from the tablet and wrote a ten thousand dollar IOU and tossed it into the pot.

"What have you got to back up that paper?" I asked.

"I've got a Porsche downstairs," said Saint, and dangled the keys in front of my face.

"Pick up the paper and drop the keys," I said; and he did it.

Cadillac Gene then lifted the keys to his LD and dropped them in the pot. I smiled for the first time since before Saint offered Angel to me. I smiled and chuckled and felt good. Saint and Gene turned over their straight flushes and I waited and let them suffer while I peeked at my last card, knowing exactly what it was—the third seven to go with my two deuces.

"Five sevens!" Cadillac shouted in disbelief.

Saint Laureate had his head down, buried in the palms of his hands. Hoping, probably, he had read my cards wrong.

"Five sevens!" Gene said again and lifted my cards to make sure.

I lifted the keys to the Porsche and tossed them to Manny.

"Give me the bank," I said to Gene, and he reached into the kitty can without taking his eyes off of the sevens and handed me the roll.

"Five sevens!"

Saint Laureate finally raised up and he had tears in his eyes and his face was drained of blood.

"You owe this chump, this square, this sucker, more than ten thousand dollars, and I don't want you to ever forget it," I said.

"What about my car?" he asked.

"Manny's got the keys. Tomorrow morning, if you don't give him the money, all of it, he's going to sell it, and whatever he gets for it will be deducted from what you owe me. But you owe me MONEY! Money . . . and a lot more than you're worth."

I picked up my cash, the keys to Gene's Cadillac, and started toward the door.

"Hey, Lefty," Gene called. "Hey, brother, you ain't really going to take my 'sheen,' are you?"

Taking a deep breath, I explained, "I've got to, Gene. I took a taxi here, and cabs are tough to get this time of morning. I'll take good care of it. When you get the money, you can pick it up."

"Hey, baby, wait a minute," he said and stood. "Please, Lefty, I need my sheen to work with, you understand. I mean if I ain't got it in the morning, the word gets around, my name's gonna be nothin', you understand."

"I'm sorry, Gene, you should have thought about that before you bet it."

"I know, but . . . five sevens!"

"It can only happen in a wild-card game. From now on you'd better stick to straight stud."

"Lefty, please," Cadillac Gene pleaded with outstretched palms. "I ain't never done nothing bad to you."

"You were going to pull your gun on me, Gene."

"Swear to God, I wasn't. I wouldn't shoot you. There's a heap of cats I'd shoot before I'd even think of shooting you, Lefty. I swear I never meant you no harm. Now, tell the truth, when have I ever done any wrong to you?"

"You laughed at me tonight. When your boy, Saint there, was cracking on me, you laughed and thought I was a joke."

"Never! I swear on my life, I never took you for a joke. You're the best poker player I've ever seen. You're the king, the king of sharks. Hell, man, if you don't take the Big Biazarro, nobody can. Ain't that right, Saint?"

Gene, the girl, Manny, and I all turned and looked at Saint.

96

He sat at the table, and once again was burying his face in his hands.

"Tell him, Saint!" Gene shouted, and caused Saint to look up.

"Tell him what?" he said, almost incoherently.

"Tell the man how goddamn good he is at poker."

"What for?" Saint said, and lowered his head. Gene snatched him up from the table and shook him.

"Tell him, motherfucker! Tell him how good he is or I'll kill you!"

"All right. All right, he's good. He's the best fucking poker player on earth. In the universe. Shit!"

Gene placed him back in the chair, and while patting Saint's shoulder, he said simply, "You see there; now, what do you say, Lefty, leave me my sheen so I can work tomorrow . . . please?"

"When do I get the money?"

"I'm going to put all my bitches to work first thing in the morning." He turned then, and seeing the pale girl standing there, he shoved her toward the door and shouted, "Get your ass out in that street!"

The girl darted instantly out of the door.

"I swear I'll get you your money by next week. Just let me have my sheen, and please don't bad-mouth me to the fellas."

I looked at Manny, who shrugged and smiled, and then I tossed Gene's keys to him. Manny, in turn, tossed Saint's keys on the table.

"You've both got a week," I said. "Manny will collect."

"Thanks, man," Gene said, almost in tears.

"You want me to take a finger for each week that goes by?" Manny asked me.

"Take what you want."

"Okay."

As Manny and I started for the door, Saint called to me.

"What do you want?" I asked.

"I want to tell you I'm sorry."

"What does that mean?"

"I guess it means I respect you. And you can do me a big favor when you play against my father . . . kill him, will you? He's a bigger asshole than I am. When you meet that bastard, you'll see what I'm talking about."

Looking around the pimp's palace and feeling the awesome negative vibrations of the room, I finally understood why Ace didn't want me to play in games like that. I finally understood and swore to myself this would be the last one.

From now on it would be big money games, class, and against the best professionals in the world on my way to the Big Biazarro.

# 17

The rain had stopped falling and West Fifty-sixth appeared shiny, wet, and clean. As we stepped outside, Manny asked if I would like to share a cab. I told him I would rather walk for a while, and he agreed.

I loved walking in New York. I loved the vibrations one feels when being involved in that city. The strength of New York, the size, the smell, the excitement, the instant people everywhere, and the danger. Yes, the danger—it's what gives Manhattan its pace. People move fast. They don't have time to stop and talk. There is always something else to be done. Something of importance happening somewhere besides where they are at the moment. No one wants to get caught in one spot too long, so you must keep moving.

Only the addicts, the winos, the street hustlers, and the hookers stand around trying to score. Everyone else is on the move.

As we crossed Times Square, it entered my mind that midtown Manhattan must be the center of the universe. Where else could it be?

We continued across Forty-second, walking east past Grand

Central Station and on over to First Avenue. There we decided to grab an uptown cab to Sutton Place. Manny asked if it would be all right for him to drop me off on First Avenue. "Sure. I can walk the one block to the brownstone."

Strolling along Sutton Place I felt a chill as the cold, late night winds began to find their way up from the East River. I also felt a drop of rain splatter against my forehead, and I knew it would pour again before long. And then I felt the steel pipe hit me on the right temple. And I felt the size thirteen shoe bury itself agonizingly deep into my stomach, and the pipe crashing against the back of my head sending me facedown to the pavement. They lifted me, these two who came in harm's way to do me in, and threw me against a parked car. A huge, burly fist then went deep into my left side and I could feel my ribs crack under the blow. The steel pipe hit me once more, and I fell again to the pavement.

"That's enough," one of them shouted.

"No!" I cried out and reached for them, only to receive another swift, deadly kick to the chest.

I must have blacked out then, because when I awoke, the front of my leather jacket and beige shirt were covered with blood I had spit up without realizing it. I managed somehow to muster up enough strength to push myself up against the parked car. Looking up, I saw a crowd of seven people, three whites, two blacks, and, standing in the center, two nuns. My vision was blurry, so I squinted to make sure of what I was seeing. They were there all right, all seven of them, and when I reached out for help, they suddenly had other places to go and other things to do—so they dispersed, and I fell back to the sidewalk and passed out.

The next thing I knew it was late the following afternoon. The next things I felt were the hospital sheets covering me, and the awesome pains in my head, ribs, and chest. The next voice I heard was Ace White's as he stood outside in the hospital hallway. He was obviously furious with John, the chauffeur.

"And where the hell were you?"

"I was home."

"That's nice," said Ace sarcastically. "I trust you were comfortable?"

"I said I was suppose to go with him, but he told me not to," John explained.

"I thought *I* was paying your salary," Ace shouted. "What are you getting—money under the table from Lefty or something?"

"Mr. White, please!" a feminine voice pleaded.

"I'm sorry, Nurse."

"This is a hospital. Keep your voice down."

After she was gone, Ace continued his tirade against John through clenched teeth.

"I thought I told you to watch that kid day and night. Didn't I tell you that?"

"Yes, sir, and I was watchin' him, but he said he didn't want me to. And I warned him about goin' to them kinds-a poka games. I told him—"

"You told him! You'd better tell me something, because I didn't realize I was paying you two hundred and fifty dollars a week to give out advice. If you're smart enough to give out advice, what in the hell are you doing wearing that gray monkey suit? Why don't you set up an office and get yourself one of them fancy blond stenographers?"

"Mr. White, it ain't my fault."

"It ain't, huh? Then whose is it?"

"I told him—"

"I don't give a good goddamn what you told him. But I'm going to tell you something. If that kid dies, you'd better find yourself a deep hole to hide in. Because if I find you, I'm going to break both your arms and put you back in a cotton field, and then I'm going to sit there and see how you make a living. Now get the hell out of my sight!"

After that, things were quiet again and I think I fell asleep for a while. I don't know for certain how long, but it was Ace's voice that woke me again. He was talking to one of the doctors in the hallway.

". . . the nurse said you were the doctor in charge."

"Yes, I'm one of them."

"How is he?"

"He's very lucky to be alive," said the doctor. "He has two fractures in his skull, probably a deep concussion, and there are broken blood vessels around the right temple. Three of his ribs were broken and one went through his left lung, that's why he was spitting up so much blood. But the luckiest thing of all was that the bruise on the chest, probably from a kick, fractured a breast bone right in front of the heart. It just missed it."

"I want to know his chances, Doc. The truth."

"Right this minute, I'd say they're about fifty-fifty. If no blood clots form in the head area, he's got a damn good chance."

"And if they do?"

"Depends where, of course. But if we can get them in time, he'll be all right."

"Say he makes it, how long will it take him to completely recover?"

"He's young. Strong. I'd say eight months. A year at the most."

"I don't know whether you know about him or not," Ace began to whisper confidentially, "but he's probably one of the best poker players in the world. Will this affect . . . you know?"

"To be honest with you, Mr. White, in some cases it has slowed the person's reactions up, but the patient is young and strong. We'll just have to wait and see."

"Thanks, Doc."

"You're welcome."

Ace walked cautiously into my room and smiled when he saw that I was awake.

"What's the password?" I managed to utter.

"I came a million miles to see you, kid, and I forgot it."

"Shame on you," I said. "Well, if you remember it, look me up."

"Come on, kid, give an old guy a break. They told me you'd be willing to take on an old, talented goat like me and mold me."

"Who have you beat?" I continued to whisper to him.

"All of them, except you."

"Then you don't need me, and I sure won't need you anymore."

"Who's going to steady my knife when it comes time for me to cut the mustard?"

Trying to ignore the fierce pains all over the top half of my body, I said, "I never knew what cutting the mustard meant. I don't even like mustard."

"How do you feel?" Ace asked, sitting next to the bed.

"With my hands," I said and frowned.

"Look," said Ace, "I don't mind my partner taking a day or two off, but we're supposed to be doing equally, sharing equally, working equally, or not at all, remember? So what do you say you quit this loafing around, get yourself well, so we can meet 'em, greet 'em, jam 'em, and beat 'em."

I started to cry then as an intense pain gripped my right temple. Ace grabbed my hand and squeezed it as the severe twangs bellowed up and down the right side of my head and in and under my skull, as if my head was going to explode.

"Hold on, kid, hold on," Ace pleaded.

"I can't. I can't make it, Ace."

"Yes, you can."

"I can't!" I screamed and felt myself passing quickly away.

During the night—truly a night to forget—I dreamed I was drowning, only to wake up choking with my mouth filled with blood. Coughing and gagging, I turned abruptly to the right to spit and unwittingly ripped the intravenous needle out of my left arm. I felt the skin tear and I cried out as loudly as I could. Someone grabbed me, probably Ace White, and within minutes there were several people all around my bed, holding me down, changing the sheets, reinserting the glucose needle, and cleaning the blood from my face and body.

Once all of this was finished, some heavy-handed doctor started forcing a thin rubber tube up my nose that curled down through my throat, while he kept telling me to "Swallow! Swallow!"

Straining against the tube that was plodding, catching, and retching its way down my throat and the hands that were holding me to the bed, I could feel the throbbing, awesome throes beginning to build and convulse in my head. The violence of those moments became so intense that, after bearing it all for as long as I possibly could, I fortunately passed out again.

The early morning sun, the pungent odor of ether, the uncertain atmosphere of the hospital, and the usual morning noises of the city woke me. Sitting next to my bed was a very shabby, unshaven, anemic-looking Ace White. He had obviously been there all night.

"How was the trip?" he asked.

"It left a lot to be desired," I squeaked out.

"How much did you win?"

"It was a penny-ante game."

"Would you like to try again?"

"I'll pass."

"Seriously now," Ace said, "it was awful, wasn't it, kid?"

"What makes you think it's over, old man?"

"Who do you think did it?" he asked.

"I don't have the slightest idea."

"Did you recognize him?"

"No, but I know it was two of them."

"Manny Robertson and I checked out all the people who

were at the game, and I don't think any of them had anything to do with it."

"They didn't."

"Then it was him," Ace said and grimaced.

"You don't know for sure, Ace. And you should be sure about things like that."

"I'll find out, and if he did this, I swear to God I'm going to kill that sonofabitch!" Ace said with tears in his eyes.

"Don't you know that revenge is the most worthless of causes?"

"That's childish bullshit and you know it."

"We've got things to do, Ace. Seventy-seven will be here before you know it."

"I bet you *he* won't see it."

"You go after him, Ace, and we're through."

"Are you crazy? You think I'm going to just let him walk over us like this?"

"I don't care. I want this to be the end of it."

"But it can't be, Lefty. I won't be able to sleep at night, and you know I love my sleep."

"You go after him, Ace, and we're through, and I swear to God I mean it."

Ace stared at me, and then realizing I fully meant what I said, he nodded and whispered, "Okay, partner, okay."

# 18

For the next five weeks or so, I began a slow and painful, but steady, recovery. The soreness in my ribs and chest was subsiding rapidly, but the twinges in my head and temple were still constantly with me. The pain pills helped, of course, but they made me sleep more than I cared to.

I had many visitors. Some people I didn't even know, but they all claimed that I did, and had definite stories to prove it.

It was nice of them to visit anyway, even though they had ulterior motives. They were harmless, but Ace White would always chase them away.

Ace came by every day, and I had a few visits from Fast Eddy and Manny Robertson. And one afternoon, I was pleasantly awakened from a nap by Bessie Poindexter.

"I told you," she said, looking down at me with despair in her eyes. "I told you this world was going to eat you alive, tear your heart out, and stomp you into the pavement before they'd let you be."

"Gee, it's really nice of you to come by and cheer me up, Bessie."

"I'm just telling you like it is, baby. You're too nice for this messed-up world."

"Well, I'm not planning on leaving it just yet, so we'll just have to find out."

"Be careful, baby . . . please."

I took Bessie's hand in mine then and asked softly, "Why did you disappear that morning?"

"What morning?" she asked, and walked quietly out of my room.

One September Sunday, Saint Laureate and Angel DuPont paid me a visit, and it was all too obvious that everything wasn't great in paradise. Angel, while they were in my room, didn't say a word, glance, or show any emotion whatsoever toward Saint. She stood very close to the bed and was holding my hand all the time they were there.

"How are you guys doing?" I asked.

"Oh, we're just fine," Saint answered.

"How many fingers do you have, Saint?"

He chuckled, and held up his hands.

"I see you paid all the money to Manny."

"I paid him the last thousand yesterday."

"So that's why you're here."

"No, we were planning to come anyway, right, Angel?"

"How are you feeling?" Angel asked me while ignoring him.

"I'm getting better."

"Do you know who did it?"

"No, and I don't care who did it."

"Did they rob you?" Saint asked.

"That's not what they were after. They were after me . . . and they got me."

"But why?" Angel cried.

"There could be a million reasons, but I really don't care about it. I just want to get well, and start playing again."

"How does Ace feel about it?" Saint asked.

107

"You obviously know the answer to that, or you wouldn't have asked."

"You're right. I guess I do."

Angel was holding my hand so tightly that it was beginning to hurt. Seeing tears were about to burst from her eyes, I asked Saint to wait out in the hall.

"All right, Angel, what's wrong with you now?"

"What makes you think something's wrong?" she asked and began to cry.

"Come on . . ."

"I don't know, Lefty, I'm just unhappy."

"Why in the hell don't you do something about it?"

"What?"

"If you're unhappy with him, why don't you leave him?"

"Where would I go?"

"Anywhere! Just get the hell out."

"I wouldn't know where to go."

"Angel, you've got to stop doing this. You're killing yourself, and it's not doing me any good either."

"You're damn right it isn't," Ace said bitterly as he came into the room.

"She's my friend, Ace, and I want her here."

"It's all right, Lefty," said Angel. "Saint's waiting. I'd better go."

"You don't have to go."

Angel leaned over and kissed me, and then, while crying, lingered her cheek next to mine while whispering into my ear, "I love you. I love you. I swear to God I do. Please forgive me." She turned then and rushed out of the room.

"Angel . . ."

"Let her go, Lefty," Ace pleaded.

I wanted to call to her again, but an intense pain shot through my head and I could only lie there and writhe in agony.

Ace squeezed my hand, and after a long, desperate minute, the pain eased up, and I breathed in relief.

108

"Ace . . . you've got to do something for her."

"All right. All right," he said, "I'll see what I can do."

"Swear to me you will."

"I swear I'll go see her, and anything she wants, I'll get it for her. If she wants a trip, an apartment, anything. If she wants to live at the brownstone, she's got it. Now, will you relax, okay?"

"If you don't do what you promised me, Ace, I'll never speak to you again."

"You have my word on it, Lefty."

Turning away to hide the tears that were about to swell in my eyes, I said, "You don't understand, do you?"

"No, I don't. Because I know you don't love her. But it doesn't matter. You're my partner and partners have to stick together. I just don't want her to mess things up for me."

"She won't—if you help her."

"I'll help her—if she lets me."

Continuing to look out at the city, I could feel Ace's puzzled eyes staring at me—begging for an explanation.

"One time," I began, "when I was a kid up in Ferno I went out in the woods and while there I found this baby rabbit. He was so pretty, so cute, but he was wild. I brought him home to keep as a pet, but he . . . insisted on getting sick and dying. I bought him everything, the best lettuce I could find. A pet bunny to keep him company. Everything, but he died anyway. Do you understand?"

Ace paused, and then said, "She's not a rabbit, Lefty, and she's not a pet, and she's not going to die."

"I know. I know . . ."

A few days later, Ace reported to me that he had taken Angel to lunch, and she agreed to let Ace help her as soon as she figured out what she wanted him to do.

He also said that Hilda had orders to allow Angel into the brownstone any time she showed up.

"Okay?" Ace asked.

109

"You do have a heart, Ace," I said and my head hurt as I tried to smile.

"A heart, yes, but a brain is debatable."

"If you're looking for an argument, you'd better get a different subject."

"I can tell you're getting better, Lefty," said Ace.

"I do feel a lot better. Say, do you happen to know what they put in those pain pills? I've been having some weird dreams lately."

"Good ones, or bad ones?"

"Some good, some bad. But last night I had a dream you wouldn't believe. There was this beautiful woman who was giving me . . ."

Just then a young, spry, permanently smiling doctor entered the room wearing the usual white smock with the inevitable stethoscope hanging out of the pocket.

"Good morning."

"Who are you?" I asked, not exactly friendly.

"I'm one of your doctors. My name is Moore."

"More what?"

"Dr. Harvey Moore."

"What are you doing for me?"

"Well, we hope we're making you well."

"I don't care about getting well," I said. "I just want these pains to go away."

"It's all part of the process," he said indifferently, and handed me a paper cup containing two pain pills. "Take these, you'll feel better."

"Those pills just make me sleep."

"That's better than lying awake and suffering, isn't it?"

I turned to Ace and asked, "Where did you find this quack?"

"He comes with the room at two hundred dollars a day."

"Let's up the price and get rid of him."

"You'd better take this," said Moore, "or you'll wish you had in about an hour."

110

"You're going to need them in about a minute, if you don't get out of here."

Dr. Moore shrugged, placed the paper cup down, and, while departing, said, "No one listens to me anymore. No one. That's why they're all dying like flies, because no one listens to me."

"Is he a joke?"

"No," said Ace, "just an intern from Yale."

"I like his sense of humor, if that's what it is."

"Forget him. Tell me about the woman in your dream," said Ace.

"Oh, yes, I had this dream where this gorgeous, dark-eyed, brown-skinned girl, probably Spanish, or black, or maybe even an Indian chick, was giving me this bed bath. Really soothing, you know. And while she's scrubbing me here and there, she's sort of paying extra-special attention to the vital areas. I mean she was washing me all over with this sponge thing and water and all these soap suds. And it was the soap suds that did it, Ace. You know what I mean?"

"No, not exactly."

"I mean she had all these suds and they kept . . . foaming up. You know?"

"You mean she was jerking you off?"

I started to giggle and nod.

"So?" said Ace.

"What I mean is, it was so real. So real that when I woke up this morning, I felt relieved. Sexually relieved."

"So you had a wet dream. What's the big deal?"

"That's the point—I didn't have a wet dream, because when I woke up this morning, there was no mess."

"So you just had a dream."

"I know, but it was so real," I said, "and good."

"Do me a favor, will you?" said Ace. "From now on, keep your dreams to yourself."

"You're just jealous."

111

"You want to have weird dreams sometime, try mushrooms."

"Why?"

"You'll see."

"I liked it anyway," I said.

"Good," said Ace, while shaking his head. "But from now on, keep them to yourself."

"It was better than some of those nightmares I've had."

"Well, at least you're feeling better now," said Ace. "And it's a good thing, too, because if you had died on me, I had one hell of a good plan to get even with you."

"What was it?"

"If you had died before we got a chance to take the Big Biazarro, I was going to visit the nearest bar and drink five gallons of beer and then go and stand over your grave and pee on it for an hour."

I started laughing so hard I was ignoring the pain that was wailing away in my head. Ace sat smiling at me, very glad that I was feeling well enough to laugh again. But I stopped laughing when the door opened and in walked the gorgeous nurse in my dream.

"It's you . . . !" I said without thinking.

"Hi," she said and came over to the bed. "How are you feeling today?"

"Fine. How are you?"

"Okay."

"What's your name?"

"Lola Maldonado."

"Lola Maldonado meet Ace White."

"Pleased to meet you, Señorita Maldonado."

"How long have you been my nurse?"

"For the last three nights," said Lola, "and now I'm switching to days."

"That's a shame," I said. "I mean that's really a shame. It's a crime and a shame. It's a sin and a shame."

"Perhaps Señorita Maldonado prefers the day shift," said Ace.

"I like them both," said Lola.

"But the night affords you more time to see New York as it should be seen . . . with the bright lights."

"Hey, Ace," I called.

"I don't get out much," Lola complained.

"Well, we can take care of that. My chauffeur will pick you up here when you get off and take you home. Later, we'll get together at one of my favorite little cafes over on the East Side."

"Hey, Ace."

"What time did you say you get off?"

"At four-thirty."

"Good. My man will be on time."

"Hey Ace," I called louder as Lola left the room.

"Yes, Lefty, what *is* it?"

"I saw her first!"

"Yes, but only in a dream, kid; only in a dream."

# 19

I was scheduled to go home from the hospital on the twentieth of October—four months to the day after the incident. At my request, Ace had hired Lola Maldonado to be my live-in nurse until I completely recovered.

Lola had me dressed and waiting when Ace, Manny, and a black stranger dressed in a gray chauffeur's uniform came to pick me up.

"Where's John?" I asked.

"Who the hell knows?" said Ace. "Last I heard, he was up in Harlem shining shoes."

"You'd better go find him, Ace, because either John drives me home, or I'm not going."

"Come on, we haven't got time to go look for that idiot."

"Make time!"

"Time is money, Lefty. We're not running a home for chicken sleepers. We have important things to do."

"Not without John."

"I fired that jerk because I couldn't depend on him."

"Then hire him back for the same reason, but I want him behind the wheel of that car, or I'm not going."

Ace exhaled a breath of exasperation. "Percy," he began to introduce the new chauffeur, "I want you to meet Mr. Lefty Wilson, the man who has just placed you back on the unemployment line."

"How do you do, Mr. Wilson?"

"I'm sorry."

"Easy come, easy go, Percy," said Ace, as he ushered the man out the door.

"Hurry back," I called to them.

Three hours later they returned with John, all cleaned up and dressed in a uniform. He came in and smiled at me for the very first time. "It's good to see you, Mr. Wilson."

"It's good to see you, John."

"I want you to forgive me, sir, for what I did."

"I want you to forgive me, John, for what *I* did."

"It'll never happen again, sir."

"God, I hope not, John. I don't think I could stand it."

Brownstone houses are nice to live in, but even nicer to come home to. Hilda, Ace's housekeeper, who gave me a big, warm hug, had huge logs ablaze in the fireplace, and a delicious beef stroganoff heating up for dinner.

The first thing I wanted to do was to lie before the fire and rest. The second thing I wanted to do was play cards. Assuming this, Ace had taught Lola to play five hundred rummy. The four of us formed partners, and Ace and Lola played against Manny and me. Ace was a good teacher, Lola was a fast learner, and every game ended with both teams right around the five hundred mark.

After dinner, Manny asked if I would like to play a few hands of head-up poker. I assumed correctly that Ace had put him up to it.

"I'm a little tired. Maybe tomorrow."

"Okay," said Manny. "I'll drop by in the afternoon to see how you feel."

After Manny was gone, I told Ace he could stop worrying. "I'm going to be okay. My brain is going to function properly and I'll be playing as good or better than before."

Ashamed of himself for asking Manny to test me, Ace said, "I'm sorry, Lefty. I'm just a shit sometimes. Believe me, you're more important to me than the Big Biazarro."

"Well, you don't have to go that far, Ace."

We both laughed then, and it was good to be home again.

For the remainder of the winter and on into the spring of '75 I concentrated on just two things—getting my health back to normal and preparing for the Big Biazarro. Ace managed to get complete dossiers on all the men who had played in previous Biazarros and were planning on playing in '77. Sporados would be there, of course. Deeds, the former champion, had not committed himself yet, but Ace believed he was merely stalling. Peter Sampler, the German car manufacturer, part of the Mercedes family, would return for a second try, as would Oliver Attenborough, better known as Lord Lichfield in England.

Ace had also gotten word that there were two other newcomers preparing to make a try at the game. One was a girl out of Grosse Pointe, Michigan, by the name of Linda Grizzard, whose millionaire father had been training her for the Biazarro since she was six. Linda, of course, hadn't had any rough action, and the plan was to get her out of suburban Detroit and to pit her against stiffer competition for the next two years.

The other young newcomer was C. K. Langershim from the Bel Air, California, fortunes.

Ace felt that the two newcomers wouldn't reach the game, and when I asked why, he said, "They're both looking forward to playing you, and that'll be the end of them."

"Do you really have that much confidence in me?"

"Kid, I think you're the best poker player in the world, bar none. You've got one big problem. You're soft. This girl, Linda Grizzard, is a cute little eighteen-year-old virgin with soft, glassy eyes, and if she starts crying at the table, you'll probably let her win."

I laughed and said, "I'm not that soft!"

"What you have to do, Lefty, is want to win at all costs," said Ace. "You've got to have the killer instinct in order to make it to the top. It's a terrible thing to say, but after I knew you were going to be all right, I was hoping that the beating you received would make you tougher."

"That *is* a terrible thing to say."

"I know it is, but you need to pay some dues, Lefty, or otherwise Deeds and Sporados and those guys are going to tear you apart."

"I don't believe it."

"All right," said Ace. "What do you think you have that they don't?"

I thought for a moment, and said, "Second place."

Ace thought about it, and nodded his head, while saying, "You've got a point there."

"I've got nothing to lose, Ace, because the only people who expect me to win are the guys here in town, right?"

"Yes, but as soon as you're well, we're going to get back on the road, and the people who haven't heard about you will see you as you start to knock off the tinhorns. But you have to be tough—mean at those big tables and all the little tables in between. What do you think would have happened if I had been pitted against Linda Grizzard when she was six years old?"

"You would have taken her dollies."

"You goddamn right I would, and everything else they laid down on that table. For two reasons. One, they would have me there to bleed me dry if they could, and I'm always going to do it to them before they do it to me. Two, she would learn an important lesson from taking a beating. That's your problem, Lefty, you're too soft. You give too many things back. You gave the money back to those actors. You gave back a Porsche and a Cadillac Eldorado in one night. And God only knows what else you've given back to those suckers."

"They paid me the money, Ace."

"That has nothing to do with it, kid. We win money every day, and nobody thinks anything of it, because it's expected. But to win a Porsche, a Cadillac, a castle. Anything with a title on it is what people are going to talk about. We're expected to win money, and after a while it becomes the norm. 'Big deal, Ace White won thirty-five thousand dollars.' But— 'Ace White won six rubies, a Maserati, and Zsa Zsa Gabor's joy stick' makes news. In 1949, I won a glass eye from Lucky Louie Ludall, and to this day, people still ask me what I did with Lucky Louie's eye."

"Well . . . ?"

"Well, what?"

"What did you do with it?" I asked.

"That's not important."

"As of this minute, it is."

Ace smiled, a bit embarrassed. "There was this lovely Latin lady in Cuba during the Batista regime who had the most beautiful navel I've ever seen."

"All right. All right, I get the picture."

"You could never picture her, Lefty. She stood about five-eight and she spoke only in whispers and in Spanish."

"Getting back to your lecture, Ace . . ."

"Oh, yes," he said, coming out of his dream, "you simply have to stop being so soft. Do you want to know something, Lefty? Those guys laughed at you after you gave those things back. They snicker behind your back and call you a first-class sucker."

"They're suckers for playing with me, Ace."

"Two wrongs don't make a right, kid," said Ace. "One-up-manship is the name of the game."

Silent and thinking now, and realizing Ace was right as always, I decided to stop the embarrassing lecture by changing the subject. "You said we would be going on the road. Where?"

"Probably to Puerto Rico and around the islands. Then on out to Vegas and California."

"Sounds exciting."

"It'll be a lot of fun, kid, but a lot of work, too."

During the winter, I asked often about Angel DuPont and was informed that she and Saint Laureate were still together and had taken a trip down to the Virgin Islands. It wasn't reported whether they had seen Saint's father.

It was a long, tedious, cold but beautiful winter, and Lola Maldonado made it easy. The snow came and covered Sutton Place and hung gloriously from the trees, and then melted slowly to form little running rivers along the street. Often, Lola and I would sit and watch the early morning sun melt the intricate and beautiful frosted designs that covered the window panes. And we would see the short-haul trucks deliver the antiques, art objects, expensively tailored clothes, costly furniture and all the other goodies that only the idle rich can afford.

We would also watch the ten-year-old twin boys who lived directly across the street come home each day dressed in their blue private school uniforms, disappear into their brownstone, and then almost instantly return in warm, rugged play clothes to romp in the street. One of their favorite games was to see how high they could pile the snow up on the wire cages that surrounded and protected the neighborhood trees.

Their mother was a tall, sophisticated woman with a *Vogue* model's face that was aging to perfection. Once, but only once, after calling down to the boys, she looked over at me and smiled. Didn't wave, nod, or mouth any words—she merely smiled as if she had noticed me there at some other time. The next day, and from then on, she acted as if I had never been born, burped, bathed, bottled, bedded, or . . . beaten.

Lola Maldonado, born and raised in Tijuana, Mexico, but schooled in San Diego, California, was a marvelous nurse, a beautiful and warm human being, a fantastic lover, and a recuperator personified! Probably the very best recuperator in the entire world. Lola had a way about her that could make a man recuperate almost instantly; either that, or make you want to remain ill for a very long time.

During the months she nursed me, she would wake me each morning with a massage. Hilda would prepare a breakfast for us, and then Lola and I would take a bath together—soak in the tub until our fingertips were like dried apricots. And then we would wrap ourselves in huge fluffy towels and lie before the fireplace while listening to the snow and the wind wisping against the windows, and the logs crackling and popping in the fire.

At first we weren't lovers, and then one day we kissed. That did it. Lola loved kissing. It was her specialty, kissing. She would kiss anywhere, anytime, and I loved it. And I also loved the smell of her body. It is indescribable at this very moment, other than to say it was clean and Castillian. If she were here I could probably run my face over her arm, her cheek, or her thigh and tell you what it is really like, but unfortunately, she's back home in Tijuana.

But as our winter funned on, Lola took the time to teach me everything she knew about making love. She was a twenty-three-year-old expert. She would point out her erogenous zones, and then, when I would touch or taste them, she would fall apart and attack me.

I loved it. She explained to me the value of making all kinds of love. Letting no place go untouched, no spot unkissed, no moment unlived, or unloved.

"You have to taste all the sweet wines and bitter herbs, Chico," she whispered to me one night. "Me, I want to make all kinds of love before I die. I want to feel all sorts of good things—in and on my body. Anything, anything at all that makes me climax, I want to do it. And do it often."

Until Lola, I never suspected that gorgeous, intelligent women spoke this way.

"I want to walk in the rain with you, Chico; swim in the nude. Have you rip my clothes off and tie me to the bed, or just take me gently while I sleep. I want you to want me, to love me, to need me, and take me. To make me know I am yours and you are mine. If there is something we haven't done, I want you to tell me about it, because I don't want to leave any doubts in your mind about the way I feel. Is there anything we haven't done, Chico?"

"I don't know."

"Well, let's start from the beginning again and mark them down this time."

Each and every day, Lola and I would bathe together, lie together, and love together. We would love and lie before the fireplace and kiss and hug and give each other "head" without giving it a second thought.

Hilda, the hippest and coolest old chick alive, would bring our meals to us there on the floor, and one day Lola and I were so involved in a new experiment that Hilda, bless her sweet heart, had to clear her throat seven times before she was able to get our attention.

One warm afternoon, much to my chagrin and amazement, Lola asked Hilda if she would like to join us. Hilda, always calm, unruffled, and cool, said, "Thank you. It's very thoughtful of you to offer, but I have found that I am very susceptible to colds."

Lola and I fell out on the floor laughing as the great Hilda walked nonchalantly back into her kitchen.

Many people would have called Lola Maldonado a sex freak. I wouldn't. I think she was fantastic. She was an exciting, sensual, and, without a doubt, the most inventive woman I have ever known. Take for instance the day she brought me an ice pack to wrap around my erection while she lay with a steaming hot towel between her long, luscious legs. When my penis was as cold as a polar bear's dong, and her vagina was as hot as a stoking oven, she said, "Are you ready?"

Not knowing exactly what to expect and being a little afraid, I didn't answer.

"Ready or not, here I come, come, come," said Lola, and she did, did, did. She sat on me, and, as my fudgesicle went

121

slowly up into her hot tamale, she went completely insane. She started screaming, sweating, shaking, crying, and coming. She was always an ardent and responsive lover, but never like this.

To be honest with you, I found it different, but I wasn't nearly as enthralled with it as Lola was. She confessed later that she climaxed at least a dozen times.

As our vital area temperatures began to cool down and coincide, Lola finally relaxed. Rolling off, she took a deep breath and said, "I think I came out of every pore of my body. We'll have to do that again; again soon, okay, Chico?"

"Of course."

I watched her as her large, round breasts heaved with every breath. Her shapely body perspired lightly, and her blue-black hair was mussed and lay sensually over her eyes.

"Chico . . . I'll talk to you later, okay?"

I pulled her to me then, and held her in my arms. She cuddled closer and whispered something incoherent as she buried her lips into my neck.

# 20

Christmas day of 1974 Ace sent Lola Maldonado home to Tijuana for the holidays, and John upstate to bring Jack and Della, my father and mother, down for the day. I have never seen Ace White so nervous. He wanted to impress them, I guess. Perhaps to convince them that their only child was in good hands.

Jack and Della were severely independent people. They were old now, in their late sixties, quiet, unassuming, and more than anything else, and as always, completely devoted to each other. That is why, I suppose, I was allowed so much freedom to choose my own way. It could have turned out badly, of course, but it didn't as far as I'm concerned. But don't get me wrong, they were always there when I needed them. They were there with their love, their patience and care. I was never jealous of their love for each other, because I never felt I was being shut out. More like I was caught, nicely, in between them.

There were nights when I, like all young children, would fall asleep while reading, or watching television, and Jack would lift me in his strong arms and carry me into bed. Della,

123

like all mothers, had that sixth sense when things were not quite right with me—and she would take the time to stop and forget about her own problems, chores, or activities of the moment, and touch me, talk to me, or even silently put her arms around me. And if that ain't loving you, baby, I don't know what love is.

In their twilight years, Jack and Della were old and quiet, but it wasn't always like that. They had put in their long decades at work, Della at the pocketbook factory and Jack at the cement plants, and the time had etched those hard working hours on their lovely faces. Time had also taken their youth and their energy and left two calm, small-town, happy people with vivid memories of when they used to laugh, sing, drink, and dance all night with their feet never touching the floor.

During dinner, Ace White led most of the conversation. Della would smile and sort of look and lean toward Jack after every joke Ace would make. Most of the jokes were, of course, about me, and we all thoroughly enjoyed them.

It was sad what happened after dinner. Ace had been fine up until then. Almost as if he was the star who dropped the ball just before crossing the goal line, he announced that *we* had bought a farm upstate for Jack and Della. They looked at Ace, frowned slightly their disappointment in him, and lowered their eyes.

At that moment the only thing you could hear were the tinkling noises of Hilda in the kitchen as she prepared to serve dessert.

"I think it's time for us to start back," said Della.

"Yes, it is," Jack said more firmly, and stood.

Ace tried desperately to say something, but there was nothing to be said. The unfortunate damage had been done.

I walked Della and Jack to the door while Ace remained at the table, buried in his faux pas.

"Thank Mr. White for everything," said Della smiling, as if nothing wrong had happened at the table.

"Yes," Jack agreed.

"Good luck in that game of yours," said Della. "We've been hearing about it."

"We had an idea you were heading in that direction, Lester," added Jack. "Glad you turned out to be so good at it."

"It's what I like doing best of all," I said.

"Well, from what we hear, you're real good at it," Jack said proudly.

"Why don't you send us a post card from some of those places you go?" Della inquired.

"I will. I promise."

They both smiled at me, and then, holding hands, they started down to the street where John waited with the limousine door open. I was glad, very glad at that moment, that they had each other.

Returning to the dining room, I found Ace with a pained and perplexed expression on his face. I sat and when Hilda brought the coffee, I nodded for her to join us.

"How old do I have to get, Lefty, before I grow up?" Ace asked.

I didn't answer.

"I was just trying to . . . to . . ."

"It's all right, Ace. They understand."

"I'm glad someone does, because I didn't realize I had done anything wrong until I said it, and then it was like a bomb hitting me. Where in the hell did I get the audacity to think that I, in my dumb-ass capitalist thinking, could buy my way into their beautiful, private lives?"

"You meant well, Ace."

"Meant well, my ass. I'm almost as old as they are with half their common sense. How could I be so goddamn stupid?"

I said, "There are some things you just can't buy, Ace."

"Hah, I've heard that so many times, a million times . . . but only now do I believe it."

125

Lola Maldonado remained in Mexico for the entire month of January and part of February. I spent most of the time studying the dossiers on my possible opponents in the Big Biazarro. Ace and I would sit and he would throw questions at me. I began to feel as if I had known each of them for years.

Ace seemed to be concerned about only three people: Sporados, the present champion, Linda Grizzard, because he thought I would take it easy on her, and C. K. Langershim, because we had very little information about him. Ace sent Izzie Rodriguez out to California to get as much poop on C.K. as he could.

We weren't the only ones doing this. Manny and Fast Eddy reported to Ace that at least four different investigators were running around New York City and up to Ferno to learn as much as they could about me. But New Yorkers, being the coolest people in the world, weren't giving out much information for one main reason: they all intended to bet on me coming out a winner in "the Big Game."

Manny Robertson, Fast Eddy, Ace, and I would play poker almost every night. Fast Eddy was constantly annoyed by the way I would change my style of play. Ace loved it, but Eddy would cry, in his static way of speaking, "Goddamn it, Lefty, first you are bluffing, then you are playing like a pensioner. Then you are betting like a wild man, and then like a teacher. Why in the hell will you not make up your mind?"

The three of us would laugh and this would make him even angrier and his freckled nose even redder.

One night Manny called and said that a champion, a nineteen-year-old kid from south Philly by the name of Roland Lamacco, wanted to come along and meet us. Ace insisted Roland come without friends. He had heard about Roland, and knew his backers were training him for the Las Vegas Championship that year with a possible eye on the 1982 Big Biazarro. Ace wanted me to play against him, feeling I could take him easily, but wanting me to try something different. He

126

suggested I put a time limit on the game, four hours, and allow Roland to win for the first three hours, and then see if I could take him in the final sixty minutes.

The five of us, Manny, Fast Eddy, Roland Lamacco, Ace, and I each bought five hundred dollars worth of chips and began to play straight five-card stud.

Roland was a good, hard, cautious player. I can't remember him bluffing one hand, which, of course, I believe to be a mistake. Even if you lose, you should at least establish that you might bluff. It naturally and automatically gives another dimension to your game. Many don't agree on that, but I have found it works for me.

As fate would have it, not only was Roland winning that night, but so was Fast Eddy; so, by the time the final hour began, the money was spread out between the two of them.

Ace whispered for me to forget about Fast Eddy and to go after Roland. I shook my head and continued to play with both men in mind.

Fast Eddy, wanting to go out a winner, was beginning to goof up the game by folding every hand, regardless of what he had. I was really ticked off at him for playing that way, but with only twenty minutes left and Roland still two thousand dollars ahead, I had to concentrate on him and I took him on a eight hundred dollar raise that turned out to be an excellent bluff, because I started raising from the first card. He almost called me, but decided that he wanted to keep his last money for better cards. I managed to get what he had left with a pair of aces in the next hand.

"I guess I should have called that bluff," Roland sighed.

"You play a good game of cards, Roland," I told him.

"Yeh, sure."

"No, you do. You just haven't got the nerve you need yet. You can't let the money scare you. People make mistakes when the money becomes more important than the game. Don't think money. Think *poker*."

"Thanks," he said. "I'll remember that. And the next time we play, I'll try to give you more competition."

"I'm sure you will."

It is difficult to understand why it happened, but when Lola Maldonado returned from Mexico on the tenth of February, things had changed between us. My mind was entirely somewhere else, and hers also. She wouldn't admit it, but something, or more likely, someone, happened to her while she was in Tijuana.

She remained at the brownstone for another week, and then, we and the doctors decided that it wasn't necessary to have her around any longer.

It's odd, but Lola and I didn't even kiss good-bye. Perhaps both of us were afraid it would start up again, or place some heavy memories on us. We simply smiled our farewells and that was the end of it.

On April 28, 1975, she called from Kennedy Airport to tell me she was on her way back to Tijuana for good.

My time, my winter of contentment with Lola Maldonado, was priceless and I will never, ever forget her. I swear I won't.

# 21

It was a rainy May afternoon when Izzie Rodriguez stood just inside the door of the brownstone in a waterproof trench coat speaking quietly with Ace White. I came out of the kitchen just as Izzie said softly, "He hasn't been seen in town since that night. Some say—"

"Who hasn't been seen?" I yelled bitterly across the room.

"Hi, Lefty," Izzie said quietly. "Well, I've got to be going."

"Not yet!" I shouted, and Izzie shrunk against the wall. "Ace, are you looking for Stan Kondor?"

"Who's Stan Kondor?"

"Don't jive me, Ace. We're supposed to be straight with each other, remember?"

"All right, I was just wondering where he was, that's all."

"Since when do you care?"

"Do you want to know the truth? I don't care. I couldn't care less about a Stanislaus Kondorwicz."

"Izzie," I said, turning to the Computer, "the next time you give any information to Ace about Stan, I'm going to have John and Manny give you a haircut and a shave . . . all over your body."

Izzie frowned his concern, nodded, and rushed out of the door.

Ace had his head down, shaking it from side to side. Disgusted with him, I threw my glass of chocolate milk down on his shaggy off-white carpet before going to my room.

The doctors were more than pleased with my recovery—so much so that Ace and I, dressed in our tailored, dark mohair suits, decided to venture out on the town for dinner.

The Caravelle is one of the most subtle and elegant French restaurants on the East Coast, though you can no doubt find yourself several good arguments on which French restaurant has the best cuisine. When Ace and I entered, Raoul smiled and showed us to one of the best tables. No sooner had we sat than we were accosted by this nervous little fat dude who claimed he represented some massive nationwide corporation and stated that he had been authorized to guarantee us one million dollars a year if we would sign with him lock, stock, and bodies. He said the deal would be federally certified and airtight, and that they would more than match any other offer we might receive. He went on to explain that they would pay us a million a year and put up the table stakes at all games, and collect all the winnings. Plus, we would be given an almost unlimited expense account. And finally, Ace and I would become immediate and full-fledged partners and members of the board of this massive corporation; which he wasn't at liberty to name, I must add.

While the little fat dude caught his breath, Ace asked him calmly, "Do you know what a 'wonder' is?"

"No, I don't," he answered.

"I'll tell you," said Ace. "You stick your finger up your ass and then you smell it. If it doesn't stink, it's a 'wonder.' I think that's what you're looking for, a 'wonder.' And I want to tell you, I think you've got a better chance of finding it up your ass than you do with us."

It took the little fat dude a few moments to fathom what

130

Ace meant, and then he said, "Oh, of course. Excuse me. Good evening, I'm sorry. Good, good, good night."

Watching the little man moving quickly across the room, Ace and I burst into laughter.

"I would love to be there when he explains it to his bosses."

"That would be worth any price of admission," added Ace.

Sitting across the room from us was the notorious Jason Muldaur, a millionaire playboy who got his kicks playing against noted gamblers and top-rank sharks in head-up black-jack.

Jason was an effeminate and luxurious dresser who stood at least six-foot-three with an affected air and a permanent smirk on his pasty face. He was never seen anywhere without one of New York's top fashion models on his arm. Every girl I saw him with was immediately recognizable, having recently been on the covers of *Seventeen, Vogue, Cosmopolitan,* etc.

This one, Bergen Romaine, had just climbed into the six-figure category. She stood five-foot-ten and looked as if she weighed less than ninety pounds. She had the usual high cheek bones, light auburn hair, and a dead-pan expression on her silky smooth face.

Jason, seeing Ace and me across the room, pranced over to our table. He stopped, smiled at Ace, and then frowned at me.

"I say, Horace, you do enjoy the minorities, don't you?"

"What do you want, Muldaur?" Ace snapped at him.

"Your money, of course. At your age, what else could you possibly have to offer?"

"Lefty here plays blackjack."

"I bet he does," Muldaur sang, "but unfortunately, I'm not in the charity or relief business this week."

"You know something, Jason," said Ace. "You're an insult to every gay person in this country, because you're trying to pass as one and you're sickening."

"Sticks and stones, Horace. Do you want to play tonight or not? You can bring your . . . friend with you if you must."

"You know damn well who Lefty is, Jason, now why don't

you jump down off your pastel horse before I jump up and kick your plastic ass?"

"Promises, promises, Horace, you know how violence excites me to tears."

"Why don't you play him, Ace," I said. "Play him and beat his brains out, if he has any."

"Stay in your place, bubbles," he said to me, and Ace almost didn't. I had to grab his arm to hold him down.

"I'm having a party tonight at ten," said Jason calmly, "if you're interested, we can play at twelve."

"We'll be there," I said.

"Would you like to play at twelve, Horace?"

"I'll play at ten or not at all," said Ace.

"Feisty old goat, aren't you?"

"That's why he wins," I said.

"He won't tonight."

"You want to bet?"

"I intend to. More than his rusty old ticker can stand," said Jason, and walked back to his table.

"What an ass he is," Ace uttered as we watched Jason slide in beside the model. After drinking a bottle of '61 Pommard and eating *aiguilette de canard au Médoc,* we had John drive us over to Jason Muldaur's East River Drive penthouse apartment. The duplex was huge and a cross between a *House Beautiful* article and one of *Playboy* magazine's "Playboy Pad" features. The elite of New York's most gorgeous East Side people were there. Several, much to my surprise, said they had heard of me. It was pleasant to see that all of Jason's guests were much nicer than he could ever be.

Ace didn't care about the party, he wanted to go directly into Jason's game room and start playing blackjack. We left the noise of ice and booze-filled glasses, pretty people chatting, and the sound of the many-speakered stereo playing Chicago's latest album.

Ace and Jason sat opposite each other and cut for the deal. Jason won, used a joker to seal the bottom of the deck, and started dealing a thousand dollars a hand.

I sat silently watching as the cards were falling against Ace. At the end of the first hour, he was twenty-one thousand dollars in debt, and hadn't been able to catch a single blackjack.

I looked at Ace, he smiled and shrugged, and I decided to go back to the party for a while. Stepping out into the huge living room, which was becoming a solid mass of people, I found Bergen Romaine waiting for Jason.

"Hi," I said.

"What's going on in there?"

"Jason's winning."

"He always does," Bergen said as if she was bored with it, and him.

"Let's get a drink."

"Okay," she said and took my arm.

After working our way through the noisy crowd over to one of the three bars, we ordered two scotch and milks and decided to move out onto the terrace. From there we could see the East River directly below us with the lights from Rikers Island sparkling and dancing on the water as a lonely tug boat chugged laboriously along, heading north toward Harlem. Looking downtown, we saw the Empire State Building with its tower bathed in light and reaching up into a black sky ladened with little white star dots.

"Jason says you're a great poker player," Bergen spoke first to break the silence.

"Are you and Jason tight?"

"Sometimes."

"Now?"

"Yes," she said, and turned away from me and looked back into the party.

"Do you love him?"

"I wish I knew what love was all about."

"You'll know when it comes. Do you think he loves you?"

"No, but don't ask any more questions, okay, because you're going to get personal."

"Are you ashamed of your personal life?"

"I might be if I talked about it."

133

"It's better to talk about it."

"Perhaps . . . to a shrink, or a priest, or my mother, but never to a two-bit hustler."

"I've never hustled for two bits in my life. Two bucks, maybe, but never two bits. Besides, I assumed we were going to be friends."

"Besides sex, give me two reasons why you want to be friends."

"Give me two reasons why I shouldn't."

"You don't even know me."

"That's one, but it's easily rectified."

"And . . ." She couldn't think of another.

"You see," I said.

"One's enough."

"Not in my book of rules."

"I know what you're getting at, Lefty, and I've heard it all before, and I don't care to hear it again right now. You're going to try and open my eyes to what Jason is and the kind of life I'm living, and I just don't want to hear it. If you really want to be my friend, then speak to me of fairy tales and fantasies. But don't bother to tell me facts. Lie to me if you want to, but keep it light. Keep it gay. Life is much too short for anything else."

After a pause, I said, "Shall we see how the game is going?"

"Are you giving up?" she asked.

"No, I just forgot how to talk to sweet, young children."

"You could have said something a lot meaner," she said, and turned to me. "But you're not like that, are you?"

"Shall we go in?"

"Only if you really want to."

"I think I really do."

"All right," she said sadly and took my arm.

Walking back through the crowd and into the game room, I could see that Jason Muldaur's luck was continuing. Ace was down about thirty-five thousand dollars now and Jason still had the deck. Bergen and I took seats at the table.

"Be careful of him," Jason said to Bergen, "that stuff rubs off."

"Deal!" Ace snapped at him.

Jason dealt and he hit an ace and a nine to Ace's eighteen.

"Falling bad for you, huh, Ace?"

"Right now they are, but Lady Luck isn't prejudiced."

"Do you play?" I asked Bergen.

"I love it."

"Deal us a hand," I said, and looked at Ace. He knew immediately what I was trying to do—change the order of the cards and perhaps Jason's luck.

It worked. Bergen and I hit a blackjack on the third hand after winning the first two.

"Who wants to buy the deal?" I asked.

"Why don't you deal, hot shot?" said Jason.

"Deal's up for sale," I said.

"I'll give you a thousand for it," Jason said coldly.

"A thousand? You're a cheapskate, ain't you?"

"I'm sure that's more than you get for washing windows, or scrubbing floors, or whatever manual labor you people are good at this year."

"Ace, would you like the deck for eleven hundred?"

"All right," said Ace.

"I'll give you fifteen hundred," Jason shouted.

"Sold to the . . . man in the violet shirt."

"What do you say we up the bet to two thousand a hand?" Ace asked.

"Make it three if you want to, Moses," Jason quibbled.

"It's three," said Ace.

"Us, too," I said and waited for Jason to deal.

Bergen and I won six out of the next eight hands, and Ace won five out of the eight. Jason was beginning to sweat. I split the take with Bergen and suggested she play on her own.

The deck was not only cold for Jason, it was freezing, and almost frozen. The only person he could beat was Bergen, and when she went broke, she got up from the game, excused herself, and went back to the party. But the damage had been done. The three of us played for another two hours, Jason lost eighty-six thousand dollars, paid us off in cash, and went stomping out into the party.

"Thanks," said Ace.

"For what?"

"You saved my bacon, kid."

"Nah. Your luck would have changed and you would have gotten him by yourself. I just saved us a little time."

Suddenly, we heard loud screams coming from inside the party.

"I bet it's the model!" Ace said and we both rushed from the room. Going out into the duplex we saw an open space in the middle of the crowd, and standing over Bergen Romaine was a very bitter Jason Muldaur with blood on his hands. Bergen's face was a mess. Her lips were busted, her nose broken, and one eye battered shut. I was certain he must have hit her at least a half-dozen times with his fists. Taking a handkerchief from my pocket, I started toward Bergen.

"Don't touch her!" Jason screamed at the top of his voice.

It was enough to stop me.

I took another step and he shouted, "You touch her and I'll kill you."

I said, "I don't believe it," and walked over and bent down to Bergen. I felt Jason's strong hand grab the shoulder of my jacket and I looked up just in time to see Ace's fist going flat, fast, and flushed into Jason's pointed nose. Ace, moving like a bantamweight, ripped a quick left hook into Jason's stomach, which staggered and knocked the wind out of him, and then Ace danced in for the kill, paused, and put Muldaur away with a hard right cross that might have staggered Muhammad Ali. Jason fell out on the floor, his arms stretched to their limit, and his eyes went up into his head.

Helping Bergen to her feet, Ace and I rushed her out of the party. At Mount Sinai Hospital they put over thirty stitches in her face, and it was all too obvious that her great modeling career had come to an instant conclusion. Disfigurements do not sell.

That night we called her parents, who lived in Minneapolis, and when they flew in the next morning, John met them at the airport. While waiting for Bergen to get well enough to travel, Mr. and Mrs. Romaine, lovely, warm people even during this crisis, stayed with us at the brownstone.

Another tragedy of a sort happened their second night in town. The four of us were dining at O'Henry's Steak House in Greenwich Village when Angel DuPont walked in on the arm of the most obvious out-of-town trick ever to hire a call girl.

As I stared at her, I could see an enormous change. In Cannes, she was like a child, a nineteen-year-old drifting sparrow desperately looking for a place to land. Now, she was dressed in satin. Satin was wrong for her. Completely wrong.

Her hair, once shiny and draped long over her shoulders, was now teased and winged out, and curled around. It looked cheap and horrible.

She must have felt my eyes on her, because she suddenly became concerned and searched around the room before finding me. And when she did, she immediately rushed up from the table and ran out of the steakhouse with her date directly behind her.

The Saint had turned the Angel into a bona-fide whore. It wasn't a surprise . . . it just hurt to see her that way.

Two days later, John drove the three Romaines to the United Airlines terminal and they flew off into the sunset never to be seen again. Within forty-eight hours we received a bouquet of long-stem roses accompanied by a beautiful thank-you note.

"Lefty," Ace sighed at dinner that night. "I think it's time we got on the road, don't you?"

"I think it's past time we got on the road."

"No regrets, kid. What's done is done."

"Don't you feel bad for Bergen?"

137

"She made her bed, Lef. She knew what the gig was when she took it."

"And that's it."

"That's it, kid."

"You feel more than that, Ace, or you wouldn't have punched him the way you did."

"Oh, that," he said. "That was nothing. I just needed the exercise."

I looked at him, and he couldn't hide his smile.

"Let's start packing," said Ace, and rose from the table.

# 22

There is something terribly exciting about airports. Especially if you love to travel, as I do. John dropped us off at the curb, and Manny and Fast Eddy, carrying our luggage, walked us into the Pan Am terminal. As I checked in our bags, Ace was giving them instructions on what he wanted them to do while we were away. "Keep your eyes and ears open. Cover all bases, including and especially Harlem. They know things up there they don't even hear about in other sections. Anything sounds important, call us immediately."

Izzie Rodriguez had returned from California late the previous night and was supposed to meet us at the airport with the information he had gathered on the Coast.

While waiting for Izzie, the four of us stood around laughing and joking. We were kidding Fast Eddy about being from Georgia and arriving in New York City with straw in his hair and cow dung on his shoes. We kidded Manny about being either the tenth, eleventh, twelfth, or thirteenth ground-gainer in the country while playing college football. And, of course, the joke on Ace was his age, and on me it was my youth and squareness.

139

When there were fifteen minutes left before take-off, the Computer jumped from a taxi and ran inside.

"Sorry I'm late," said Izzie. "Got caught in a traffic jam. I got some great news and I got some bad news. Which do you want first?"

"Give us the bad," said Ace.

"Okay. Sporados was in California while I was there, and he has announced two things: one, that all of the players who will play in the 1977 Big Biazarro will be selected by June of 1976. One year from now."

"How is that different from other times?" I asked.

"More players. More money around and more people interested in playing," said Ace. "Up until now, there were only a select few who knew about the game who cared to invest that kind of money. Now, with three new players this year, those seven seats are going to be hard to get."

"The other thing," said Izzie, "and get this—the game will begin one minute after midnight on New Year's Eve. The very first minute of 1977. He hasn't decided on the location yet."

"I think he's running scared," said Ace. "I think he's trying to get you before you're ready. Either that, or have the game before you get your five master markers. He knows we'll have the money, so it must be the markers."

"It's a year and a half," I said. "That should be enough time."

"You're right," said Ace, "if you can stay out of fights."

"I will."

"Okay, Izzie, what's the good news?"

"Here is the folder on C. K. Langershim, but I don't think you're going to need it because Linda Grizzard beat him royally two nights ago in L.A. She is really something else! First of all, she is one of the most gorgeous girls you will ever see. Some say she's a virgin, but I don't know about that. When she sits down at that table with that pretty little smile of hers, and that silky, long, reddish-blond hair, and those blue-green eyes —wow, how any man can concentrate on cards is beyond me.

Well, anyway, she ripped C. K. Langershim apart. Took her three hours, that's all, and he was ready for a shower. Told me after the game he didn't know what hit him. She toyed with him. She played with his mind. Played with his ego. Had him thinking he was the salt of the earth, and then socked it to him with a full house that must have fallen from the ceiling, because he didn't see it coming. She's good. She's fantastic."

"Do you hear that, Lefty?" asked Ace. "Are you going to let her play with your head, your ego? She can stop you. Stop you dead."

"Let me tell you the rest," said Izzie. "This is great. They're having a hi-low session in San Juan this weekend, and guess who's going to be there?"

"Who?"

"Everybody. C. K. Langershim, though I don't understand why. Malcolm Laureate. Linda Grizzard, Sporados will be there Saturday and then he's leaving for Greece. And there's even talk that George Palmer Deeds will be there, and a few other Poker Masters. We could make a big hit over this weekend."

"What do you mean, we?" Manny kidded him.

"I'm on the payroll."

"We're all on the payroll, but Lefty's got to do the playing."

"Kid, do we meet 'um, greet 'um, jam 'um, and beat 'um?" Ace asked.

I had noticed something about Izzie that had been bothering me since he arrived. For some reason, and it was frightening, he had refused to look at me. He kept talking around me, over me, under me. He was speaking to Ace, to Manny, and Eddy, and avoiding my eyes at all cost.

"Izzie . . . look at me and tell me something."

Ace, Manny, and Fast Eddy lowered their heads and I knew something horrible had happened—probably to Angel.

"Izzie, I'm right here. Now look at me. Quit avoiding my eyes, and tell me something. I'm not afraid of Linda Grizzard or anybody else because I know poker and I know people, and

141

I know goddamn well you're avoiding me and I want to know why. Right now!"

Tears were already in my eyes and the four of them gathered around me to shield me from the public's eyes. Izzie, too, was almost in tears, and he looked to Ace for help.

Pained, frustrated, and angry, Ace said, "Tell him."

"Oh, no," I moaned. "What happened to her?"

Izzie, sensitive and shy as always, began to tear as he said, "I'm sorry, Lefty."

"What happened?" I screamed.

"She's . . . she's in a coma."

"Oh, God, no."

"I'm sorry, Lefty," Izzie cried. "She shot herself."

"Oh, God, oh, dear God. You all knew and nobody would tell me."

"It happened the night she saw you at O'Henry's," Ace explained. "She ran home and shot Saint in the head five times while he was asleep and then put the last bullet in her own brain."

"Oh, Jesus. Oh, sweet Jesus, no!"

"There's nothing you can do, Lefty," Manny said softly.

"How do you know?"

"She's in a coma. There's nothing anybody can do but wait and pray. We didn't want to worry you about this."

"Broads like that are always killing themselves, Lefty," Fast Eddy complained. "It is just something they do."

"I could have saved her."

"It is impossible. It is impossible to save them. Besides—they do not want to be saved."

"Come on, kid," said Ace. "We got a plane to catch."

"I'm not going."

"Oh, Christ!"

"I want to see her."

"Lefty," Ace pleaded. "She can't see you. She can't talk to you. She won't even know you're in the room."

"She'll know I'm there."

142

Angel's room was large, sunny, clean, sterile, and filled with dozens of colorful flowers. There was a vase of long-stem yellow roses on her night table and a card that read, "To Angel. Love, Lefty."

Angel lay there in the bed, so still, so sad, so quiet, with only a slight breath to indicate she was still alive. Taking her soft, frail, lifeless hand in mine, I pressed it to my cheek.

"Oh, Angel, my friend, my dearest, my love, forgive me. Forgive me for not helping you. For not building you a cottage with an iron, white picket fence. Oh, baby, what is this joke that goes on and on, so painfully on? What is this silly melodrama, this travesty that must have been written by some hack living in the Chelsea Hotel?

"Live. Please live, Angel darling, and I'll give it up. I'll give it all up for you."

At 11:36 A.M., June 25, 1975, three days after I learned of the incident, Angel DuPont passed quietly away without ever recovering from her coma.

Death. Death. Death is such a drag. It's so unreal, cruel, and permanent. It's so final. There's no reprieve. It's an eternal good-bye. It's capital punishment. It's farewell, my lovely. Death. Old Man Death—the shadow-maker, the heartbreaker, the soul-taker, stay away from my front door.

Angel DuPont was gone, and all that she was would be gone forever. There are no questions to be asked, because there is no Angel to answer. Everything I know of her now is all that I will ever know. That's what death does to knowledge.

Sitting at her bedside moments after the doctor had pulled the sheet up over her face, I could feel the air of death creeping over the room. I wanted to run, to flee, and never be part of that moment again, but I sat there. Sat there looking at Angel's cold, hard form under the sheet. It was a heavy and impossible moment. Impossible, because there was nothing I could do but sit there.

When they came to take her away, I moved back to the wall and stood flush against it. They wheeled out the entire bed, leaving the room even more sterile.

That's it. That's Angel's show, folks. She came, she talked, she danced, she cursed, she smiled, she loved, she lost, and she died. That's Angel's show, folks. She brought nothing and she left nothing but this gaping hole of guilt in my heart that I do not understand. That's Angel's show. That's Angel DuPont's show, folks.

She gave very little, that is why there were few to mourn her. Few who cared. Few who understood.

The postman would ring a door bell somewhere in Delaware and say, "Got a package for you. It's your daughter coming home at last."

Angel didn't exactly like Delaware, but it can't be a bad place to rest. There is no bad place to rest. To rest, to call it a day. To lay back and say, "Fuck it, I've had it. It's your turn to carry the ball, baby, I don't like the game."

Walking over to the night table, I took a rose from one of the vases.

"I hardly knew you, Angel, hardly knew you at all, and yet you took such a large piece of my heart. . . ."

# 23

Fast Eddy Youngblade was sitting in the lobby of the hospital reading the Monday racing sheet when I came down.

"Hey, Lefty, how goes it?"

"She's gone."

"Oh, wow, man, I am sorry. I am really sorry."

"Let's take a walk," I said and we strolled over to Fifth Avenue and started downtown. This was the beginning of what might be the longest walk ever taken on the island of Manhattan. We took Fifth Avenue all the way to Washington Square Park in Greenwich Village.

At times we were silent for blocks and then one or the other of us would say something.

"Did you know I came from Macon, Georgia, originally?"

"If you're from Georgia, how come you don't have a southern accent?"

"That is the first thing I left down there."

"What was the second?"

"Mary Lou Beckworth. The prettiest Georgia piece you had ever wanted to see. Red hair from head to toe. Freckles and red hair. All that girl ever talked about was having babies.

145

Having babies. Shit! Scared me to death. Had to get my hat, Lefty."

"What have you got against babies?"

"I have nothing against little roast beefs and crumb crushers, but I just was not ready for it. I was eighteen years old and the best poker player in Macon, Georgia. No-bet Harris and Lawdy Roberts came through town one night and told me about the big money to be found in games up here. I could not wait to get on the next Trailway heading north."

"Did you at least say good-bye to Mary Lou Beckworth?"

"Not exactly. I, ah, called her once I got here."

"What did you say?"

"I said, 'Mary Lou, I have come up to Yankeeland to make my fortune. Once I do, I will either send for you, or come and get you.'"

"Did she believe you?"

"I do not know."

"Did you mean it?"

Eddy paused for a moment, and then said, "I do not know."

Walking through Greenwich Village, we stopped at one of the Italian sausage stands for an afternoon snack.

When we finished eating, Fast Eddy said he had to make a phone call.

"Not yet," I told him.

He looked at me, choosing his next words carefully. "Oh, it is not what you think."

"It's exactly what I think."

Eddy stood there scratching his head and frowning, "Well, you see, I placed this bet—"

"Shut up, Eddy, I don't like to be lied to."

"Who do you think I am calling, Lefty?"

"I know who you're calling. But let's just walk for a while and then later I'll let you call him."

"Lefty, I swear, I am calling my bookie."

"Does your bookie happen to be named Ace White?"

Fast Eddy frowned and kicked at the street. "How did you know?"

"It doesn't matter. Come on, we'll walk for a while and then we'll get in touch with him."

Walking on Sixth Avenue, we started uptown. We passed through Chelsea, the garment district, Times Square, and were walking on Central Park West as the sun, which had been hiding behind thick layers of clouds all afternoon, finally broke through to save the day, just before disappearing somewhere into the Jersey swampland.

"You know," Fast Eddy said, as we rested on a street bench, "I have been trying to get up enough nerve to go back to Macon. I have had more than enough money for over a year now, but I would not know what to say to her."

"You could start with, 'Hi, how are you?' "

"Suppose she is married now? I mean, it has been six years. I called three years ago, and she said she was still waiting. I do not know if I love her anymore. I mean, a lot of water has gone under the bridge, you know what I mean?"

"There's only one way to find out."

"Say, you do not mind me talking about this, do you?"

"No."

"I mean, it has been six years and I am sure she is changed, and I have changed completely. The thing that bothers me the most is that, of all the broads I have screwed, none of them have . . . touched me the way Mary Lou did. Do you know what I mean?"

Thinking of Angel, I nodded that I understood.

"I guess it was because we had so damn much in common. Growing up together and everything. You have to have stuff in common, don't you think, Lefty? I mean, what do you talk about if you do not have things in common?"

"You'll find something."

"You really think so?"

"I know so, Eddy."

Going on, we walked into Harlem and straight up Eighth

147

Avenue to 118th Street. Crossing over to Lenox, I rang Bessie Mae Poindexter's bell. I realized then that at 9:00 P.M. she would be on the stage at the Apollo Theatre.

Going back downtown, we cut over to the East Side of the park. Fast Eddy had a small flask of Bourbon, so we stopped to drink and remained there on a bench until after midnight.

"Do you think I will ever be as good as you, Lefty?"

"What do you think?"

Fast Eddy thought for a moment, and then, shaking his head, he mused. "No, I guess I won't. You are the best. But I am getting better, don't you think?"

"At least your nose doesn't get red anymore when you get a good hand."

"Aww, come on, I stopped that years ago."

"How did you learn to control it?"

"Toughness. Got in a couple of fights. Got the shit beat out of me once. Not as bad as you did, but I bled. You know, you pay the dues, you grow up. One night I got a straight flush and the guy thought I was bluffing because my nose was not red. I killed him with a six hundred dollar raise. Ever since then I have been okay."

"Let's do it again," I said.

"Do what?"

"Walk to the Village and back."

Fast Eddy looked at me skeptically, and then said, "Let us drink on it and get moving."

We both took two large swigs of the Bourbon and started on our way again. We walked back over to the West Side, and at Broadway and Fifty-sixth Street we saw the police arresting two Times Square hookers for shop-lifting. At Seventh Avenue and Forty-ninth Street, we watched an oriental guy jump into a karate stance and then get the shit kicked out of him by a notorious street fighter named Jimmy Edmonds.

As we passed the George M. Cohan statue on Times Square, three homosexuals approached us, asking for cigarettes.

"Get lost, fruits!" Fast Eddy shouted at them.

"Neither one of us smoke," I explained nicely.

"You're cute," said the smallest one, rubbing my arm.

"If you do not take your hand off of him, you are going to lose it, scum bag!" Eddy said, shoving the boy away from me.

"Oh, tough man, tough man," the little guy sang, as the three of them continued uptown.

Crossing Forty-second Street between Seventh and Eighth avenues, we saw a familiar face on a drunk in the doorway.

"Hey," said Fast Eddy. "That's Gats Brown."

Rushing over to Gats, who was smelly, dirty, and ragged, we shook him to wake him.

"I'm goin', I'm goin'," he said, probably thinking it was the law.

"Hey, Gats, it is us. Lefty and Fast Eddy."

"Eddy," Gats said, squinting through eyes that had been made heavy by cheap wine. "Lefty. Lefty Wilson, is that you?"

I told Eddy to help me lift him, and we took Gats into a pizza parlor and ordered black coffee and a large pizza.

"What happened, Gats?" Fast Eddy asked. "You were always so together."

"What do you *think* happened?" said Gats. "It was a bitch! It's always a bitch. Bitch told me she loved me. Gave the bitch everything. And what I didn't give her, she took. Ran off with some conk-head nigger from Raleigh. Told her he was gonna take care of her. Said he had a house and shit. Nigger didn't have nothin'. Had himself a line, that's all he had. Bitch called me up sayin' she wants to come home. 'Oh, daddy, I'm so sorry.' I said, 'Bitch, if you bring your scroungy ass back here I'll kill you.'"

Gats stopped talking and laid his head on the counter while crying. Fast Eddy and I looked at each other, and Eddy shrugged.

"So what happened, Gats?" Eddy asked.

After catching his breath, Gats cried, "She didn't come back. She didn't come back and she ain't called, and I don't know what to do without her. I don't know what to do without her."

149

"Why not forget about her?" Fast Eddy asked simply.

"Oh, God, I wish I could. I swear on my mother, I wish I could."

"Why don't you go to Raleigh and find her?" I suggested.

"I wouldn't know how to start. Sides, I ain't got no money."

"You've got friends."

"Shit, I ain't even got no friends worth nothin'."

"What are we?"

Gats looked up at me, and then over at Fast Eddy, and started to cry like a baby. "Oh, no."

"Oh, yes," I said. "Come on."

For the next two hours we shopped in the all-night clothing stores along Forty-second Street.

An hour before sunrise we put two hundred dollars in Gats Brown's new suit pocket and placed him on a south-bound train for Raleigh, North Carolina. I gave him the address of the brownstone and told him to write me.

Fast Eddy and I went to the Village and returned nonstop through Midtown. We were walking back into Central Park when the sun was high enough to light up the entire city and chase away the nighttime chills.

"You know, it is funny," said Eddy. "You, me, and Gats are all going through a thing with broads right now, right? You with Angel, me with Mary Lou, and Gats with his woman. Wow!"

"What did he say her name was?" I asked.

"Bitch," Fast Eddy answered simply.

"That's right . . . bitch," I said, and thought how sad their lives must be.

We entered the Central Park Zoo just as an attendant was feeding the seals and we stopped to watch.

"I love this town," I said, "but I've got to get out of here for a while."

"You have to from time to time," said Eddy. "New York is the best, but if you do not escape once in a while you will go nuts."

"Let's walk."

We moved over by the orangutan's cage, where we saw a bunch of young kids spitting on this huge, fat ape who sat close up on the bars, and was occasionally spitting back at the kids. Finally, someone chased the kids away. Fast Eddy and I stopped and looked at the orangutan and, sure enough, while we were standing there, he sat there chewing on something, and then all of a sudden spit a spray of saliva right at us. We ducked out of the way and laughed.

We decided then to stand over on the side and watch what would happen. The orangutan remained close to the bars, patiently chewing, and when some unsuspecting stroller would pass by the cage, he would let him have it.

This one Madison Avenue-type guy, dressed in a suit and tie and carrying a brief case, came rushing by with a grin on his face as if he had just sold Manhattan Island, when "splot" —the ape hit him square in the ear.

Fast Eddy and I were laughing so hard we would have fallen over if we hadn't been holding each other up.

Next came this up-tight, snooty old private school teacher with her five prize students. They were all practicing their Latin. The teacher, closest to the cage, was explaining that our friend was a *"Pongo Pygmaeus,"* and was found mostly in Sumatra and Borneo and—"swat"—caught her right between the eyes.

The students were laughing as much or more than we were.

Finally, one of the zoo attendants came to hose down the cage and the drain. Our friend kept chewing patiently, but had the wrong angle on the attendant, so he leaned slightly to the right, and when he had the angle—"ssvit"—he sprayed him right on the back of the neck. The attendant immediately turned the hose on our friend and chased him into the house.

Fast Eddy and I decided to grab a bite at the zoo cafeteria. We found a table out on the terrace, and Eddy excused himself to make his phone call. A half hour later, Ace White and Manny Robertson joined us. They both said they were sorry about what had happened, and then Ace said, "If you want to go down to the funeral, we can spare the time."

I thought about it for a moment. "No. Like you said—what's done is done. Let's get on with the game."

"That's best," said Manny.

Ace said the word from Puerto Rico was that Linda Grizzard was still undefeated. She beat Malcolm Laureate, C. K. Langershim again, and had a stand-off with George Palmer Deeds.

"Wasn't Sporados there?" I asked.

"He was there, but he didn't play."

"How many markers does Linda have?"

"I don't think she has any, but it doesn't matter. Sporados feels the markers were just a way of keeping the game segregated. Now the rule is, if you defeat a Master for a hundred thousand dollars or more, you can consider it a marker. Sporados says to call it a 'ganar.' So, you've got one ganar for having defeated Duxbury."

"Did you talk to Sporados?"

"Yes. He came to New York after leaving Puerto Rico. He wanted to meet you, but I told him you were unavailable. I didn't think you would want to meet him under the circumstances."

"Where's Linda Grizzard now?"

"No one knows. She left San Juan about a week after the tournament for parts unknown. She, ahh, hinted that you're ducking her. When asked why you were rejecting the offer to play her, she said, 'Why would the hot dog reject an offer from the meat grinder?'"

"She didn't say that, did she?"

"Izzie said he heard it with his own ears."

"She really said that about the hot dog? She called me a hot dog?"

"Said you were ducking her. Afraid to meet her on a poker table."

152

"She said that, huh?"

"That is what Izzie said."

"Maybe we'd better find out where she is."

"I'll get Izzie right on it."

"Are you okay, Lefty?" Manny asked, concerned.

"Yes. Thanks, Manny."

"Okay, partner," said Ace, "we leave for Puerto Rico tonight."

# 24

Even though it was late in the evening when we arrived in San Juan, the heat was intense. Ace and I picked one of the many cab drivers who stood around beckoning to us in Spanish. Once again, my bags, even though Ace's luggage was checked in with mine, came out last.

Ace had booked a large suite for us at the Americana, one of San Juan's finest, and we arrived at the hotel only to be greeted in the lobby by Malcolm Laureate, Saint's father.

"How are you, Horace?" he asked and shook hands with both of us. "You're Lefty Wilson, I assume."

"You assume correctly."

"I understand you knew that ridiculous son of mine?" he said to me.

Perplexed by his statement, I said, "Are you aware your son is dead?"

"Yes, I heard. It didn't come as a surprise, knowing the kind of low-class women he hung out with. I'm surprised he lasted as long as he did."

"You're screwed, mister, you know that?" I said. "Your son said you were a shit, but I had no idea he could be so right. I don't like you, so you'd better stay out of my way."

Malcolm Laureate was taken aback by me and turned to Ace for an explanation.

"I hate to tell you, Malcolm, but you are a shit," said Ace. "You always have been. I've never told you before, because I didn't want to piss you off. I mean, it's been so easy taking money from you all these years, but you are a shit! Probably the biggest and ugliest turd I have ever met."

"You're going to be sorry you said that, Ace."

"Why? What are you going to do to me? Talk behind my back?"

"I don't have to take insults from you or him," said Malcolm, nodding at me.

"If you're really offended, Malcolm, you know goddamn well you're welcome to step outside."

"I'll do my fighting at the poker table."

"For as much chance as you've got against Lefty, you may as well take a swing at me now."

"We'll see," Malcolm said and walked away.

The next morning after breakfast, Ace and I sat out by the pool and learned that neither Sporados, Deeds, nor Linda Grizzard were still in Puerto Rico. Other than Malcolm Laureate, there were two other Poker Masters: Hank Boswell of Chicago and Kenneth Martin Jacobs of Atlanta.

Hank approached us about a hi-low game. We agreed. That afternoon Ace and I rented a car and took a tour of old San Juan with its narrow streets shadowed by Spanish balconies that hung out from every building. We had lunch at La Mallaquina, one of Puerto Rico's oldest restaurants, visited the mammoth fort known as El Moro, and walked inside a quaint little chapel where a Puerto Rican wedding was taking place. We watched for a while, and I winked my congratulations at the bride and groom as they rushed down the aisle and out into the sunlight to face the world together.

Back at the Americana Hotel, we had dinner sent up to the room while I rested and Ace made a few phone calls. After dinner, Boswell, Jacobs, Malcolm Laureate, and I sat down with two amateurs to play seven-card hi-low. Within a couple

155

of hours, I was eight thousand dollars in the hole. Ace White was very concerned.

During the break, he pulled me on over to the side for a chat.

"What's wrong, kid?"

"Nothing," I said nonchalantly.

"Do you have some plan that I don't know about?"

"No plan, Ace. I'm just not that adept at playing hi-low yet."

"Yet? What do you mean, yet?" Ace asked, suddenly alarmed by the fact that I knew little or nothing about the game. I knew that the highest hand and the lowest hand split the pot at the end of the game, but other than that I didn't know at the time you could have a great high hand and go low and win half the pot—if no one beat you, of course.

"I really haven't played that many times."

"How many?" Ace asked, raising an eyebrow.

"Once or twice, I think."

"That's it, we're out of the game."

"Trust me, Ace. I'll catch on."

"Lefty, there are three Poker Masters out there who have been playing this game for years, and you think you're going to learn it in one night."

"Poker's poker, Ace."

"There's something you don't understand here, kid. *They* know the game, and I guarantee you, they know you *don't* know the game."

"That's good. Because they're going to keep thinking I don't know the game, but before the night's over, I *will*."

"What makes you so sure?"

"I don't know. I just know I can do it."

We had been playing for five hours and I was now fifty-two thousand dollars in the hole.

"Lefty, can I speak to you for a moment?"

Taking me by the arm, Ace led me over into a corner. "Kid, I really don't think this is your night, your game, or

156

your town. What do you say we call it quits and take off for one of the other islands?"

"Trust me, Ace. They're not touching me."

"Lefty, we're fifty-two thousand dollars in the hole. Somebody's touching you."

"Ace, do me a favor. Take some money and go downstairs to the casino and try out your thermostat. I guarantee you by the time you get back, I'll know the game."

"You might know the game, but we might be broke."

"Would you like to place a bet?"

"What bet? What are you talking about?"

"I'll bet you any amount of money you want that I take these guys before the night's over."

Ace looked at me, felt my forehead for a temperature, and asked, "Are you feeling all right, kid?"

"I've never felt better."

"I'm not going downstairs," he said. "I want to see this."

We went back to the table and within another hour I had lost another ten thousand dollars. The two amateurs called it a night and I was left with the three Masters.

I can recall catching only a total of four royal flushes in all of the straight poker hands I have played. The one in Puerto Rico came in the nick of time. I was close to eighty thousand dollars in the hole, Ace White was breathing heavily, and Malcolm Laureate had a kings over full house and dropped a thirty thousand dollar bet on the last card. I called and raised, and he raised me another thirty thousand. I raised back, he lost, and pulled out of the game without a word.

Boswell, Jacobs, and I continued to play. The early Friday morning sun was sending its warm rays into the suite as the game wore on. We had continued to play hi-low even though it is almost a ridiculous game with only three players. The funny thing was, no one suggested switching to stud. It was as if we all felt that hi-low was going to do it for us. Of course, I didn't want to switch because I was learning the game. I kept getting low cards, and I remembered Cooncan Bill once told me that if I ever played hi-low to play the game for low. So, to be honest with you, I was going low almost every hand, regardless of what I had.

An hour later, Malcolm Laureate, who had already dropped about a hundred thousand, returned to play. Ace handed me a cup of black coffee and whispered in my ear, "I want Malcolm to think I'm telling you something profound, but I really have nothing to say, but nod your head anyway."

I nodded my head, but I was laughing so hard I almost spilled my coffee on the table. I looked up at Ace, who stood there with an exasperating look on his face.

Boswell said, "Why don't you let us in on the joke?"

"Yeah, what about us?" Malcolm snapped bitterly.

"It's a personal joke," said Ace. "You wouldn't understand, right, Lefty?"

I was still laughing so hard, I couldn't answer.

Malcolm Laureate bought back in the game for twenty thousand dollars, and Ace and I looked at each other with the same thought—that Malcolm was running short of cash. Kenneth Martin Jacobs was also running low, and when I beat his seven–six low hand with my seven–five, he called for a break.

Within seconds, Ace and I were back in the corner, arguing. "Forget the markers, Lefty, we don't need them anymore."

"But I want them."

"What are you going to do with them, wipe your ass? I told you, we're not playing for markers anymore, we're playing for ganars, and, as of this moment, you've got three with Duxbury, Laureate, and Jacobs. Let's quit."

"Quit? Are you out of your mind, with all that money left on that table? Besides, I want to bust Laureate."

"I've got news for you, kid, I think he's already busted."

"So, maybe he'll play for his castle."

"What in the hell would you do with a castle?"

I thought a minute and said, "I don't know."

158

"You know, of course, you could easily start losing."

"It's possible, but not likely," I said.

It was possible, and likely, and I did. I lost the next six hands and over fifty thousand dollars. Boswell was killing the three of us. On the next hand all four of us caught some good cards, the pot was worth over eighty thousand dollars, and Boswell and I split the pot.

Laureate had about three grand in front of him now and a concerned look on his face. Hank Boswell placed the cards down for Laureate to cut and he proceeded to deal the weirdest and most unbelievable hands I have ever seen in all the hours I have spent in smoke-filled rooms. As you know, the game was seven-card hi-low stud. On the last card (Jacobs dropped out on the fourth card) Boswell had the ten, jack, king, and queen of spades up; Laureate had three aces and a nine up, and I had, believe it or not, four fives up. We all looked as if we were going to declare high. My four fives gave me the honor and the task of betting. I dropped in ten thousand dollars. Laureate was now writing markers. He called and Boswell raised me twenty thousand. Ace White, standing behind me, swallowed awfully loud. I called Boswell's twenty and raised him back fifty. Laureate wrote a marker. Boswell called and raised me back fifty. I just called. Laureate wrote his final marker.

It was time to declare, and we all knew that if there was one winner, he would ganar the other two. We each took three chips into our hands and placed our hands under the table. At this point you put either one, two, or three chips in one hand and bring it up. One chip represents "low," two is "hi," and three means you're going "hi and low." All three of us were trying desperately to figure out what the other two were going to do. It's not what your hand reads, but how you declare. I had the best high hand on board with my four fives and Boswell had the best low hand with his ten, jack, queen, and king —the fact that they were spades meant nothing at this point.

159

Malcolm Laureate was stuck right in the middle with his three aces and a nine.

When all three of our fists were frozen about six inches above the table, ready to declare, Boswell said, "This gets down to what this game is all about, doesn't it?"

Kidding, I said, "We could always split the pot three ways and start all over again."

Boswell chuckled, but Laureate didn't think it was very funny.

"Come on, drop them," Malcolm snapped.

"I think my hand's stuck," I said, and Boswell laughed while Laureate glared.

Boswell then opened his hand and a single chip fell flat onto the green, felt-covered table. Laureate stopped breathing, opened his hand, and his one chip fell on the table right next to Boswell's. Slowly, I moved one finger at a time and opened my hand, but nothing fell because the palm of my hand was so sweaty it was holding tight to the single chip. Finally it, too, fell, rolled around the table, and dropped over, symbolically covering a portion of their two chips. We all were going low and that meant there was going to be *one winner*.

Now, everything depended on what we had in the hole. To go with his ten, jack, queen, and king of spades, Boswell had another jack, ten, and king, so he ended up with a pair of tens for his low hand.

To go with his three aces and a nine, Laureate had a pair of eights and another nine, so he ended up with two pair for his low hand. He, of course, assumed that Boswell and I were both going high. To go with my four-up fives, I had a six, two, and four in the hole, so I ended up with a pair of fives for my low hand and it was the very best low hand in the history of poker—as far as I am concerned.

"How in the hell could you possibly go low with four fives?" was Boswell's question.

"I don't know," I said. "It just seemed like a good idea at the time. You were looking very much like a straight flush."

"You telling me!"

Malcolm Laureate was crushed and in debt to Ace and me for over a hundred thousand dollars. "I don't believe it," he said, and looked up at me. "You don't look like a poker player, you don't talk like a poker player, you don't act like a poker player, and you sure don't play like a poker player. You're an amateur; but that's your thing, isn't it? People take one look at you and they're sure they can beat you. And even when you're beating their brains out, they take another look at you and still don't believe it."

Ace was smiling as he leaned over to count up the chips, cash, and markers.

"Where did you find this kid, Horace, on Mars?"

"No. He comes from a little jerkwater town called Ferno. They raise them up there. Raise them like they do horses in Kentucky, peanuts in Alabama, and beautiful women in Sweden. Hundreds of them up there."

Boswell and I were laughing as Laureate stared at Ace as if he was taking him seriously.

"It's the truth," said Ace. "Just go there and pick one out. Knock on any door and you'll find a kid who doesn't look like a poker player, talk like a poker player, act like a poker player, or play like a poker player, but he'll beat your brains out. Oh, incidentally, Malcolm, you owe us amateurs one hundred and thirty-seven thousand dollars . . . when do we get it?"

161

# 25

The following afternoon, Malcolm Laureate delivered a cashier's check for one hundred and thirty-seven thousand dollars to our suite and, as he handed the note to Ace, he looked over at me and shook his head. "You just don't look like a poker player," said Malcolm.

We had a late lunch while waiting for Izzie to call us from New York. The phone rang just as we were finishing up and packing to go to St. Croix for a week. Izzie reported that Linda Grizzard didn't return to Detroit and he was still desperately trying to find out where she was hiding. George Palmer Deeds announced in Dallas that he would definitely participate in the next Big Biazarro, but he would play neither Linda Grizzard nor me before that time.

That was all Izzie had to report, and he said he would check in with us later. When I asked Ace why we were going over to St. Croix, he said it would be a good place to rest after all we had been through in New York. He also said that schoolteachers flocked there during the summer and we could probably have a lot of fun.

"Schoolteachers!" I said. "I would think they'd be below your level of acceptance."

"To be honest with you, they always have turned me off with their June frustrations and September anxieties, but they're . . . easy. Easy to be with, easy to talk to, and easy in other ways."

As always, Ace's information was absolutely correct. The teachers were there in droves.

The Comanche Hotel in Christiansted was a well-constructed plexus of ramps, bridges, and archways leading to and from unique, comfortable rooms of all sizes, shapes, and colors. The rear of the hotel faced the harbor, where there was always a rich variety of seacraft: everything from weather-beaten banana boats to sleek pleasure vessels resting in the quiet blue waters. Down by the shoreline there was an old, gray, stone lighthouse reserved for "honeymooners only" and booked up far in advance. All of the rooms were moderately priced and we rented a beautiful two-bedroom suite overlooking the bay.

We got lucky and scored almost immediately as four of the schoolmarms were checking in across the hall.

Our first pair of suitor-tutors were from Newark—where else? They were loquacious chicks with slightly simian faces, but with bodies that looked as if they had been carved out of freckled marble and sanded to sheer perfection. Mine was a kindergartner, Meryl Miller, who bragged, even while making digital love to me, about how cute her little urchins were. What they said to her: "Why is your chest so big, Miss Miller?" What they brought her: ". . . everything from apples to aspirin." And how nice their parents were to her, except little Joey Stillman's father, who goosed her right in the ass during Parents' Day and right in front of little Joey and several other children.

Talking constantly wasn't Meryl Miller's only annoying habit. If there's one thing that turns me off, it's women who wear curlers, anywhere and anytime. Meryl Miller wore curlers everywhere and almost all the time. We met for lunch and she wore them, I took her to a secluded little club called Magic Isle for an afternoon of snorkeling and she wore them again. She did, luckily for her, take them off for dinner. But she put them back on before we went to bed. Believe me, they aren't very romantic. But as Ace always said, "A bird in the bush is worth two in the tree," or some damn thing.

After only four intensive days and nights of boobing around with the schoolmarms we were bored to death and anxiously looking for something different.

The Comanche Hotel's swimming pool sits just off the open-air dining room where we would sun each afternoon, order a chilled bottle of Tavel and one of their delicious boat salads, which consisted of sliced ham, swiss cheese, cole slaw, potato salad, chicken salad, olives, pickles, slivers of carrots, tomato slices, lettuce, and a spicy french dressing, all fresh and uniquely arranged on colorful straw baskets.

I'm positive the Comanche Hotel will one day become world famous for either its boat salads—*or* the gorgeous black waitresses who work in the dining room. There was one, a fox named Peggie, who automatically caught everyone's eye.

She was one of those long-legged stallion types who could conjure up all sorts of sexual fantasies just by passing in front of you with those round muscles in her backside working overtime to deliver the message. I had been trying for days to get her attention, but she never served in our section of the dining room. I kept asking Ace to switch tables, without telling him the reason. One day she was finally serving us and I couldn't believe her. She had a narrow face with pretty bright eyes and a warm and inviting smile. But it was her body that was sheer perfection. Every man in the restaurant usually stopped whatever he was doing when Peggie crossed the room.

"Boy, isn't she something?" I said to Ace as I watched her.
"Oh, I've seen better," he said unenthusiastically.
"Where?"
"Everywhere, kid. There are gorgeous women everywhere."

164

"As gorgeous as she is?"

"Definitely!"

When Peggie brought us our after-dinner coffee, I said to her, "Why don't you join us when you're finished work?"

"Okay," she said, and then to my chagrin, but not complete surprise, she turned to Ace and said, "Thanks for the roses. They were beautiful."

Ace smiled and nodded but kept his eyes down on his coffee cup. After counting to ten, I said, "So you've seen better, huh?"

Ace shrugged and toyed with his coffee.

Soon, our one week hiatus in St. Croix had turned into a four-week bonanza of dining, wining, and winning. During this period, Ace was completely taken up with Peggie, and I with envy and switching from teachers to nurses, secretaries, college students, and then finally back to schoolmarms—Meryl Miller to be exact, who was by this time brown as a berry but still as loquacious as ever. Two hours with Meryl and her mouth and her curlers was more than enough for me.

Peggie, as I am certain you can imagine, turned out to be a hell of a lot more than just a perfect body. I got to know her when the three of us would dine together and found her to be one of the sweetest, nicest, and most delicate women I have ever met. She had a wonderful personality, a broad-minded sense of humor, and a great deal of charm, class, and intelligence. She spoke very little and it was a welcome relief from the chatterboxes. The three of us had some great times together.

Finally, it was time to leave. We insisted on doing only and exactly what Peggie wanted on our last night in St. Croix. All she asked was to have dinner at La Terrace, an elegant little restaurant in Frederiksted (a smaller town on the opposite end of the island), and a drink at the Stone Balloon, her favorite bar.

The food at La Terrace was superb, but the fifteen-mile ride back to Christiansted was a complete and silent disaster, because Peggie was so sad about our leaving.

We entered the Stone Balloon, a dimly lit corner bistro near the Comanche Hotel, and found three seats at the bar. After toasting each other and swearing to be together again, the farewell pressures began to wear me down so I made a polite but quick exit into the split-level room off to the right. In the square, denlike hall there were a dozen small black tables where you could read, drink, or play cards. Finding an empty one, I sat and ordered three large double-rum punches. I finished the first, was sipping on the second, and watching the third cool it when this young, white, ugly, rich-looking teen-age kid sat uninvited at my table.

"Do you play five hundred rummy?" he asked brashly.

I couldn't believe he was talking to me, so after looking around, I pointed to myself. He nodded and said, "Yes, you, stupid!"

Within moments, a bevy of faces was smirking at me as if I was Santa Claus. Then some of them began to pull up chairs and sit around my table. Of course, of course, I said to myself, this kid, this toad of a boy, was evidently the island champ.

"Do you play, or don't you, asshole?"

I nodded quickly that I did.

"What rules?" it asked me.

"Yours. Yours, of course."

"Okay," it snapped. "You can deal nine, eleven, or thirteen cards. You can go out with a spread; that is, you don't need an extra card to throw away. Aces count fifteen up or down. The winner gets paid to five hundred only. Do you understand?"

"I think so," I said. "If not, I'll catch on as we go along."

"How much do you want to play for?"

"Whatever . . ." I said.

"Can you afford a dollar a point?"

Oh, God, did I want to castrate this little delinquent—and

166

his entire entourage, who snickered with every puny remark he made.

"A dollar a point is rather cheap, isn't it?" I said.

"All right," it said. "How about ten dollars a point? You don't look as if you can afford much more than that."

Again I looked around in disbelief. I had heard that on some of those islands they still practiced voodoo. I also checked my glass and smelled it. Could this be true? Little Lord Fauntleroy jacking up the price on me? And on my "road game"?

I spied Ace and Peggie in the crowd of faces, and coming up in front of them was this tall, wealthy-looking gentleman who was evidently the kid's father, or uncle, or whatever, but most certainly his backer, because he leaned over and whispered something into the kid's ear. It must have been something smart-ass, because the kid sat up, wet his lips, poked out his chest, and began to shuffle the cards. "How much can you afford to play for?" it snapped.

I was so shocked by this entire dreamlike sequence that I wasn't able to answer.

"How much? You're wasting my time," he shouted.

"I'll try ten dollars a point," I said, looking at Ace, who winked his approval.

We began to play, and Steven, that was the kid's name, played a straight, hard-driving game, but he lacked experience and he also played much too fast. Five hundred rummy, like most card games, has to be thoroughly figured. The cards have to be remembered and your gambles should be as certain as possible. Steven failed to figure out my style of play, not that it mattered, because I would have switched styles and confused him. This was probably his most amateurish move, although he made many others. But he was intelligent enough to learn from it, his father was paying the tab, and I can assure you, Ace and I would collect.

I lost the first game 500 to 465. The second and third games by lesser points. Rising from the table amidst loud cheering

167

and a few well-meant salutations, I held my seat out for Ace to sit and play.

Walking into the bar, I ordered three more rum punches. After gulping down the first, I lifted the second and heard a whisper, "I've seen better acting in grade school." I lowered my glass very slowly. Turning, I saw a yellow, slant-eyed devil smiling mischievously at me and I copied the smile. Pulling her miniskirt up high on her smooth, round thighs, she slid next to me. I immediately placed my hand on her bare knee and said, "There ought to be a law!"

"Against me wearing my skirt so high?" she asked.

"No. Against you wearing it any lower."

Demurely, she shoved my hand away, leaned over, and kissed me on the ear. "You *are* going to buy me a drink, aren't you?"

"Of course," I said.

"As many as I want, aren't you?"

"Why not?"

"Champagne!" she shouted vociferously.

Grabbing her hand, I guided her quickly over to a corner. Her name was Cricket Lang and unfortunately she had heard of us in New York. Her answer was negative when I asked if she had been following us. Then she ran her story down for me. She had been a well-paid prostitute in Chicago, a poor whore in New Orleans, and a high-class call girl in New York. After spending four and a half months in the house of detention because of a political shake-up, she decided to go straight—so she turned three quick hundred dollar tricks and stole away on a midnight flight to Puerto Rico. Harry, her former employer, followed her, caught her in a Condado Beach Hotel, beat her up, broke her nose, made violent love to her—and then fell asleep.

Cricket took advantage of this respite, tied Harry to the bed, gagged him, put the "Do Not Disturb" sign on the door, and caught the first flight leaving Puerto Rico—"for anywhere."

168

Caribair, a fly-with-us-if-you-dare airline, brought her to St. Croix.

I told Miss Cricket that I would ordinarily cry over such a sad tale, but I was too happily drunk. She informed me that I could probably sober up rather quickly and cry very easily if she announced to the barful of Cruzans that Ace and I were professional gamblers who were taking complete advantage of little Steven.

"All right, Cricket, what in the hell do you want?"

"Company," she answered simply.

"What company? Whose company?"

"Yours!"

"Mine! Why mine?"

Then she explained. Harry had got out of the hotel, checked at the airport, and followed her to St. Croix. He was at that moment out in the dark streets of Christiansted looking for her.

"So what do you want from me?" I asked.

"Just let me stay with you," she said. "Harry's a coward. As long as I'm with someone he won't say a word to me."

"Why don't you call the police? I don't want to get mixed up in any family arguments."

"You don't have any choice," she informed me politely enough.

"That's not entirely true," I said. "All I have to do is go in there and stop that game and *your* game is right out the window."

Cricket smiled and then said, "Go ahead."

If there's one thing I can't stand it's running into a smart-ass kid and a smart-ass broad in the same night—so I decided to get drunk. It wasn't long before Cricket and I had killed two bottles of Piper-Heidsieck, were the best of friends, and stoned out of our minds. Ace, now twenty thousand dollars richer, thanks to Steven and his dad, and Peggie joined us on the next two bottles. By 1 A.M., the four of us couldn't begin to pass a sobriety test; and there, sitting quietly at the end of the

169

bar with a rhinoceros face and the anger of ten smoked hornets, was Harry.

"There he is," said Cricket, finding it extremely difficult to point at him.

"There he is," I said.

"There he is," said Peggie.

"There he is," echoed Ace. "There *who* is?"

"Harry, of course," said Cricket.

"Harry, of course," repeated Peggie.

"Oh, of course, Harry," said Ace. "Who in the hell is Harry? Let's invite him over and find out."

"Let's not," said Cricket.

"Is old Harry a friend of yours, Cricket baby?" Ace asked.

"Not exactly."

Leaning over, I whispered into Ace's ear, "Harry is a P."

"You're kidding," he laughed; then leaning over to Peggie, he giggled, "Harry is a P."

This caused a chain reaction of laughter and we all began to sing, "Harry is a P. Harry is a P. Harry is a P-P P-P P."

"What's a PP?" Peggie asked innocently.

"A PP, my dear," Cricket said very properly, "happens to be a pink Protestant."

"Oh, really," said Ace. "I thought it was a pink pussycat."

"Peter Piper," shouted Cricket.

"Pickled peppers," laughed Peggie.

"Pepperoni pizza," said Ace.

"Perfect period," added Cricket.

"Hold it. Hold it," I interrupted, having sat quietly by while the others carried on the burden of disdain. "How's this? Perforated prophylactic?"

"Bad! Bad!" said Ace.

"Purple pimp," Cricket cried bitterly, staring directly at Harry.

Then we all turned and in a voice shouted, "Harry is a pimp!"

This drove poor Harry right out into the street and we were forced to carry on alone until closing time.

I don't remember passing out, but the morning sun, rising and flooding the suite with its brilliance, woke me. Through hung-over, shrouded eyes I saw Cricket lying nude beneath the sheet. I took off my clothes, jumped in and out of a warm shower, and crawled in beside her. She instantly cuddled up to me and we kissed. It's odd, but she looked exactly the same as she did the night before. Her eyes, like ink dots on ivory balls, sparkled and were darker than her hair, which hung long, glowed shiny-black, and smelled of jasmine. I brushed a strand back from her face and kissed her again. Fully this time.

Her slanted features and narrow mouth were childlike and sultry. Her body was long, curvy, and extremely soft and pleasant. Cricket was Chinese, patient, and lovely.

Unlike Meryl Miller, who made love as a sort of collusion of stealth, a frantic concentrated attack of bodies, a shouting revival meeting, and a don't-touch-me-now-that-we're-finished soap opera, Cricket was *amoureuse*. From start to finish, she was yours—completely and proficiently yours. A professional with charm and warmth and yet a slight shyness which gave me the feeling she was still a child. And I suppose she was in many ways, when you consider the fact she was the same age as I, twenty-three years old at the time.

I cannot recall one second of our hours together when some part of Cricket's lovely body wasn't touching mine, be it her hips, hands, or whatever—and that's nice. Very nice. In a word, Cricket was beautiful.

For the next few weeks, the four of us were inseparable. Peggie took a vacation from the Comanche and we partied. Champagne and love flowed all over the island. It was one of the better times I have had in my entire life.

On August 8, 1975, the telephone woke us as Izzie was calling from New York.

"I've got some bad news for you, Ace."

"What is it?"

"Your place, Schiffron's West, burned down last night. No one was hurt, but the building was completely gutted."

"Fuck it. Where's Linda Grizzard?"

"But, Ace, did you hear what I said?"

"Did you hear what *I* said? Where's Linda Grizzard?"

Izzie, shook by Ace's indifference, muttered something under his breath and then reported that Linda was over in Berlin playing the German Champion Sampler. She was supposed to be leaving from there, but Izzie didn't know of her destination.

"Keep on it," said Ace. "We're on our way back."

We had booked seats on a late afternoon plane for San Juan. There we would catch a flight for New York. The sun was gliding low, crimsoning the sky from top to bottom as we waited for our plane to board. The four of us, Ace, Peggie, Cricket, and me, stood silent and sad watching the day and our good times slip away. Finally, Ace pulled me over to the side and said, "What do you think you're doing?"

"What do you mean?"

"Cricket is what I mean."

"She's got nothing to do with us."

"You're taking her with you, aren't you?"

"Yes, of course, but it's got nothing to do with us."

"Listen, silly," he snapped. "Can't you see the spot this puts me in with Peggie? Look at her, she's about to cry. It's bad enough leaving her here, but with you taking Cricket . . ."

"Take her with you," I suggested calmly.

"And do what?" said Ace. "I had it all worked out that we'd be back in a month or two; now you make me look like a creep and a liar."

"Don't worry, she'll be all right," I said. "Look at old Harry over there. He's just waiting for us to get on that plane. Old Harry, I didn't want to mention it before, Ace, has been eying Peggie for some time. I think he's pretty well forgotten all about Cricket. Like I said, she'll be fine. Harry will see to it."

172

Ace looked at Harry, was about to charge after him, when I grabbed his arm and pulled him over to the women.

"Ladies," I said, "Mr. Ace White, of New York City and all points north, has a grand announcement to make."

"I do?"

"Of course you do."

He looked quizzically at me.

"About the party."

"The party!"

"Yes, the party for *four!*"

"What party?" Ace shouted, perplexed. "I don't know anything about any damn party."

"Yes you do, now say it!"

He frowned at me and I nodded my head toward Harry. Ace looked at Peggie and, grimacing, began reluctantly, "Me and my . . . partner here have decided to take the party to New York, champagne and all."

Cricket cheered and kissed Ace, then hugged and kissed me. Peggie moved over to Ace, touched him, and said, "It's all right. You don't have to take me. I'll be all right and I'll understand."

"I'm glad somebody does," said Ace, "because I don't."

He reached into his coat pocket and pulled out a ticket with Peggie's name already on it.

"Why, you old phony!" I shouted.

"I'm a gambler," said Ace. "Now if anything goes wrong I can always hold you responsible for talking me into it."

"I didn't talk you into it—she did . . . and without saying a word," I said, pointing to Peggie, who was all but in tears.

Ace turned to her then and did something that was very unusual for the old hardnose. Right there in broad daylight he took Peggie in his arms and kissed her. He whispered something that made her smile. And to this day—to this day, even though I've asked many times—I still don't know what he said.

# 26

It was great to get back to New York and the brownstone. John couldn't believe his eyes when he met the four of us at the airport. Hilda, always cool, wasn't shook up at all about having two new women in the house. Peggie and Cricket, being the kind of women they were, managed to win John and Hilda over within a few days.

The party that had begun in St. Croix carried over into New York. Peggie, of course, had never been to New York City, and Cricket admitted she had never seen Manhattan the way we showed it to her.

Three weeks passed and the party was coming to its inevitable end. It's one thing to be down on a tropical isle with nothing to do but drink, love, dance, and forget the rest of the world is out there, but New York is facts. The city is a grown-up's town. Manhattan is an island of realization. You can play only so long and then you've got to get down to business. And my business was playing poker. And right now my main business was finding Linda Grizzard and sitting across a table from her.

"Sporados feels," Ace said, as the five of us, Ace, Manny,

Izzie, Fast Eddy, and I, sat having a meeting in the living room one afternoon, "that it's between you and Linda now. He feels the other six players will probably be himself, Deeds, Hank Boswell, Peter Sampler, Jimmy Palusso, and Lord Lichfield. There are others who want to play, of course, but Sporados being the champion gets to call the shots and the other Masters have pretty much agreed to it."

"Did they poll all twenty-seven of them?" I asked.

"No one knows for sure," Izzie said.

"Why is it a choice between Linda and me?"

"I think it's a lot of reasons," said Ace. "You've both been winning like crazy. You both have four ganars, and you have money behind you. Besides, Sporados would like some fresh blood in the game. He's the one who has been pushing for you kids. A lot of the others don't want anything to do with you—for a lot of reasons. Mainly because they're afraid of you."

"I think it is ridiculous that we have a little over a year to go before the Biazarro and only a broad is standing in our way," said Fast Eddy.

"She's good," said Izzie.

"Where is she?" I asked, and looked at Izzie.

"She has to play you, kid," Ace confirmed. "She has to play you or she can't get into the game either."

"Then why aren't they looking for me like we're looking for her?"

"It's no secret where you are, kid."

"Why are they stalling?" I asked.

"Maybe she's afraid of you," offered Manny.

"Are you afraid of her?" Ace asked.

"No. It's not the fear, it's the curiosity that's getting to me."

"Have you been studying her dossier?"

"Backwards, I know that dossier. You could blindfold me and bring her into the room and I'd know she's here. I know what she looks like, talks like, and smells like, and I've never been within a thousand miles of her for all I know. I want her worse than I want the Big Biazarro right now."

175

"Don't get too anxious," Ace warned. "You'll misplay your game."

"I've got a feeling she's going to stall as long as she can, so you may as well relax, Lefty," suggested Izzie.

"Relax? How can I relax?"

"You know you can beat her," said Fast Eddy. "You can beat everybody. Especially a broad. Broads always get emotional. You may as well get ready, because when you beat her you can bet she will turn on the waterworks."

"I don't know about that, Eddy," I said. "She's played a lot of hands. She didn't cry at those stand-offs, and I don't think she'll cry if she loses."

"You act as if you respect this broad."

"He has to respect her," Ace said firmly. "You underestimate a player of her caliber in one hand and you can blow it all. Every poker game gets down to one hand and you play a shark cheap in that hand and you might as well give your soul to Jesus because your ass is going to belong to the shark."

"I cannot believe this broad is that good!"

"You don't have to believe it, Eddy, just as long as Lefty is aware of it," said Ace.

"I'm aware of it."

"Stay that way," Ace advised. "And now for the rest of you; we're forming a corporation. You're all going to be a part of it, so let's drop the fancy sport clothes and casual duds. From now on, it's going to be dark or pin-stripe suits with dress shirts and ties. Now, if you're wondering why I've decided on you, it's because it's almost impossible today to find men you can trust. I could surround myself with lawyers, but within a year I'd be signing everything over to them. I could surround myself with hoods, but hoods can be bought. And then there's always relatives, but they usually turn out worse than hoods with some of your blood running in their veins, and on their hands. Besides, I don't have any close relatives that I know of. So, I have decided to take a chance on friends. If you can't trust your best friends, you may as well hang it up, right?"

176

"We'll stick with you, Ace," said Manny. "And if any of you three guys cross him, you're going to have to answer to me."

"What about if you cross him?" asked Fast Eddy.

"I had nothing to begin with and I'm not looking to set the world on fire," said Manny. "I'm perfectly satisfied with what I've got with Ace, and I'll bust anybody's back who tries to mess it up."

"Do not look at me," said Fast Eddy. "I had less than you did when I came up here from Georgia."

"All right, that's enough," said Ace. "Just as long as we know where we stand. The plan now is to split up and look for Linda Grizzard. Izzie, you're going to England. I booked you a suite at the Dorchester, and a chauffeur to drive you around. Manny, you're going out to California. Linda's father owns a lot of property in the Malibu Colony area. I've rented a house close to theirs. All you have to do is keep your eyes open.

"Eddy, you'll be in Detroit. You'll be staying with a friend of mine in Grosse Pointe, a short distance from the Grizzard estate. If she comes back there, I want to know immediately. And that goes for all of you. Lefty and I will be staying here for a while just in case they want to find us. But let me emphasize this—from this point on, you are all wealthy men. See that you act like it."

Manny Robertson, Izzie Rodriguez, and Fast Eddy Youngblade hit the road, and Ace White and I hung around the brownstone and the high-brow places of Manhattan.

Peggie and Cricket were still with us, but after three months of the big city life, pretty Peggie began to long for the fresh, clean openness of the islands. Who could blame her? So, after several long and tearful discussions on the subject, we put Peggie on the plane for St. Croix right after the holidays.

Cricket and I really dug each other, but, as with all my relationships, my mind soon drifted to my obsession, the Big Biazarro. One night, lying before the fireplace, Cricket cuddled up to me and I ignored her as I had been doing lately.

177

"Things ain't too good between us, are they, Lefty?" Cricket said sadly.

I shook my head in agreement.

"I know you're hung out on the game, but I don't need much of your time, or your love. I don't bug you, do I, baby?"

"No."

"I mean, I would do anything in the world to please you. You know that, don't you?"

"Yes, I know, but there's nothing anyone can do."

"Gee, Lefty, I don't understand what's happened to us."

"Nothing's happened to us, Cricket, it's just that the party is over. It doesn't mean we're through or anything, it just means I've got to get down to business and start preparing myself for the game."

"It's not only the game, Lefty, don't you know that?"

"It's the game, it's always the game, and it will always be the game."

Cricket was crying now and I couldn't find any words to comfort her.

"Are you going to kick me out?"

"Of course not, we just can't go on partying anymore for a while."

Continuing to cry, Cricket said, "Oh, Lefty, you never, ever loved me. And every day I fall more and more in love with you."

She kissed me and cried even harder. "Oh, God, I wish I was Angel DuPont."

Pushing her away and shaking her, I stared at her to get her meaning. She was frightened and wide-eyed.

"You'd better be glad you're not her, because she's dead and you're alive. Think about it."

I got up then and went to bed.

I have to admit when Ace announced the next day that he had heard from one of the guys that Linda Grizzard was planning on being in California in a couple of weeks, I was greatly relieved.

178

"I might not be here when you get back, baby," Cricket said sadly at the airport. "I mean, I might be somewhere else. Like maybe London, or Paris, or . . . Newark. It doesn't matter, does it, baby?"

"Of course, it matters."

Cricket stared at me and I turned away.

"I guess we're eighty-six, ain't we, baby? The party's over, the curtain's coming down, and we've had our last hurrah," said Cricket. "Does it matter if I die, Lefty? Oh, baby, you were so sweet to me. Hold me. Hold Cricket one last time like you did that first night in St. Croix. Touch me, feel me. Don't forget me, Lefty. Don't forget me. And when you think about us . . . please think about the good times. Only the good times are important."

I never saw Cricket again, but I never forgot her either and I never will. You see, she was right—only the good times are important. And we, she and I, had a hell of a lot of them. So be it.

The word was that Linda, her father, mother, and twelve-man entourage were in South Africa and weren't due in California for at least a week. Ace decided that we would make a stop in Las Vegas. I had never been there, but like everyone else I had heard it could be a fun town.

Three men in dark business suits met us at the airport and Ace didn't seem too pleased about it. When I asked who they were, he said he would tell me later.

They took us to one of the main Strip's tallest hotel-casinos. Ace was really in a bad mood, and he told me to wait downstairs while he went up to "The Tower."

Pointing his finger at my eyes, he said, "Don't play anything until I get back. Now, I mean it. It's very important that you just watch until I come back."

"Okay. Okay."

Ace disappeared with two of the three gentlemen while the

third stayed with me. I took the time to send Jack and Della a post card and then walked into the gaming rooms.

The casino was moderately crowded for a late afternoon in the middle of February. I walked over, watched the action at a dice table for a few moments, and when I got an urge to place a bet, I remembered what Ace had said and walked away. Blackjack was next, and unless you're playing, it can be one of the most unentertaining games to watch. Next were the roulette wheels, and I stood there the longest, trying to figure a sequence. The high numbers were riding for a few turns and then the middle numbers came up five out of the next six times. Then, all three of the twelve sections started to fall. And, finally, zero and double zero came in consecutively, and that can kill you.

The big money game that Wednesday evening seemed to be baccarat. They were betting hundreds on the possible *nine* game. It's not one of my favorites to watch, so I mozied on, heading irrevocably toward the poker tables. Of the twelve available, three were in action. One each of the fifteen to thirty dollar, the three to six dollar and one to three range. At the last table there was something rather humorous going on. At one end of the table was this huge, very up-tight, midwestern-type blond lady with an expensive beehive hairdo and a holier-than-thou look on her snooty face. Down at the other end of the table were these two old, little Jewish ladies playing their cards close to their chest. Let me tell you, the two old "bubahs" had the snooty chick in a vise. They had her jammed up and jelly tight. And Miss Snooty was so busy looking around the casino to see who was looking at her that she wasn't even aware of what was going on. The grandmas were betting her from side to side. And they were serious, too. Neither one of them cracked a smile. Just kept playing those cards for all they were worth, and raking in the chips.

I decided to sit down at the center of the table and watch, but no sooner had I taken a seat than two other men sat on either side of me and ordered chips from the pretty, dark-haired dealer who talked with a Texas accent.

A pit boss whispered something in her ear about me, and she gave me one of those knowing smiles and a pile of chips. I said, "No thanks," but she wouldn't take them back.

Soon, all of the chairs were filled. A man had taken Miss Snooty's chair and another had taken one of the old bubah's chair, but the smaller of the grandmas refused to budge.

A thin, curly-haired youth was pulling on her arm, trying to pry her out of the seat. "Please, Nanna!"

"Allen, get your hands off me. This is my lucky table."

"The game is changing, Grandma. Please let me have the seat."

"I'm going to hit you, Allen, if you don't get your hands off of me!"

He continued to pull on her and she whacked him with her purse so hard he backed off for a moment. Just then, the kid's father rushed up to the table and pleaded with her, "Mother, please, let Allen play for a while."

"I can play better than Allen and you know it."

"I know, dear, but he needs the experience."

"No!" she yelled as each of them took an arm and lifted her bodily from the chair. "Leave me alone. Somebody help me!"

Right then, Ace came running up to the table and pulled me away.

"I thought I told you not to play."

"I wasn't playing! I was watching."

Ace was angry, but not all of it was directed at me.

"Come on, we're getting the hell out of this town."

"We're going?"

"And right this minute," he said.

"Can't we see a show or something?"

"No!"

We went out to the main desk where our luggage was still sitting. I looked back and the three dark-suited men were still with us. Ace and I grabbed a cab and started for the airport.

181

"You want to quit huffing and puffing and tell me what it's all about?"

"They want you to play their boy."

"Who's they, and who's their boy?"

"Don't be naïve, Lefty. Their boy is named Vincent Romero and they want you to play him so he can start getting a rep."

"Can't I beat him?"

"In a straight-up game, yes. But who in the hell knows what they're going to pull. Besides, at this point, you have nothing to gain and everything to lose by playing anyone except Linda Grizzard."

"Gee, Ace, I don't like running like this. Why don't I play him and beat his brains out and teach him a lesson?"

"For the simple reason, kid, they would love to get into the Big Biazarro, and a match with you would start them on their way, and I don't want to be responsible for letting them get their grubby hands into that game."

"I think you're taking this thing too seriously, Ace. After all, they're just businessmen like anyone else."

Ace looked at me then with a deep, concentrated disappointment. "Kid, I never actually knew until this very moment how goddamn fucking stupid and naïve you are."

I started to say something and he put his hand over my mouth and said, "Don't say anything more, or I might throw your ass off the plane."

# 27

Arriving at the Los Angeles International Airport at 3:00 A.M., we rented a car and Ace told me to drive to the Beverly Hills Hotel while he lay back to get some sleep. I don't know whether you know L.A., but there is no one on the streets at three in the morning. After an hour of driving around like I was lost, which I was, and being completely exhausted, I decided to stop at the first resting place I came to, which turned out to be the Rancho Motel in West Los Angeles near Century City.

Ace was asleep by the time we got to the motel, so I parked the car and walked up to the office window and rang the bell. A skeptical-looking dude with buggy eyes and a crew cut stepped cautiously up to the window.

"What do you want?" he asked quickly.

"A room," I said. "What else?"

He peeked out into the yard and asked, "Who's with you?"

"My partner. He's asleep in the car. Look, we've been traveling all day and night. Can we please have a room so we can get some sleep?"

"How long do you want it for?"

"Just for tonight."

"That'll be forty dollars."

"Okay."

"Each."

"Each!"

"That's right."

I looked at the motel. It wasn't that impressive. "All right," I said, "but that room better look better than the rest of this place."

"That'll be three days in advance."

"What are you talking about? You pay as you go!"

"Not here. And not you. You look suspicious. So does he. You're black and he's white; that looks even more suspicious."

"Screw off, jerk," I said and turned away just as Ace came up to the window. "What in the hell are we doing here?"

"I couldn't find the damn place!"

"So what's holding us up?"

"This guy says we look suspicious and he's trying to stick us up."

"As tired as I am I probably look a lot worse than suspicious. Pay him and let's get some sleep."

Reluctantly, I reached into my pocket, pulled out the cash, and handed it to the jerk, who gave me the key to Room 18. The room was small, barely large enough for the twin beds and the huge color TV set that sat high on a shelf staring down at us. By 4:15 we were fast asleep, but at 5:00 A.M. somebody was pounding on our door.

"Who is it?" I shouted.

"It's the police! Open up!"

Ace and I gave each other perplexed looks, and then I got up slowly and walked to the door just as they began to pound again. Standing there were two of the world's biggest and ugliest cops and a short, fat, middle-aged couple who looked as if they hadn't made love in years—she in her nightgown and he in his shorts and T-shirt. All four of them gaped at Ace and me as if we had burned the American flag, peed on an apple pie, and crapped on the White House lawn.

"Can I help you, Officers?"

"What are you doing in this room?" the short man asked.

"Sleeping."

"Don't be a smart-ass," snapped one of the cops. "These people were burglarized tonight and we want to know how you got the key to this room."

Ace and I looked at each other, and I said, "And he thought *we* looked suspicious!"

It took us an hour to convince the cops and the couple that we had been ripped off right along with them by the burglar, and had nothing to do with the crime. The policemen finally allowed us to go back to bed, but Ace announced that we had decided to move into the Beverly Hills Hotel, and this, of course, made the police wary of us again. But as Ace explained it, "Never put off till today what you can do . . . what you can do . . ." I don't know; one of them damn sayings.

Anyway, we changed from our pajamas into our street clothes and drove to the Beverly Hills, which towered out of the thick, green foliage lining beautiful Sunset Boulevard. A front portion of the hotel was painted green to blend in perfectly with the landscape, but the main lobby I found rather bland and very disappointing for such a luxurious hotel. There were also a lot of little dudes dressed in green running around trying to help the customers. Two of these little green dudes grabbed our bags and rushed them up to our third-floor suite—which was five times larger than the motel room. Within minutes, we were fast asleep again, and this time for good.

When I woke up at 2:15 in the afternoon, Ace was gone, but had left a note that read, "Gone to see Manny. Will check back with you later today. Behave yourself and stay out of trouble."

After showering and shaving, I ventured down to the Polo Lounge and found it pleasant enough, but crowded and a bit stuffy, so I moved out onto the terrace. The waiter came over, smiled, took my order of sausage, scrambled eggs, milk, and toast, and then informed me that the tree in the center of the yard was an African pepper tree. I thanked him for his ethnic information and told him I wish he would move his ass because I was starving.

The terrace was made of white brick, and each glass table had a fresh bouquet of daisies and a pink and white umbrella overhead to block out the sun. As my waiter poured the coffee, I gazed around at some of the other guests. There were about fifteen people sitting and eating, and the couple that caught my eye were seated at the back lounge table. He was trying to look important while gabbing loudly on the telephone about getting Steve McQueen for two million dollars to play in his next film; and seated next to him was this young blond girl who appeared a mere sixteen but her tits were at least forty-two. As he puffed on a cigar, looked around the room, and continued to shout into the telephone, she sat there with an infantile, witless look in her pretty blue eyes, and a molded smile on her lips. She caught me looking at her, stared back, and when I refused to turn away, she lifted a huge red lollipop from her plate and licked it. I turned away.

Appearing suddenly in the doorway was a midget dressed in one of those red, button-lined military jackets, and he began to call out, "Telephone for Mr. James. Telephone for Mr. James." He obviously knew who Mr. James was because he walked directly across the room to the back table where Mr. James continued to shout into the phone while his companion continued to lick the huge red lollipop with long wet strokes.

Have you ever noticed how you can be looking one way and a person can enter from another direction and light up the room so much with her presence it can startle the hell out of you? Well, evidently there was a fashion show just starting in the Polo Lounge and the models would all come out and take a turn around the terrace.

She, this vision, was about five-foot-eight, svelte, black, and super-gorgeous. I'm certain she was wearing something fantastic, but even burlap couldn't look bad on her. My eggs came and I ignored them. My waiter asked if there was anything else, and I acted as if he didn't even exist.

"Come on, baby," I whispered to myself as she stopped in front of each table, did a turn, smiled, and walked away. Finally, she was there. Right there in front of me, did her turn, smiled, and started away.

"How much is it?" I asked quickly to keep her near me.

"Two hundred and eighty dollars," she said, and her voice sounded like a wisp of sand.

I was so taken by this creature that I couldn't think of anything else to say, so I said, "Why don't you give up this ridiculous life and sit down here and have some eggs?"

She chuckled and walked away. I watched her every move until she disappeared into the Polo Lounge. Calling the waiter over, I soon learned he didn't know her or even her name—that she was hired by the dress designer. Some cat by the name of Blackhole or something.

I almost died holding my breath until she reappeared in the doorway. I was hoping she would at least look at me as she entered the terrace, but she was doing her job, which wasn't to entertain me personally.

"What's your name?" I asked, and she said, "Carrie," and floated away. "Carrie." I said the name over and over again to myself. What else would her name be but Carrie? It's such a pleasant name for such a marvelous woman. As I continued to watch her do her turn around the terrace, the waiter came up and blocked my view, asking, "Is there something wrong with your eggs, sir?"

"If you don't get the hell out of my way, there's going to be something wrong with you!"

By the time Mr. Efficiency got out of the way, Carrie was once again disappearing through the door and into the lounge.

There were also other models coming in and out, but I found no difficulty at all in ignoring them.

Again the long wait until she returned. I decided to take a wild shot because I knew sooner or later she would stop coming through that door.

As she approached me, I said, "I'm in Room 328. I'll see you there after the show."

She smiled, did her turn, and kept going. I sat there trying desperately to fathom what her smile meant. Did it mean she would be there? Or that I was a silly dilly with the nerve of an elephant and the brains of a mentally deranged turkey. Then I thought to myself her smile could have meant she liked me, but was debating with herself whether or not it was a good idea. Then on the other hand it could have meant she thought I was an obnoxious pain in the ass with the audacity of a tiger and the mental capacity of a feeble-minded flounder.

It suddenly dawned on me that the show was over. More than enough time had elapsed for Carrie to return and she hadn't. I quickly dropped a ten dollar bill on the table and dashed off the terrace as if I had been gripped with a sudden attack of diarrhea. Running through the lobby to the elevator, I almost stepped on the midget who once again was calling out, "Telephone for Mr. James."

As I got off the elevator on the third floor, I was stopped by the sight of my door being open. In New York that would more than likely mean that a second-story man or a dope addict was relieving you of your valuables. Out of force of habit, I didn't even think how ridiculous the thought was. I merely crept up to the doorway and peeked in. Bending over and revealing the most beautiful pair of legs and fantastic round bottom was a maid dressed in a short brown smock. Before saying anything, I looked around the suite to see if Carrie had arrived.

"Pardon me, but did a young lady come here looking for me?"

"*No hablo inglés,*" the Chicano woman said and smiled. She was young, no more than twenty-five, and even though my thoughts were somewhere else, I couldn't help noticing how pretty she was. As I stood there trying to figure out what to do about Carrie, the maid assumed I was waiting for her to leave, so she picked up her dust rags, went into the bathroom, and came out with a large scrub pail containing. two mops.

I said, "Hold it," pointed to myself, and then to the door. "I go. I go. You stay. You stay." Stepping out into the hallway, I had to laugh at myself for thinking I would be able to cop a woman like Carrie just by giving her my room number. I continued to chuckle at myself as I walked to the elevator and went back downstairs.

"Let's see, I'll have some scrambled eggs and a sirloin steak rare. Better give me some coffee, too."

The waiter stood staring at me as if I was more than a little strange. He wanted to ask me something, but decided not to, and just walked away.

"Telephone for Mr. James."

I turned and saw that Mr. James was still on the telephone and sitting next to him was the young blond girl still licking her candy.

It took me an hour to finish my steak and eggs, and I had a couple of coffees with honey before calling it quits. While I sat there, I kept gazing up at the doorway hoping against hope that Carrie would come floating through. Needless to say, it was in vain, so I got up and returned to the room. As I opened the door, I expected anything but what I saw. Carrie, dressed in a chic, beige pantsuit and a black turtleneck sweater, was sitting on the bed. All I could say was "Hi."

She smiled and said "Hi" also.

And then someone else said "Hi." It was Ace; and by the smirk on his old, pale face I could tell he had already got in his best shot.

"Have you two met?" Ace asked.

"I thought you were going to see Manny?" I said bitterly out of the side of my mouth.

"I dropped in, said hello; he had nothing to tell me, and that was it."

"Too bad."

Ace then introduced us and I wanted to die.

"Carrie and I are going to have dinner at one of the best places in town," he said. "What's it called, baby?"

"Scandia," she said, as she and I kept looking at each other.

"Can I come?" I asked like a little boy.

"Lefty . . . ?" Ace chuckled at me.

"But I saw her first."

Ace laughed and I realized how silly it sounded, then the three of us laughed together.

"I'm not busy tomorrow night," Carrie said to relieve my agony.

"Right now you think you're not," I explained, "but by the time this old nudge gets through brainwashing you with that 1932 dialogue you won't want to see anybody but him."

Ace put on his suit jacket and straightened his tie. "How do I look?" he asked, pouring salt into my wounds.

"Like shit. Any other questions?"

"Yeh. What are you going to do tonight?"

"I'm going to try to think of a hundred ways to kill you."

"Let's go, baby," Ace said, taking Carrie by the arm.

Right then an extraordinary thing happened. As Carrie passed me, she paused, looked into my eyes, then leaned over and kissed me fully on the lips. I closed my eyes to savor the kiss, and also to keep from seeing her leave.

For the remainder of the afternoon, I rested and read a few chapters of *Games People Play*. When it was time to eat again, I got up, took a shower, dressed, and went down alone for dinner.

# 28

On my way to the main dining room I saw the famous Mr. James and his girl friend talking with a dapper-looking gentleman with dark hair, and my hustling instincts went into form.

"Excuse me. Are you Mr. James?"

He smiled proudly at the recognition and said, "Yes, I am. Can I be of some help to you, sir?"

"I hope so," I said as if a bit embarrassed. "I'm only in town for a few days, and when I mentioned to some of the people over at Paramount that I was staying here, well, they said right away if I wanted anything I should check with you."

He grabbed the bait. "Paramount? Who do you know at Paramount?"

"Barney and I hung around together during the film festival last year in Cannes."

He said "Excuse me" to the black-haired gentleman, took my arm, and guided me into a corner.

"You don't mean Mr. Hiller?"

"He's Barney to me."

"Right, right," he said, pausing while trying to figure how to use me. "My name is Foster James. Everybody calls me Fuzzy. You can call me Fuzzy."

"Thanks, Fuzzy."

"Can I buy you dinner?"

"No, that isn't necessary. What I wanted to know was if you knew where there was any action?"

"Girls? Don't worry about girls. I'll get you girls."

"I appreciate that and I'll keep it in mind," I said, "but what I was looking for is some gambling action. Cards. Poker, five hundred rummy, gin. I'm on a losing streak and I'm trying like hell to break it."

He stood there with his eyes bugging out of their sockets, staring at me as if I was something good to eat.

"Cards . . . ?" he finally uttered.

"Yeh, you know, something to pass the time away."

I flashed my bankroll on him then and he almost fainted.

"What do you do for a living?" he gasped.

I chuckled, lowered my head, and said, "Well, let me put it to you this way because I'm sure you'll understand what I mean. Two years ago I had to change my citizenship from American to French." I winked then and he got the message. Whatever it meant to him, I don't know, but it did the trick.

After eating a top sirloin New York steak and stuffing myself on some pie à la mode, all on Fuzzy's bill, the four of us, Fuzzy, the chick, the black-haired man, and I, went to Fuzzy's room to play five hundred rummy—my road game.

There is no bigger favor a person can do for me, and no greater harm they can do themselves, than mark a deck of cards. Because the first thing a hustler does is check to see if the cards are marked, and once I saw they were, I began to use them, too. With my knowledge of cards it was just a matter of time before the money began to swing my way.

Frank, the black-haired man, lost four thousand dollars, paid me off in cash, and called it quits. Fuzzy was six thousand dollars in debt to me, but said his luck would change and he wanted to keep playing. Not being a hard man, I suggested he give it up because once my luck started running good it didn't stop. But he insisted, and by midnight, the chick, Candy, was fast asleep on the sofa, my eyes were getting tired, and Fuzzy owed me twenty-seven thousand dollars.

"Just let me get out the old checkbook," he said, trying to sound jovial about his demise.

"No checks, Fuzzy. Cash on the line just like your friend."

"My checks are good."

"I don't doubt it, but I have no use for them. No place to cash them. You understand."

"I don't know if I can come up with that much cash."

"You don't, huh?" I said cold enough to scare him.

Fuzzy smiled, hoping I would do the same and say that I was kidding. But I stared him straight in the eye and said, "Get it up!"

He reached into his pocket and pulled out forty-two dollars in cash. "This is it," he explained. "I pay for everything with my credit cards. I'm broke."

"What have you got that's worth anything?" I asked, taking a gold watch off his arm and a five-carat diamond off his finger.

"You're not going to take them, are you?"

"Of course not," I said. "I'm just going to hold them until you get my money. Let's see, this junk should be worth a couple of thousand, maybe."

I looked around the room and saw nothing of value, except for one thing—I went over and woke up Candy.

"What are you going to do?" Fuzzy asked.

"I don't know, maybe I'll buy her a bigger lollipop. Don't worry, Fuzzy, the minute you come up with the cash, you can have her back."

"I could have you arrested for kidnapping."

"I suppose you could, except that being a French citizen, I'll probably fall under the protection of diplomatic immunity."

"You're no diplomat."

193

"Neither are you, so we're both left without any protection. Just get the money, Fuzzy, and you and I will be friends forever."

Candy sat up and peered at us through sleep-filled eyes. "What's up, Fuzzy?"

Fuzzy looked at me, then walked over and sat on the sofa next to Candy, who lifted a lollipop from somewhere and stuck it in her mouth.

"Ahh," Fuzzy began to explain, "this gentleman wants— would like, ahh; honey, I hate to ask you this and I know you're not going to want to do it, but would you consider going with this gentleman until I handle some business?"

"Okay," Candy said simply and started across the room.

Fuzzy sat stunned on the sofa as Candy opened the door, turned back to me, and said, "You coming?"

I chuckled to myself and followed her out of the room.

When we got to the suite, I saw that Ace's bedroom door was closed and I feared the worst—that he and Carrie were in there getting it on. I told Candy she could have my bedroom and I would sleep on the living-room sofa.

"Why?" she asked, wrinkling up her nose.

"You're a little too young for me, honey."

"Oh, that! I just look young. I turned twenty last week. Fuzzy gave me a dozen roses and a hundred big sugar daddies. Do you like candy?"

"I like it, but it's not that good for you. Bad for your teeth and some people say it makes you violent."

"Violent," she giggled. "I'm never violent, except maybe in bed."

"Yeh, well, ahh, why don't you go to bed and get some sleep while I sack out here?"

"You're weird," she said. "Where you from?"

"New York."

"Are you a gangster?"

"No, I'm a spy."

She laughed and it sounded more like a loud cackle than

194

anything else. Within seconds Ace came charging out of his room.

"What the hell was that?"

Seeing Ace in his black silk pajamas, Candy asked, "Is he a spy, too?"

"Ace White meet Candy. I won her in a five hundred rummy game."

"Is this what they play for out here?"

"It's not what they play for, it's just the way they pay off."

"Where's the game?" said Ace anxiously.

"'The Game' is running around town trying to scrape up twenty-seven thousand dollars so he can get her back."

"Oh, one of those," said Ace.

Trying to look over his shoulder into the bedroom, I asked, "Did you guys have a nice time at Fandia?"

"It's called Scandia; and yes, we did have a nice time, and stop stretching your neck, she's not in there."

I smiled and sighed openly in relief, but only for a moment because Ace said, "She just left five minutes ago."

"Don't tell me about it," I pleaded. "Please don't ever tell me about it."

"I don't intend to." Ace laughed as he walked back toward his bedroom. At the door he turned and said, "Good night, Miss Candy. Good night, Lefty."

"Don't you like him?" Candy asked while moving over to sit on the sofa.

Staring at Ace's bedroom door, I said, "No, I don't like him. I *hate* him. He's old and he's wrinkled and he shouldn't be able to pull girls like that. I don't know one other wrinkled old man in the world who pulls young chicks the way he does. Damn it, he must be using some kind of dust or something. He probably sprinkles it on them. Throws it up their noses and they just do it to him. I bet that's what he does. Throws the dust at them and they just do it to him."

"What in the hell are you talking about?"

"About him!" I said, pointing to the door. "You see how old he is?"

"So what?"

"Just this—he goes to bed with some of the most beautiful women I have ever seen. Now, how many old men like him do you see making out with beautiful women?"

"Not too many," Candy explained, "but maybe he does better than you do because he doesn't get so up-tight."

I looked at her and shouted, "I'm not up-tight!"

"Then shut up."

Not knowing exactly how to take it, I glared bitterly at her. In the meantime, she stuck the lollipop in and out of her mouth and leaned over to kiss me.

"Did you taste the candy?" she asked.

"I think so."

She kissed me again, sending her tongue deep into my mouth.

"Did you taste it that time?"

"Yes, yes I did."

Getting up, I walked over to the bar while asking her if she would like a drink. She said she preferred her lollipop.

Looking across the room at Candy while fixing a scotch and milk, I don't mind telling you she was beginning to turn me on.

"What do you want to do with your life, Candy? Suck it away?"

"I can think of worse things, can't you?"

"I guess I can think of better things, too."

"You're right," she sighed. "I'm going to be a songwriter. Fuzzy's helping me. He knows all these people in the record business and he's making appointments for me starting in two weeks."

"Why not now?"

"Well, he's got this big movie deal cooking and he doesn't have time right now."

"What kind of songs do you write?"

196

"The best. Country Western."

"Sounds great."

"You'll hear of me, I guarantee it."

We were silent for a moment, and when I walked back over to her, she stood up, smiled, and said, "I think you're kind-a nice. Do you like me?"

"You're okay."

"Just okay?" she said, and placed her lollipop down on the end table.

"What do you want me to say?"

"Not too much I hope, because I like a man of action," Candy said while kicking off her shoes.

"Is Fuzzy a man of action?"

"He's okay. He's just a little fast on the trigger," she said, pulling the ribbon out of her hair.

"Are you sure you're twenty years old?" I asked as I began to unbutton my shirt.

"Cross my heart and hope to die," she said, stripping off a bracelet.

"Tell me quick, what year were you born?" I said, unfastening my belt.

"Nineteen-fifty-six," she said, slipping her dress over her head.

When we were both nude, we took the time to look at each other. She was the typical, plain-but-pretty California blonde— just like the hundreds you see on the orange crates, on the billboards, and in the suntan lotion ads. She had long, straight yellow hair, darling lips, and volleyball tits that were much too large for her small body.

At that point we both must have been horny as all hell because it was a toss-up as to who attacked who. There was no romance, no tenderness or caring. It was just two sex-hungry individuals fucking the hell out of each other without an ounce of concern about the other person.

And after our first, fast, furious flight, we both fell out on the floor trying to catch our breaths. When this was accomplished we looked at each other, smiled, growled a little, and were about to start another round when the telephone rang. It was Fuzzy calling to tell me he was very close to getting the money.

"You're a little late, Fuzzy."

"You said I had until morning."

"Right. Would you like an extension?"

"No, no, I'll get it."

"Right."

"How's my girl?" he asked.

I looked over at Candy lying nude on the sofa and sucking her lollipop, and I said, "She's just great. Just great."

"Okay," said Fuzzy. "I should be there within the hour."

After hanging up the phone I walked over to Candy just as she pulled the lollipop out of her mouth.

Ten minutes later I was in the bathroom carefully gripping a pair of scissors while trying to cut a sugar daddy out of my pubic hairs. Out in the living room, Candy was humming and singing while making up some different words to go to the tune of "Streets of Laredo."

Her version said:

"I had my first blackie
"I didn't turn khaki
"I'm still bright and white
"And filled with delight . . ."

I was laughing so hard I almost cut off my left nut.

By the time Fuzzy arrived with my money, Candy and I were dressed and waiting. Before he came, she asked if it was absolutely necessary for her to go with him. When I offered to give her enough money to return to Orange County, she said, "You know that's not what I mean."

From then until Fuzzy came, we just sat silently holding each other. Outside, the dark morning sky was hazing a shade toward blue as the late night hours were about to give way to day.

It was then that Fuzzy knocked on the door.

For some reason, after they were gone, I remained there on the sofa and slept until the middle of the day. The pretty Chicano maid woke me as she attempted to clean without disturbing me. When I said good morning, she corrected me by saying, *"Buenas tardes."*

I knew that meant "afternoon," but out of consideration for her and any other Spanish-speaking person I might run into, I had picked up a Spanish vest-pocket dictionary. Taking it in hand and flipping to the back where there was a list of "Useful Phrases," I tried to carry on a conversation. She was a darling girl who kept laughing at each sentence I tried to construct.

*"Como se llama usted?"*

She controlled her laughter just enough to answer, "Juanita."

"Good, good," I said. "Me llama is Lefty."

"Lef—"

*"Si.* Lefty."

She finally got it out and laughed herself into the bends. Then she took her left hand and held it up in the air. I nodded my head, laughing along with her. Then she made her left hand into a fist and playfully punched me in the nose. I stopped laughing.

We continued having fun like this for an hour or more. I sent down for lunch and she joined me. She just sat right there in her brown smock uniform with her mops sitting in the center of the room in the scrub bucket, and we ate lunch.

At about three o'clock, Ace called from somewhere over in Beverly Hills and said he and Carrie were on their way back to the hotel to change clothes, and then they were going to spend the rest of the day and the evening on the town. He also said that *"if"* I could get a date they would like for me to join them.

I looked Juanita up and down and decided I would take her.

"Of course I have a date," I said.

"Who is she?" Ace asked, half kidding. "Some ninety-year-old waitress from down in the soda shop?"

"Don't get smart, Methuselah. I date only ladies," and looked over at Juanita to make sure she didn't understand what I had just said.

"All right," said Ace. "We'll be there in about fifteen minutes. Have yourself and your lady ready to go."

After getting off the phone, the first thing I wanted Juanita to do was to get those damn mops out of the room so Ace wouldn't discover she was a hotel maid. The second thing I wanted her to do was to change into something better than that brown washwoman's smock. With signals and all sorts of Spanish and English jibber-jabbing, I finally got her to understand that I wanted her to get rid of the mops and go down to the dress shop, buy an entirely new outfit, and charge it to my room.

Juanita wasn't out of the room thirty seconds before Ace and beautiful Carrie entered.

"Where is she?" Ace said, but I couldn't hear him while I stared at Carrie.

Finally coming back to earth, I said, "She'll be here. You just go change your rags."

As Ace walked into his bedroom laughing, Carrie and I looked at each other. After a moment she asked softly, "Do you hate me?"

"No," I said. "I hate him. But I love you."

She smiled and shook her head. "No, you don't. You don't even know me."

"Give me the chance, Carrie, and I'll know you like you've never been known before."

"I bet you would."

"All kidding aside, I would really like to see you."

"All right."

"Did Ace tell you about the game?"

"Yes."

"We'll probably be in New York until then, if you want to come, I'd love to see you there."

"Ace has already invited me."

"So, you'll come?"

"Yes."

"To see me, or Ace?"

"You . . . if you still want me."

I reached over and touched her cheek and said, "I want you, baby."

When Ace came out of the room I warned him to remember that my lady Juanita didn't speak English. And I asked him to please be on his best behavior.

Soon the knock came at the door and as Juanita walked into the suite all three of us were taken aback at how gorgeous she looked.

*"Buenas tardes,* Señorita," Ace said and kissed her hand.

*"Buenas tardes,"* Juanita said, as I took a closer look to make certain this was the same person who went downstairs. It was, but what a fantastic change had taken place. She was gorgeous. She made me very proud as she came over and took my arm. I looked at Ace, hoping to detect at least a twinge of jealousy, but there was none because Carrie was on his arm.

"Shall we go?" said Ace.

"Good idea," I said.

"Where shall we eat?" Carrie asked.

"Why don't we try The Bratskellar," said Juanita in perfect English. "I've never been there."

"Hold it!" I said, throwing up my hands. "Excuse my English, but somebody has just put some stuff in the game."

Ace began, "I thought you said she—"

"Hold it. That's what I'm talking about. All right, Juanita, let's hear it."

"What's to hear? You think you two are the only hustlers in town? I needed a new dress, and I honestly have never been to the Bratskellar."

We were all silent for a moment and then Ace said, "It makes sense to me."

"Me, too," Carrie agreed.

"Okay. Okay, I'll make it unanimous," I said, and then, turning to Juanita, "but I'm warning you, lady, I'm going to keep my eye on you every minute."

Juanita cuddled up close to me and said, "I wouldn't have it any other way."

# 29

The next morning at eight the phone rang three times before I was wide awake enough to answer. I had to lift Juanita's arm off my chest to get to it. "Hello?"

"Good morning," a soft feminine voice beckoned.

"Who is this?"

"Did I wake you?"

"No, I always get up thirty minutes after going to sleep."

"I'm sorry," she continued to whisper in that angelic voice of hers. "Would you rather I called later?"

"No, I'm awake now. What is it?"

"Wouldn't you like to know who I am?"

"It would help if I did."

"Would you like to take a wild guess?"

"Okay, Lucille Ball. Is that wild enough for you?"

"You're not even close."

"Oh, shucks. Do I lose my driver's license, or what?"

"How would you like to meet somewhere for breakfast—you and I, and the ocean?"

Coming more to my senses, I was shocked as I assumed correctly the person I was talking to.

"Are you still there?" she asked.

"Yes, I'm here."

"Do we have a date?"

"Why are you calling me?"

"Because I want to see you. I want to meet you and get to know you."

"But why?"

"Do you think you know who I am now?"

"You're Linda Grizzard."

"My, you are bright. They say you are. They say you're a genius when it comes to cards, is that true?"

"You'll find out sooner than you'll want to."

"Oh, now, don't become hostile. I'm serious about breakfast. That's why I'm calling so early. I thought perhaps you could slip away from your people and I'd slip away from mine and we'd meet on equal grounds, so to speak. I had my chef prepare this marvelous breakfast and I thought we could have a morning picnic. Please, Lefty, I really would like to see you before we go into . . . combat."

I thought for a moment, was completely intrigued by her voice and the thought of finally meeting her, and decided I would do it. "All right, I'll meet you. But if there is just one inkling of a trick, baby, you've had it!"

"They neglected to tell me about your being violent. Is this a new side to your nature?"

"It's something I learned on Sutton Place one night."

"Oh, yes; a lesson well taught by Stan Kondor, I understand."

"I see you've been studying my dossier."

"Yes, I have, and I find you a very fascinating man. One whom I would very much like to meet under different circumstances one day."

"I'll keep that in mind after I eliminate you from the game."

"What would happen if I eliminated you? Would you hate me terribly?"

"If you win, Linda, it'll be a fluke. One of the biggest in the history of the world."

204

"I love a man with confidence."

"From what I understand you've never loved a man. That you are as chaste and untouched and as virgin as a newborn babe."

There was a pause when all I could hear was her soft breathing.

"I was hoping we could meet without any animosity."

"I'll go along with that, but we've got to have truth, baby, or the meeting will be worthless."

"But we don't have to be bitter at this point, do we?"

"I'm not bitter, Linda, I just don't understand why you're calling me. The only real reason we have for seeing each other is to play poker and we can surely do that without eating ham and eggs on a sandy beach at nine o'clock in the morning."

"You didn't understand anything I said, did you? I want to meet you on separate and impartial grounds. I'm sorry, but I merely assumed that, you being a Moon Child, you would be more romantic. Have more of an adventurous spirit. I was hoping your curiosity about me would equal mine of you."

"I'm sorry, but it doesn't, so that's that, right?"

"No, it can't be. You've already said you would meet me. Please, don't change your mind."

I thought about it again, knowing full well I was dying to jump out of that bed, get dressed, and fly down to the beach to meet her in person. Actually, the only thing that was holding me back at this point was the sound of her voice, some of the things she was saying, and the fact that Ace would want to kill me for going, but I really dug talking to her.

"You come straight west on Sunset Boulevard," she said, "and I'll be waiting for you at the beach. You'll know I'm there when you see my white Mercedes convertible at the curb."

The second she hung up, I was out of the bed and half-dressed. Once I was ready to leave, I bolted out into the living room to find Ace White sitting on the sofa next to an extension phone.

"Please, please don't tell me you were listening."

"I was listening."

"I asked you not to tell me that."

"You were actually going to go down there?"

"Why not?"

"Suppose it is a setup? Suppose there is a professional killer waiting for you? With you dead, Lefty, Linda is automatically in the game. You think they wouldn't kill you for the kind of money that's going to be in that game?"

"Come on, Ace, you really believe that that eighteen-year-old girl is setting me up?"

"She's twenty now."

"That doesn't answer the question."

"All right, no. I don't believe this is a setup to kill you, but I'll bet you a million dollars it wasn't her idea. And I'll bet you anything, she has been bugged and watched."

"You really think they would go that far?"

"Lefty, we're talking about millions of dollars!"

"But they already have millions of dollars. It can't be for the money, it's got to be the championship, just like us."

"What do you mean, just like us? You think I wouldn't like to have the twenty-two million that was lost and won at the last Biazarro?"

"Be honest, what is more important to you, Ace, the money or the title?"

"All right, I'll say the title to make you happy, but one without the other wouldn't mean much."

"I don't know," I said, becoming disgusted. "Why can't it be fun? Why does it have to be all this cloak and dagger jazz. Dossiers, spying, and bugging. Just put me on an honest table with her and let us go head-to-head and the best player wins."

"Kid, if it was up to me, that's the way it would be, but they're afraid of you. And they're going to do everything they can to beat you simply because they know they can't head-to-head on an honest table."

"So what do we do now?"

"First we get some sleep," said Ace, "and then we go down to Manny's beach house and we'll see what he's got."

We arrived at the Malibu house at 12:30 and found Manny lying out by his pool with two UCLA coeds: a black and an Oriental.

"What in the hell is this?" Ace shouted.

"Friends I met at a party last night. They're from the Midwest and they had never seen the ocean."

"Fine. They've seen it. Get rid of them."

"Don't be angry, Ace, you told me to relax."

"I told you to relax, but I didn't tell you to die and go to heaven. Get rid of them."

"Okay," said Manny. "Come on, I'll show you Linda Grizzard."

We followed Manny up the stairs to the second-floor hallway and up a ladder to the attic. There, Manny had put in a two-way mirror and had rigged up a pair of electrical binoculars for extreme close-up viewing.

"She's not out there now, but she usually takes a walk on the beach right after lunch."

"Alone?" Ace asked.

"She walks alone, but there are a pair of gorillas always close-by."

"Who else is with her?"

"Her parents, and I've counted nine other guys. Some look like lawyers with their big black brief cases and others look like advisers and backers."

"Does she have a boy friend?" I asked.

"If she does, it's the best-kept secret in the world. The only time she's ever with anyone else, they stand at least three feet away from her. Her only personal contact is with her mother. You know, they hug, they play on the beach. The father sometimes, too."

"How long have they been here?"

"They arrived two days ago. It's the blue house three doors up," said Manny.

"I wonder how they knew we were here?" I said.

"How do you know they do?"

"Lefty here got a phone call from Linda this morning."

207

"You're kidding!"

"She invited him to breakfast."

"Why didn't you go?"

"There was an old petrified rock standing in the way."

"Man, let me tell you," said Manny, "when you see her, you're going to wish you had pushed that rock, shoved that rock, or anything else to get to her."

"We're not here to flip over Linda Grizzard. We're here to beat her," said Ace, and then turning to Manny, "Get rid of those teeny boppers."

"You see anything?" Ace asked as I had my eyes glued to the binoculars.

"Nothing yet."

"You want to stay here?" he asked. "I'm going to go down and pull Izzie home and Eddy out of Detroit."

"All right, I'll wait here."

I continued to look through the glasses and watched the quiet, four-foot breakers roll in and crash against the shore, flatten out, and then creep smoothly up on the apron and then slide gently away followed by the ever-searching sandpipers. The midday sun was at its peak and sending its rays directly down on the curve of the waves, causing them to look like huge rolls of blue crystal glass. Three hundred yards from the shore were a half-dozen white sailboats dipping and slanting as they sliced their way through the rocky, wind-swept surface of the ocean.

Panning back to the shore, I looked again at the terrace of Linda Grizzard's beach house and saw four chairs sitting there, empty, and a planked wooden table sitting bare except for a Bee deck lying there alone with its seal unbroken.

Someone passed in between the deck and me and I focused to see who it was. It was Linda. Yes, yes indeed, it was Linda. All they had said of her was true and understated. She moved, she flowed out across the terrace and onto the sand dressed in a tiny blue bikini that barely covered the vital areas. Her body was superb. Magnificent, large, lean, statuesque, and curvy

208

with an exceptionally small waistline. Her legs were long and shapely. Good legs. Very good legs. She had large, full breasts that moved when she walked. Her skin was clean and blemish-free as if she had been fed the proper diets and massaged and milk-bathed all her life. As she walked out to the water and stopped to look, I focused on her hair. It was reddish-blond, but more reddish than blond. She turned then and started to walk my way, and I focused on her eyes. They were bluish-green—more green than blue.

I wanted to read her, to know her, to decipher and dissect her, and assess correctly the type of girl she was. She appeared to be the clean, tender, spunky, and sprite type who is usually shy and cuddly one moment and then brazen and brimming with excitement and bursting with anticipation and desire the next.

Perhaps I was wrong, but I always felt you could tell an intelligent person by their bone structure and facial features; if this was true, Linda Grizzard wasn't very bright. Although she was one of the most gorgeous and sensual woman I have ever seen, there was very little depth in her face, her eyes; almost as if she had been so protected all her life she perhaps didn't even know the war was on and over, or that the Indians were the good guys, or that a small, frail, sensual woman could make a big, strong man break down and cry.

No, Linda wasn't a woman; not yet. She appeared to be a happy, agile, prancing girl, anxiously looking forward to new-found freedoms, but as yet she was too young and much too naïve to be of any intellectual or domestic value other than to play poker, and perhaps to love.

As her long, gorgeous legs carried her closer and closer into my view, I wondered what it would be like with her. I began to wonder more and more what it would be like to make love to her. To love her. To screw her. To ball her. To fuck her. To fuck, fuck, fuck her, on a bed, a sofa, a floor, or even up against the wall with her soft, chubby arms caressing me while her tiny, moist lips quivered fervently at my neck and her long, firm thighs rode high and pressed tightly against my hips. Her breath, terribly hot, would come in short, quick spurts and still carry a faint trace of fresh milk. She would perspire, but just a bit, with a fragrance that is as pleasing as any perfume on the open market. Initially, she would resist, almost convincingly, while teasing and then slowly, warmly, sweetly pleasing me, wanting me, craving me as she gives me all . . . all . . . all.

Linda passed out of my view as she was now walking directly in front of the house. I ran to another window to watch her.

Ace climbed up into the attic and asked, "Did you see her?"

"Yes," I answered without taking my eyes off of her.

"What do you think?"

"I think I have to go to the bathroom."

"What's wrong?"

"She's unbelievable."

"You can handle her, kid."

"I wish to God I could *handle* her right this minute."

"What's wrong with you, Lefty?"

I turned to Ace and said, "Did you see her?"

"Of course I did."

"You mean to tell me you could sit across a table from her and concentrate?"

"For six million dollars she could be naked and I'd rip her apart."

I sighed and said, "So would I; and I'd tell the rest of you to shove that game up your ass."

"Look, kid, we both love balling and we both appreciate a beautiful woman, and right now you're probably overwhelmed by her. Let's face it, it's a good thing you saw her like this. Maybe by the time you have to meet her face to face, you'll get over this infatuation. As a matter of fact, I'll have Manny move a bed up here, because I don't intend to let you out of this goddamn attic until you're sick of looking at her."

210

# 30

I honestly thought Ace was kidding about locking me in the attic, but he wasn't. At first I really didn't care, but after four days of looking at Linda, I have to admit I was getting a little bored with it.

"Are you sure?" Ace asked, raising a skeptical eyebrow.

"I can meet her now."

"All right, here's the situation. I've been on the phone with Sporados. Some things have happened. Lord Lichfield had a heart attack and has pulled out of the game. Your old friend Duxbury is taking his place."

"Why can't Linda and I both play?"

"Because there has been so much talk about the two of you meeting each other that the Poker Masters have decided to use your game for a . . . a convention-type thing. A two hundred and fifty thousand dollar head-up stand-off. Just you and her."

"And you agreed to this?"

"Why not?" said Ace. "At least every one, every one of the Masters, will be there and they are going to see you at last. It's either now or never, Left. There's no other place or time, or opponent, but Linda Grizzard."

I thought about it for a moment, and then shrugged and said, "Where and when?"

"Just an hour from here in a place called Laguna Beach. They're taking over this hotel that was built against this cliff and has a private beach and this huge third-floor terrace where the game will be played."

"I'm going to feel like a circus performer."

"You'd better get used to being watched, kid, because there are going to be hundreds of people going to the Big Biazarro this year."

"When do Linda and I play?"

"The thirtieth of May. Exactly two months from today."

"What will I do until then?"

"Prepare. Fast Eddy arrives today, and the four of us are going to play every conceivable hand of poker there is in that deck."

It was a long and tedious two months. The four of us moved into the beach house and played cards constantly. "Every conceivable hand" Ace had said, and we did it. We dealt and reshuffled and dealt again and again. We used two decks one time to see how the hands would match up. At one stretch, we dealt hands just to figure out our own odds, and they came out the same as Scarne's and every other odds-maker.

It suddenly dawned on me that I was becoming a recluse. Ace, Manny, and Fast Eddy would all ask me to go out with them at night, but I was constantly refusing to budge. Instead, I would lift the Bee deck and deal hands to make-up opponents. They were usually people I would be playing against in the Biazarro, and I began to know how each would play the hand I would deal to them. All except Linda Grizzard. She frustrated the hell out of me. Quite often I would become so angry at myself and her that I would snatch open her dossier and read it from cover to cover, trying to discover how she would bet a particular hand. It wasn't in the dossier. Sometimes I would run to the attic when it was time for her to take her daily constitutional and I would watch her, trying desperately to fathom where her head would be on "deuces back to back."

One Sunday, Carrie, one of the few people I agreed to see, paid me a visit and we took a long walk on the beach. Linda Grizzard was coming in the opposite direction and stopped to say "Good morning."

Carrie answered, but I completely ignored her. On the return walk, Linda was waiting close to the house.

"Who is she?" Carrie asked.

"My next opponent."

"Why won't you speak to her?"

"I may give something away if I do."

Linda stepped over in front of us and shook hands with Carrie. "My name is Linda."

"Hi, mine's Carrie."

"Hello, Lefty."

"Hello, Linda," I said without meeting her eyes.

"I guess this Thursday is the big day."

"I guess it is," I said.

"Good luck."

"Thanks. You, too."

"Maybe we could have a drink before the game."

"I don't think you're old enough yet."

Linda and Carrie chuckled, trying to relieve the tension of the moment.

"I'll take the chance," she said.

I decided to walk around Linda, and as we passed her I could feel her young, warm breath against my cheek.

"See you on Thursday," she said.

Carrie spent two days with me and then she had to leave for a fashion layout in Paris. She said she would hurry back as soon as possible, and I told her I would rather see her in New York after the game. She agreed.

There was something extremely pleasant about Carrie. I

213

can't explain what I needed during those days, but she filled the bill perfectly. She was the type of woman who never annoyed you. Everything she said or did was in line without being subservient. She could be the best listener in the world—for hours if you wanted to talk, or she could keep you entertained with stories of her own if you were in the mood to just lie back and cool it.

I was sorry to see her go, but she had things to do, and so did I. There was no point in trying to find someone to fill her void. There simply wasn't anyone.

Izzie Rodriguez had been staying in our suite at the Laguna Golden while we were up at the beach. The four of us moved to the hotel on Tuesday, the twenty-eighth of May. Ace decided that we would go in late at night to avoid the crowds. Waiting for us in the suite were Izzie, Sporados, and George Palmer Deeds.

"Hello there, boy," Deeds greeted me with a hug. "Ahm a-bettin' on ya. Ya gotta win for the men of this country. Ah don't want no womin in this game, and it's up to you to see it don't happin."

As I shook hands with Sporados and hugged Izzie, I heard Deeds whisper to Ace that I didn't look too good. "Is there somethin' wrong with him?"

"No, he's just tired."

"She says she's a-ready for ya," said Deeds. "Talk to her mahself this mornin' at breakfast. God, she's a pretty one, but a man can't let that stand in the way of success. Ya gotta beat her, boy. Ahm a-bettin' a million dollars a day on you from the minute ya'll sit down at that table. Ah just don't believe no womin can beat a man in a man's game."

Fast Eddy walked over to the window with me as I looked down on the terrace where the game would take place. He put his arm around my shoulder and whispered, "You do not have to worry, Lefty, it is just another game and she is just another broad."

I whispered back, "She's good, Eddy. I can't get into her mind. There's something they have beat into her head that's got me buffaloed."

"Now don't you worry none about bein' buffaloed." Deeds came running over to us after overhearing what I said. "She's only a womin. She's young, she lacks experience, and she's probably a hell of a lot more scared then you are."

I looked at Deeds and then over at Ace. He got the message. "George—Lefty is a little tired. What do you say we let him get some sleep and we'll see you at breakfast in the morning."

"Oh, yes, of course, but I don't want him to worry none."

"He'll be all right, believe me."

After Ace was finally able to get rid of Deeds, Sporados came over and stared at me as if trying to figure me out.

"Yor are afraid of her, aren't you?"

"No, I'm not afraid. I'm just puzzled by her."

"I'm impartial," said Sporados, "but I would hate for you to make a bad showing."

"Lefty does not make a bad showing," said Fast Eddy.

Sporados continued to stare at me, and then shook his head and left the suite. When the five of us were there alone, Ace, Eddy, and Manny checked the doors, windows, and balcony. Finding nothing, Ace asked Izzie if he had checked for bugs. Izzie assured him there were none.

"All right, sit down," said Ace, and we all took seats. "What have you got for us, Izzie?"

"As of this minute, the odds are heavily in Linda's favor."

"Never mind that, tell us who's here and where their heads are."

"Everybody's here except Lichfield."

"All twenty-six Masters?" Ace asked.

"All of them."

"If a bomb drops," said Manny, "so much for million dollar poker."

"Go on, Izzie," Ace said.

215

"Like I said, the odds are going for Linda at about one and a half to one against Lefty. If she wins on the first day without breaking Lefty, the odds will go up, of course. If Lefty wins, they'll probably swing to his favor."

"What do you mean *if* he wins?" snapped Fast Eddy.

Izzie ignored him and continued, "There are only four people betting on Lefty at this point. Deeds, C. K. Langershim, Duxbury, and Malcolm Laureate."

"Hmm," Ace mused. "I can understand Duxbury and Laureate because he beat them. Deeds is a chauvinist and he's trying to pass as a liberal. What's Langershim's game?"

"I don't know except that Linda beat him so badly that this might be his way of getting back at her."

"You act like you don't want anybody to bet with Lefty," said Manny.

"You damn right I don't," said Ace. "And if they do, I sure want to know why."

"But what difference does it make?"

"The more people who bet on her, the more money we'll win."

"Right," Manny agreed.

"Izzie, where do you think C. K. Langershim would be right now?"

"Probably in his room. He's not much of a night person."

"I'd like to meet him."

"I'm sure he'd be more than willing to drop over if I gave him a call."

"Is it okay with you, Lefty?" Ace asked.

"I'd like to meet him, too. Maybe he can tell us something about her."

Izzie made the call and within ten minutes the tall, handsome, black-haired California golden boy walked into our suite. He shook hands all around and was enamored at being with us.

"God, it's great meeting you, Mr. Wilson," he said, while gripping my hand with both of his.

"You can call me Lefty."

"I'd rather not for a while."

"I'm afraid I have to insist, C.K., because if you don't I'm going to be embarrassed."

"Oh, I'm sorry. I wouldn't want to embarrass you."

"Okay, it's Lefty then?"

"Anything you say."

Izzie excused himself and went out scouting information around the hotel, while the five of us sat having drinks and discussing poker and Linda Grizzard.

"May I ask you a question? Why have you decided to bet on Lefty against Linda?"

"I honestly believe he can beat her. I haven't actually played against Lefty, but I've been studying him and I don't think Linda will be able to cope with his unorthodox manner of play."

"Is that the only reason?"

"I'm not very fond of her. She's not the little angel everyone thinks she is. Underneath that perfect exterior is a vicious little cunt with a heart as cold as ice. I'm sure you heard what happened to me."

"Tell us."

"Three days before our match, she called me up and suggested we meet on a beach for breakfast, and I was stupid enough to fall for it. She had this thing all arranged in this huge picnic basket. She was wearing this tiny bikini with almost everything showing, and I want to tell you she is gorgeous. Have you seen her yet, Lefty?"

"Only from a distance."

C.K. chuckled. "Christ, she had me thinking she was falling head over heels in love with me, but it was all a sham. She had me so shook up that by the time we met across a table, I couldn't think about anything but getting into her panties."

"Did you?"

"No way! She's tighter than fish pussy and that's waterproof. Oh, she teased me with it the night we went out to

217

dinner. Even let me touch her tits, but that's as far as I got. She said she was afraid of me. Afraid I would break her heart. Hah! Well, as you can guess, by the time we got to the game, I was in love, horny, and ready for everything except poker, and she literally tore me apart."

"Did you ever talk to her after that?" Manny asked.

"Are you kidding? I played her in Puerto Rico and she acted as if I didn't exist. I spoke to her this morning in the lobby and she completely ignored me again. I'm telling you, she's a bitch! I'm glad to hear you didn't fall for the breakfast bit, Lefty."

I smiled and looked at Ace.

"Lefty's too smart for any tricks like that," Ace stated.

"How many days do you think it will take to beat her?" C.K. asked me.

"I don't know," I said and lowered my head, not feeling too sure at that moment that I could beat her.

"You're not worried, are you?"

"A little," I confessed. "A lot is at stake here, C.K."

"Don't let her looks and her sex get to you, because I can guarantee that under that skin beats the heart of a real, hard cunt. She'd do anything short of busting her cherry to win a poker game."

"Don't call her a cunt, C.K.," I said. "I don't like that word. Besides she's only doing what we're all doing, trying to win the best way we can. Do you really think we brought you down here to socialize?"

"Lefty . . . ?" Ace pleaded softly.

"We brought you down here to pump you about her. To learn as much as we can so that I'll be more prepared when I play her. We didn't give a shit about you, C.K."

He was startled and hurt and didn't know how to take it.

"But now that I've met you, I think you're an all-right guy. Would you like to hang around and play some five hundred?"

C.K. finally broke into a smile of relief and said, "I would like that very much."

218

"Okay, but you can't use that word anymore."

"I promise, I won't."

The next morning, C. K. Langershim joined the five of us for breakfast and informed us that Deeds was switching his money to Linda. Linda and her entourage were sitting directly across the room.

"Tell me," said C.K., "is it true that you actually won over three hundred thousand dollars in a hi-low game where you went low with four fives?"

"Yes."

"How could you do it?"

"I put three chips under the table and brought one up."

C.K. started laughing and I looked over at Linda and she appeared disturbed, but you could never tell with her.

That afternoon we took a tour of Laguna, a comfortable, little sunny town, but it appeared awfully white and extremely conservative. Other than being a rather nice town to look at, I didn't especially like the vibrations there and suggested we get back to the hotel.

That night, after dinner, Ace took me aside to ask if I was all right.

"I think I'm scared for the first time in my life," I confessed.

"I think it's extremely normal considering the circumstances," said Ace.

"I've thought about that, too, but there's something she's got, something she knows that I can't figure out."

"Don't worry about it, kid, you'll figure it out once you're sitting across from her."

"God, I hope so. Because if I don't, I'll probably lose the two hundred and fifty thousand as quickly as I lost that twenty-five hundred in Cannes. Remember that?"

"Of course I remember it, kid, and all the other games where you've come back after being down. And that's what can happen here, so don't worry about it. If she gets ahead, you'll figure her out."

Ace touched my shoulder then because he realized I was still back in Cannes.

"Hey, come on," said Ace as I grimaced. "Come on, kid, what's done is done."

"What happened, Ace?" I asked, trying to keep control. "Suppose I lose after not helping her?"

"You're not going to lose, kid, and what's done is done."

"Angel is done, and I can't help from thinking we could have helped her, Ace."

"We're not gods, Lefty. We're human and perhaps we did make some mistakes along the way. Angel, I'm certain, was one of them. Maybe we should have taken her with us when we left Cannes, and later we could have forced her to live at the brownstone, I don't know, but I'd be willing to bet that if she was here in Laguna tonight, she would tell you to forget about her and concentrate on that game tomorrow. You knew her better than I did; now don't you think she would say that to help you? Don't you?"

"I guess so. But it just doesn't seem right that I should be here and she should be dead."

"It was her choice. For whatever reasons she had, she made the choice."

"It just doesn't seem right, somehow."

"Who in the hell knows what is right or wrong?" Ace said softly, shaking his head. "If *I* knew, we might not even be here. We'd probably be back in the brownstone, or still down in the islands with Peggie and Cricket. Those were some good times, weren't they, Lefty?"

"Yes, they were."

"We gave them up for some reason, and the reason is the game. The Big Biazarro. And all you have to do is win tomorrow, and we're in."

"Suppose I lose, Ace?"

"Lefty, to be honest with you, I can't ever conceive of you losing, but if you do, tomorrow, in January, or whenever, I have found the best friend I have ever had, and I'm not going to let a poker game, money, or a woman, or anything ever, come between us. So if you feel like losing, lose. Just . . . just don't say good-bye, buddy."

"I won't."

"All right. Fast Eddy and C.K. have challenged you and me to a game of five hundred rummy. Shall we meet 'um, greet 'um, jam 'um, and beat 'um?"

"Why not?"

"Let's really sock it to them, partner. It'll do us good. Okay?"

"All right."

We started playing for a dollar a point at eight o'clock, and by ten-thirty, Fast Eddy and C.K. owed us over eighteen thousand dollars. When the phone rang, Manny, who was acting as spectator, answered it and said it was for me.

"Hello."

"Hi, Lefty," said Linda Grizzard on the other end. "Are you ready for tomorrow?"

"I'm ready. How about you?"

"I'll be glad to get it over with, won't you?"

"Definitely."

"What do you say we meet down in the bar and have a drink together?"

"I'm sorry, but I'm right in the middle of a game."

"Poker?"

"No. Five hundred rummy."

"Who's playing?"

"Ace and I are playing against Fast Eddy and your friend C. K. Langershim."

"Forgive my snobbery, but why do you insist on hanging out with that loser?"

"You should be very careful the way you throw those names around, Linda; you could very well be part of that club within a few days."

"Either one of us could."

"Good luck, Linda. May the best . . . person win."

# 31

Thursday turned out to be a beautiful sunny day with almost no breeze, but not extremely hot. An awning was placed over the table, which was in the center of the terrace. Seats all around the table were raised on a platform so that the Masters could have a better view of the game.

The game was to begin at noon.

Linda and I would be allowed to have one adviser. Ace would be with me, of course, and Linda's father, Harrison Grizzard, would counsel her.

Ace and I arrived on time, but Linda was ten minutes late. Ace threatened to walk out if she didn't show within the next five minutes. She appeared on the terrace and I could hear several "oohs" and "ahhs" before she came into view. She was draped in a full-length white dress that had a low bodice to reveal her healthy cleavage.

"Go get him, Linda," someone shouted. As she approached the table, Ace and I stood.

"Hi," she said, and smiled at me.

"Good afternoon."

"I'm sorry I'm late."

"I'll forgive you this time."

Linda took her seat then and we waited for Sporados to bring the cards. He walked up immediately with a brief case, opened it, and dumped twenty-four Bee decks (twelve red and twelve black) out on the green felt table. Linda and I tested them by feeling and smelling, and made our choices. She picked five, and I picked seven.

"You're generous."

"I'll probably need all the help I can get."

"No doubt," she said.

Sporados sat in the third seat. "I will be your dealer. Do you both approve?"

We nodded that we did.

"The buy-in is two hundred and fifty thousand dollars with no reprieve. You lose the two-fifty, you lose the match," Sporados explained. "During the match, you each have two break calls per day. If the match has not been decided by twelve midnight, we will recess for the day and begin the next day at noon. Do you agree?"

We both nodded, while keeping our eyes pinned on each other.

"If *I* should grow tired and would like for someone to take my place as dealer, Peter Sampler will sit in. Do you agree?"

We agreed.

"The game will be five-card stud only. I will deal from left to right and I will start with a black deck. May we have the chips, please?"

An attendant brought the chips forward and started to place them on the table. The blue chips were worth five thousand; the reds were a thousand, and the whites were priced at one hundred dollars.

As Sporados broke the seal on the deck, I could feel my heart pounding so hard it was causing my ribs to vibrate. Linda appeared completely unruffled and at ease. I wondered if it was so.

"Cut, Lefty," Sporados said, placing the deck in front of me.

᾽ I lifted the cut and dropped the cards. Sporados nonchalantly straightened the deck and placed it for me to cut again. This time I made a clean slice.

"It's only a game," Linda said and smiled.

"I'm afraid it's more than a game, Linda."

"That's right, for you it is, isn't it? You've been planning on the Big Biazarro ever since you left that . . . town you're from. What's it called?"

"Grosse Pointe," I said and looked at my hole card.

"I see you've been studying my dossier."

"There wasn't much to study."

"Your bet, jack," Sporados said to me.

"I'll pass."

"So will I," said Linda.

For the first two hours, very little happened, and there were no great exchanges of money. Linda went three thousand up at one time, and raised me twenty thou, but I didn't call. She had me beat.

By six o'clock, she had inched her way up to eleven thousand ahead just before Sporados called the dinner break.

Ace and I sat alone in our suite.

"She's not nervous," Ace said to break the silence.

"No, she's not. She's amazingly calm under the circumstances, don't you think?"

"She's not on Valium or anything. Her eyes are clear as they can possibly be."

"You know what I think it is. I think they've got her completely brainwashed into thinking she can't be beat."

"Can you use it?" he asked.

"I don't know, but I'm sure you must have a saying to fit this situation."

"Let's see," said Ace, smiling, "there must be one. Something like a person who won't be beat, can't be beat. How does that sound?"

"Schmaltzy!"

"Hmm, you're probably right, it wasn't one of my better ones, was it?"

"They're all rather bad, Ace, but that one was ridiculous!"

"Don't rub it in, don't rub it in."

The waiter entered to bring our after-dinner coffee without the honey I had ordered. Not wanting to be disturbed again, Ace told him to forget it.

"How do you feel, Left?"

"Great."

"That's the first time I've ever seen you drop the deck on a cut," said Ace.

"I've done it before."

"Okay, okay. What do you think?"

"I don't know. She's playing a good, steady, but not vicious type of poker. I expect her to increase her betting."

"Her rhetoric isn't bothering you, is it?"

"No. I've prepared myself for anything she might say."

"Anything?"

"Everything."

"All right," said Ace. "Do you think you made any mistakes today?"

"I don't think so. She hasn't tried to bluff yet. I think their game plan is to save it until tomorrow. I would really be surprised if she bluffed tonight."

"Let's face it, she's feeling you out just like you're feeling her out."

"That's what she's doing all right. I didn't notice her father saying anything to her, did you?"

"No," said Ace, while straining his recall. "He did make a sound one time."

"I heard that, too! Do you think they've got some kind of signals working?"

"Who knows? Maybe he's got a cold. Didn't sound like a signal to me."

225

"It wasn't a cough."

"I don't know what it was, but you can believe if he does it again, I'm going to have it on tape."

"What do you think, Ace? Did I make any mistakes?"

"No. And to be honest with you, on that twenty thousand dollar raise, I thought you had her beat. So did a lot of the Masters. You know, you can tell something has happened when they sort of look at each other with those half grins."

"She's not bluffing yet. She had me beat, but I expect to lose a big hand when she bluffs the first time. I only hope I read her right when she does it, so I'll know it the next time."

"Lefty, I've got to tell you, you still amaze me. When I was your age I wasn't even thinking with nearly the depth you have of poker. How did you learn it?"

"Cooncan Bill taught me. Used to let me cut his tonk and pitty-pat games for him in the back of his one-table pool hall. He wouldn't let me play. He used to call me 'the Rascal.' Used to say 'Watch 'um, Rascal. Watch the mistakes them fools makes, 'cause when it comes time for you to play, I don't want to see you makin' none of them mistakes.' I got so I could tell when somebody was getting ready to go out. And then when I started cutting the poker games, I used to watch their eyes. Then I started watching their lips and even their nostrils. Sooner or later, everybody gives themselves away."

"What about you?" Ace asked.

"I don't know, maybe I do give some things away, but if I feel I have, I switch up the next time. Besides, old Cooncan had me practicing expressions in front of mirrors. 'Get light, get light,' he used to yell at me when I had the worst hand in the deck. I'll never forget the night I was cutting the game and he was playing in it. Somebody called him outside on some business, and he said, 'Okay, Rascal, it's your turn to shine. Take my hand.' I was twelve years old at the time and there was nothing but cutthroats and professional gamblers at the table, and all at least three times my age and size. I had been playing for about an hour and winning, and I didn't even know Cooncan had come back into the place and was watching. Well, anyway, this great big mean-looking Irish railroad worker, who had a reputation for being bad, was left in this big pot with me. I had him beat and I know I had him beat, but he started talking really mean to me. Saying he liked to take little boys and bend them back over his knee until their backs sounded like a two-by-four snapping. I want to tell you, he had me so scared, I folded without thinking whether I had him beat or not. Cooncan grabbed me by the throat and dragged me out into the alley and threw me from one end of it to the other. He had me bouncing off those garage doors like I was a rubber ball. When I was crying so hard that I couldn't stand up anymore, he said, 'Now, lay there until you learn not to be scared of nobody but me.'"

"Did he hurt you?"

"No. Just my pride and the fact that he fired me for a couple of weeks. Cooncan had small games. Five dollar buy-ins with a maximum of twenty-five cents bet. I hustled up five dollars somewhere and went back and bought into the game. I broke everybody there, including old Cooncan, and he told me I was rehired. I worked for him until I was thirteen, and then I started playing on my own."

"Whatever happened to old Cooncan?" Ace asked as if he had heard of him.

"I don't know. He sold the pool hall one day to a guy named Ham something, hung around town for a while, and the next thing you know he just sort of faded away. Used to see him fishing for bullheads sometime down by the river, but I really don't know what happened to him. I should, huh?"

"Maybe not."

"I wonder . . ."

"We'd better get back," said Ace, rising from the table.

"You're late this time," said Linda as Ace and I walked up to the table at seven after seven.

"Now we're even."

"Not quite," said Linda. "I'm eleven thousand dollars up."

"I'm just going to have to see if I can do something about that," I said.

I couldn't do anything about it. By nine o'clock, Linda was twenty-three thousand dollars up and still had not found the need to bluff. She was playing perfect poker. I felt we both were, but the cards were falling slightly better for her than for me.

The first real big hand came at 11:30. She had a four-card flush, ace-king high. I caught a pair of sevens on the fourth card and bet twenty-five thousand dollars. Linda hesitated without flinching, and then called. On the fifth card, she caught something. I didn't know what, but her hand had improved considerably. High vibrations were coming across that table.

"I'll check," I said, and she looked at me skeptically. She thought I had also improved on the last card and I was waiting for her to bet so I could raise her. Linda checked and won the hand with a pair of kings.

It wasn't an error on her part, because I could have caught something. But she did one thing wrong: she didn't bet her hand. Even though she won over thirty thousand dollars from me, she had made her initial mistake. I was still clean. Her father made a grumbling sound and I turned and smiled at Ace.

"I got it," Ace said softly.

"What does he have?" Linda asked, knowing full well she had done something wrong.

"We're registering every weird sound your father makes. We intend to put them all together on a record and sell it in Grosse Pointe as a classic."

"I think the hicks in Ferno are more apt to buy it than we are."

"That's not a nice way to talk about your father's music."

"Your ten bets, Lefty," said Sporados.

I looked at my hole card and passed.

We played four more hands before midnight and I managed

to win back six thousand dollars and ended the first day thirty-eight grand in the hole.

I went directly back to the suite and found Manny changing into bathing trunks. As he walked toward the door, he asked how things were going.

"Tiring," I said. "How goes it with you?"

"I don't want to upset you, but I'm glad you're playing instead of me. These millionaires really know how to live, Lefty. You should see the food they're having shipped in here from all over the world. Caviar from Russia and lobster from Maine, and stars they're bringing in from Vegas. I mean, they really know how to live. And one guy told me they do it all the time. Wherever they are, they live like this."

"Don't you think it would get boring after a while?" I asked.

Manny chuckled and said, "Maybe so, but I sure would like to find out if it does. I sure would."

"See you later, Manny. Better watch out for that caviar, I read somewhere it makes you sterile."

"You lie."

"I don't know, I read it somewhere."

"Oh, come on, man, that can't be so."

"It's not. I'm only kidding. See you later."

After Manny was gone, I went straight to my room and climbed up on the bed with a deck of cards. I wanted to replay Linda's mistake in my head several times while picturing her face, before, during, and after the hand. Something happened after the hand. For one brief second, there was a change in her. She let her guard down. She did something wrong and she was ashamed of it. "She's a baby," I said aloud to myself. "She was hurt and embarrassed by her mistake."

Ace came into the room then and asked if I had something.

"She's a baby. They molded and trained and formed her brain into a perfect poker player, but she's still only a baby. She gets embarrassed; she gets hurt. She's ashamed of her mistakes. Almost as if her father or mother might yell or spank her in public."

"How can you use it?"

"I don't know."

"Taunt her?"

"No, she's ready for that. She's ready for insults, I found that out when I mentioned Grosse Pointe. She smiled and it rolled right off her back."

"Is she using anything on you yet?"

"No. She tested me with Ferno, but it didn't work. But it wasn't a real test. That'll probably come the first time I take a big hand from her. She wouldn't want me to become too confident. She'll try to keep me in my place."

"Lefty, I have to ask you this."

"I know what you're going to say, Ace. Yes, yes, I am ready if she throws Angel at me."

"Are you sure you can handle it?"

"No, I'm not positive, but I'm sure I won't let it interfere with the game. Maybe when she first mentions the name, it will touch me a bit, but everyone must know that. But I promise you it won't disrupt the game."

"All right, Left," said Ace, "I'll see you in the morning."

At noon of the second day, we all arrived at the table on time. Linda was wearing a tight-fitting jersey sweater that revealed every centimeter of her large, protruding nipples. I stayed with my linen suits and ties.

"Did you sleep well?" she asked.

"Very well, thank you."

"Did you dream?"

"No. Did you?"

"I dream every night."

"You'll have to tell me about them sometime."

"Do you believe everything C.K. told you about me?"

I smiled and said, "Of course not."

"You bet, king," Sporados said to Linda.

By 4:15, Linda had inched up another thirteen grand and

was now fifty-one thousand ahead. It was nothing to get excited about, and everyone knew that an advance like that could easily be wiped out with one hand. But, unfortunately for me, it wasn't. She won three hands in a row and was seventy-six thousand ahead by the dinner break.

Once again, Ace and I ate alone.

"Are you starting to worry, Ace?"

"No, I'll wait until we're two hundred and forty-five grand in the hole."

"I could still come back with the five."

"She's catching some great cards, isn't she?"

"She's playing them well, too," I said.

"She didn't bluff yet, did she?"

"No. She hasn't had to. I've got to win one big hand sooner or later."

"You're not going to with the cards you're getting."

"It'll come around. The deck's not prejudiced."

It was 8:45 of the second night when I finally caught a hand I could bet. I caught three sixes and Linda had aces over nines, but she wouldn't call my second raise so I was able to win back only thirty of the seventy-six thousand.

"Don't you feel you've missed something growing up in a town like that? It must have given you a horrible sense of insecurity."

"Not really. You see, I, at least, had a chance to grow up. No one put me in a cage with a deck of cards and told me what I was going to be. I became a gambler because I wanted to and not because my parents wanted to relive their lives through me."

Sporados dealt the hand and we both passed.

"Are you insinuating my life isn't my own? My choices aren't my own?"

"I'm not insinuating anything," I said, "I'm stating a fact. They started training you like a little monkey from the time you were six years old."

"Speaking of monkeys, is that why you're carrying that

231

sixty-year-old monkey on your back? Is that the reason you let Ace White leech off of you?"

"Actually, we leech off each other. I leech off him one day and he leeches off me the next."

"Your bet, nine."

"I pass."

"May I ask you a question?" Linda said. "Since you think you know so much about life, why is it the women you hang out with are almost always prostitutes, dance-hall girls, or scrub maids?"

"I simply do not choose my friends by their professions, but by their content of character. Perhaps someday when you're grown you'll learn that all the people who wear mink and eat caviar aren't necessarily the chosen ones. That a few of us in burlap have something of value also."

"Did Lola Maldonado wear burlap?"

"Lola Maldonado could do more with her little finger than you will ever be able to do with your entire body."

"Your bet, ace," Sporados said to me.

"I pass."

"You're passing with an ace?"

"I have a six in the hole," I said and folded.

Linda said, "Why haven't you ever become involved with a woman of class?"

"I was probably afraid she would turn out to be like you."

"They told me it would be unsportsmanlike to mention her name . . . now that she's dead. And the fact that she died the way she did, so messy and all. So tragic. The way she suffered and suffered before she died."

Sporados took a deep breath and held up the deck. Ace White placed his hand on my shoulder and I moved so he would take it away.

"If this upsets you, I won't ask you any more questions," said Linda.

"Go ahead. Knock yourself right out."

"What did you see in her?"

"As long as you live and breathe you'll never be able to understand it."

"Then why did you dump her? Why did you break her heart like that? Why did you turn her over to a pimp, and then pay a hundred dollars so she could become a whore? If you cared so much about her, if you were such great friends, why did you destroy her? Were you afraid of her? Afraid to love her? Or was it because you did love her and you would have had to give up your freedom? Your great dream to go to the Big Biazarro."

Turning to Sporados, I asked him to start dealing.

"Why didn't you go to the funeral?" Linda continued. "Your backer there sent flowers in your name. You didn't even have the guts to send your own flowers. How in the hell do you have the guts to sit down across a table from me?"

"Your bet, jack," Sporados said to Linda.

"I bet a thousand dollars," she said.

"I pass."

"You're a phony, Lefty. You claim to be a friend to this one and that one, but I bet a hundred to one you don't even know what happened to Cricket Lang, do you? Or what happened to Gats Brown after you put him on the train to go south. Or what's happening to Bessie Poindexter or why Ace White is allowing only Carrie Evans to visit you. You think I've been in a cage, they have kept you so ignorant of what is going on all around you, that the entire poker world is laughing at you. Laughing at you and that motley crew you hang out with."

I caught a pair of fours back to back and I bet them. I ended up with only the fours, and Linda caught nines and beat me for another eighteen thousand dollars.

I won't deny that she got into my mind. I thought I could handle anything she threw at me, and the Angel things didn't bother me nearly as much as the hints about Cricket, Bessie, Gats, and Carrie. I kept hoping midnight would come so that I could get my "motley crew" in the suite and find out what in the hell was going on. In the meantime, Linda went ahead one hundred and twenty-two thousand dollars.

"All right, let's hear it," I said as Ace, Manny, Izzie, and Fast Eddy met with me in the suite.

"First of all," said Ace, "everything was to keep your mind on the game. A lot of what she said was bullshit. The thing with Carrie was Carrie's idea and not mine. She liked you from the start, and you know it."

"What about the rest of them?"

Ace pointed to Izzie, and the Computer cleared his throat and began, "What Ace said about Carrie is true. Ahh, let's see, Bessie is doing fine and is supposed to come out here to see us sometime this week. She's okay, honest."

"What about Gats and Cricket?"

"I'd rather let Fast Eddy tell you about Gats, since he was with you that night."

"I would rather you tell him," said Eddy.

"Tell him!" Ace snapped at Eddy.

"It is not my fault, Ace. It is not Lefty's fault and it is not my fault."

"Tell him!"

"Gats got off the train in Philadelphia."

"And what happened to him?"

"Nothing happened to him," Eddy explained. "It was all a hustle. He hustled you and me for the clothes, money, and a ticket, which I am certain he cashed in somewhere."

"You mean, it was all a put-on?"

"From start to finish. He knew, like everyone else, what was going down, followed us around, and picked his spot. There was no broken heart, no real tears, no conk-haired nigger, and no bitch running away to Raleigh. Like they say, 'We was the takees, and he was the taker.' We was tooken."

"Son of a gun, wow! You know," I said, "regardless of what happened, I feel better knowing he wasn't really hurt. It was only about four hundred dollars, wasn't it, Eddy?"

"About that."

"It's worth it, knowing he's okay."

"That is true, that is true," said Fast Eddy. "But I think we should bust one of his kneecaps to make an example."

"Let's forget it," said Ace.

"I'm almost afraid to ask about Cricket. Should I be?"

"She is just another broad, Lefty."

"Come on, tell him," said Ace. "We've got work to do."

"Cricket," Izzie began, "is in Paris. She was strung out on heroin. We put her on the cure; she got off, and we put her in a hospital, and as far as we know, she's getting better."

"Is that the truth?"

"I swear to God it is," said Izzie.

"Is she all right?"

"Ace called this morning. He's been calling every day."

I turned to Ace, and he said, "She's doing fine."

"What else have you guys been keeping from me?"

"You're up to date," said Ace. "From now on, we tell you everything. Izzie, every morning, I want you to brief Lefty on whatever happens the previous day. I don't care what it is, tell him. You don't even have to check with me. Tell him. Tell him everything."

"Okay," said Izzie as if he didn't think it would be a good idea.

"I want to know, Izzie. I've got to know everything before she tells me at the table."

"C.K. was right," said Fast Eddy. "She is a cunt!"

The rain, hitting incessantly against my window, woke me the next morning. I crawled out of bed, and placed my face against the coolness of the pane and wondered. Wondered what they would do about the game. Where would we play? Where would Linda and I sit across from each other and say sharp, cutting things and bet and hustle and maybe even bluff. She hadn't bluffed yet, but I had a feeling that today would be the day. She was ahead. Far ahead, but not too far. The other person is never too far ahead until you are so broke that you cannot beg, borrow, or steal a dollar to keep playing. It's just like baseball, you're still in the game until you've run out of relievers, pinch hitters, and subs, and are kowtowing back to the dugout with the "boos" of your fans ringing in your ears and their tears draining the blood from your soul.

Izzie Rodriguez sat at breakfast that morning with tears in his eyes.

"What is it, Izzie?" I asked.

He looked over at Ace, and Ace said, "It doesn't matter."

"What doesn't matter?"

"Linda said today is the day," said Ace. "She told Izzie he'd better seek employment elsewhere, because he's going to be unemployed by tonight."

"You believe that, Izzie?" I asked.

"She said she knows how to break you now. Said she's got you. That it was my fault for not telling you things. That she stuck the knife in your heart yesterday and is going to twist it today and kill you."

"Izzie . . . I don't die that easy. She's got a long way to go. I haven't even opened my bag of tricks yet, much less tried anything. Do you think for one minute that I spent all those months in Cooncan Bill's lousy, filthy, smoke-filled pool hall because I liked it there? I was learning, Izzie. Studying people and poker. I spent years and years reading and reading and watching people across crowded rooms, restaurants, and parties while others would be enjoying themselves. There were those who thought I was crazy because of the way I would look at them. Questions. Questions. Questioning is something I have always done. Sometimes I would question people and friends so thoroughly I would insult them. But I wanted to know. I had to know why people did certain things."

I took a moment to catch my breath and to prepare myself for what I was going to say.

"I know why I left Angel in Cannes, and in the room at Cadillac Gene's. I know why I couldn't love her or any other woman, because they weren't the Big Biazarro. Women have *not* been my obsession. The game is! The game, always the game. Forever the game. Linda Grizzard is not a bitch, a broad, a cunt, or a fool. Especially not a fool! She knows I can beat her. She knows it better than her father, Ace, or the other twenty-six Masters, because she sat there and saw me do it. Ace, you said recently that every poker game gets down to one hand. Well, I'm here to tell you all that we, Linda and I, have not played that hand yet. I didn't come all this way to be stopped by a virgin in white lace on a beach in an up-tight town. I didn't pay all those dues and go through all that shit and shed all those tears to be fooled and buffaloed into losing one of the most important games in my life. Are you completely out of your mind, Izzie, to sit there and even give it a second thought that I might make a fatal mistake like that?"

"But she's winning!"

"She's ahead! She's not winning. She may even go further ahead, but she has to break me before she's won."

"Everybody is saying she's going to take you today. Even Duxbury and Laureate are now betting on her."

"Who are you betting on?"

"You, of course," said Izzie.

"Thank God. For a minute there, I thought I'd lost you. What about the rest of you?"

"If we don't go in '77," said Manny, "we'll just keep working and plan on going in '82. In the meantime, we're having lots of fun, right?"

Ace wasn't saying anything for a change.

"Well, old man?"

Ace sipped his coffee. "You know, they make a damn good pot of java in this hotel. Izzie, find out what it is, okay?"

We all looked at Ace, expecting something else to be said. But he just sat there, eating his toast and eggs and sipping the coffee he liked so much.

237

# 32

The third day of the match was played inside. The hotel's main banquet room was rigged for the game by the same crew and in the same way they had arranged it on the terrace. We arrived on time, and Linda was wearing a pretty, pale yellow, see-through blouse. We sat, I cut the cards, and she whispered, "I'm sorry," across the table so only I could hear it.

"Say it out loud," I said, and she smiled and shook her head.

We began to play and, unlike the other days, the game proceeded with hardly any conversation. Linda was pleasant and pretty and played poker in perfect fashion. She continued to cut into my stack and by the dinner break she was close to one hundred and fifty thousand dollars ahead. I forsook eating for a walk in the rain along the beach. It was a warm shower, but a strong wind, coming in off the ocean, was tossing huge, noisy waves against the shore and causing the rain to sweep over me and against the hotel. I walked for about ten minutes, and when I came back toward the hotel, I saw Linda Grizzard silhouetted in the darkness of her second-floor balcony and staring down at me. She stood there, expressionless, frozen in the bright light of her room while braving the wind and the rain merely to stare at me in my moment of solitude. I didn't particularly like being watched, especially in my moments of solitude.

During the second session of the third day, Linda began to play more sternly, doggedly, as if she was growing tired and wanted to end it as quickly as possible. At approximately 9:15, she pulled her first bluff; it worked, and she won another seven thousand dollars. Linda didn't say anything after the hand. She merely smiled like a child who had been spared a spanking after getting caught with her wet finger in the sugar bowl.

During this session I was able to win my share of the hands, and by the time midnight rolled around we remained where we started that morning—Linda was approximately a hundred and fifty thousand ahead.

That night, Bessie Poindexter arrived and we had a small party in her honor. C.K. came by, and Fast Eddy and Manny brought dates: two surfer-looking girls who were tantalized by Eddy's card tricks.

Bessie looked beautiful as always. She reported that New York was still standing tall and was as exciting as ever.

"I stopped by the brownstone," she said to me. "Hilda says to tell you she's got the stroganoff heating up on the stove."

"Really? At the rate we're playing, that stroganoff is going to be beef jerky by the time I get there."

"Are you all right, baby?" she asked.

"I'm fine."

"How's the game going?"

"It could be better, as I'm sure you know, but I'm still in it."

"When do you think you'll be back in the city?"

"What's today?"

"Saturday."

"Soon."

"How soon is soon?"

239

"Leave two tickets at the box office for the Apollo's Wednesday night's amateur show."

"Is that a promise?"

"Have I ever let you down?"

"No," she said, and leaned over and kissed me.

For the remainder of the night, I went to my room and studied Linda's dossier and played solitaire poker while the party continued out in the suite.

The next morning the sun was shining again and the hotel crew moved the green felt table back to the terrace. Ace and I ate breakfast alone in the suite.

"Why?" I asked. "Why do I feel she's going to spring something on me that we won't know about?"

"Careful, kid. She's got you beat psychologically. You're going into the game with your head on her, instead of on poker."

"My mind is first and foremost on poker, but I get this feeling that her people are better than mine."

"So what? All that it's going to come down to is you and her. Lefty and Linda, and who breaks who."

"If she throws one more thing at me that I'm not aware of, you guys better start running because I'm coming after you."

The fourth day started on time and Linda showed up in an even more transparent blouse.

"Good morning," she said. "The next time you walk in the rain, I'd love to tail along."

"Didn't you read the brochure?" I asked. "It never rains in Laguna."

"Really? I thought sure you were all wet last night."

"You've been thinking that since you arrived."

"True. And by the looks of your stack, I haven't been completely wrong."

"You count up when you come in and you count up when you leave, lady. Everything in between is fool's addition."

"What are your plans for tomorrow?" Linda asked and winked.

"Oh, I expect to be sitting right here, looking at your bare tits."

"If you do, you'll be sitting here alone, because I'm leaving for Grosse Pointe this evening."

"Are you conceding defeat while you're ahead?"

"No. Didn't Izzie tell you? This is your last day of poker. I'm sending you home to Ferno."

"Thank you very much, but do I have any choice in the matter?"

"Again—by the looks of your stack, not too much."

Turning to Sporados, I said, "Let's play."

Finally, the cards began to swing my way. Within the first two hours I had regained sixty grand of the one hundred and fifty I was in the hole.

Linda called her first break of the match.

During the fifteen minutes, Ace and I remained at the table.

"You know, I think this is going to be a long game," said Ace.

"You know what I'm thinking and wondering—what in the hell are they planning up in that room?"

Izzie came through the crowd and leaned over to us. "Nothing's happening. Everybody and everything is straight and good."

"Okay, get back up into that suite and stay next to those phones," said Ace. "Take Fast Eddy with you and send him down with any messages. You stay up there."

Linda returned to the table with a full smile.

"Welcome back," I said.

"You were getting rather lucky. I thought I'd slow you up a bit."

Her tactics didn't work. I won the next three hands in a row and Linda was beginning to bet cautiously. By the time the dinner break came, I was only forty-five thousand dollars in debt.

Up in the suite, I told Ace I was beginning to feel quite good.

"I never doubted you for a minute, kid. You're obviously better than she is or they wouldn't have to use all those dirty tricks."

"Do you think they're finished?"

"It doesn't matter. Only lightning could help her now."

I never would have guessed that lightning could strike out of a clear blue sky.

We were running neck and neck and then, at around seven o'clock, Linda caught on the last card and beat me on a twenty-two thousand dollar pot. She played the hand to catch, and she caught. It's not great poker, or even good poker—waiting to catch, but when you do, it is so pretty and gratifying.

When the lightning hand began, Linda was once again leading by sixty-five thousand dollars. She was looking like jacks and I was looking like a pair of tens.

Suddenly, a messenger ran up and whispered something in her father's ear, and Harrison, in turn, whispered something in Linda's. She smiled across the table as Sporados dealt the fourth card.

"God, what a shame," Linda said, shaking her head. "I bet twenty thousand."

I looked at her, not knowing what to expect.

I called the bet.

Sporados dealt the last card.

"I suppose you think you should have helped her, too."

Ace leaned up close to me.

"Bet your hand, Lefty," he said.

I barely heard him as I stared at Linda.

"Of course, you think you should have helped all of your friends, don't you?"

"It's your bet," Sporados said to Linda.

"I bet fifty," she said, and then, "What a horrible way to

go. Can you imagine, Lester? Swallowing your own tongue. Strapped in a strait jacket and gagged, and dying by swallowing your own tongue."

I turned to Ace. "What is she talking about?"

"She's bullshitting. Play your hand!"

I stood up and said I wanted a recess.

Sporados shouted, "What about the hand?" and I threw my cards at the deck.

Followed closely by Ace, I ran into the hotel. When we entered the suite, Izzie was hanging up the phone.

"I just got the call," he pleaded.

"Oh, Christ, who is it?"

"Cricket had a seizure and died in her sleep."

"In a goddamn strait jacket?"

"No," Izzie cried, "I swear to God."

"That bitch is lying to you, Lefty," Ace yelled at me. "What in the hell is wrong with you? That little cunt sits there and makes up stories and you fall for them like her mouth is a prayer book. Jesus H. Christ, what are we supposed to be, the five Disciples? We didn't come all this way to lose this game because some fucking dope-addict whore dies eight thousand miles away!"

Without thinking, I threw a vicious right hook at Ace's face, which he managed merely to catch halfway there with the palm of his hand. He did the same thing with a left cross.

Standing there, trying to pull my hands away from Ace, I could feel his hurt and bitterness because we had come to this.

"Put your hands *down!*" he said as if what I had done was the most ridiculous thing in the world; and, of course, it was.

He released my hands and I let them drop.

"It's come to this, has it, Lefty?" Ace said. "After all we've been through together, it's come to blows. All right, all right, you once told me you didn't need me, and I goddamn sure don't need you anymore, after this."

When he started for the door, Fast Eddy, Manny, and Izzie

243

followed him, and Ace yelled, "No! Stay with him! Whether he knows it or not, you're all he's got except for that pure white halo over his head."

Ace slammed the door as he left, and the four of us stood there. After an eternal minute, Izzie broke the silence by asking, "Do you want me to stay on the phones, Lefty?"

"Find him," I said to Fast Eddy. "Find him and tell him I'm sorry. Convince him."

"Right," Eddy said, and dashed out of the room.

"If he doesn't come back," I said to Manny, "you're going to have to oversee this whole thing. You're going to have to be the umbrella."

"Consider it done."

"Do you want me to stay on the phones?" Izzie asked again.

I walked over, snatched the two phones out of the wall, dropped them on the floor, told Izzie to follow me, and I walked back down to the game. Taking a seat, I asked Sporados to start dealing. And then, looking over at Linda, I said, "Your pretty ass is grass, baby, and I'm the goddamn lawnmower!"

At that point Linda was about one hundred and forty thousand ahead. By midnight, I had cut her lead in half and was playing fierce, unrelenting poker. Linda remained cool and calm, but she was aware that a completely different type of player was now sitting across from her. But, to be honest with you, it didn't faze her. She was well trained and ready for almost anything.

When I entered the suite, Izzie said that Fast Eddy and Ace were sitting in the bar. I went directly downstairs and took a seat next to Ace.

He glanced at me and then complained to the bartender about his type of clientele.

"I'm playing poker the way I should have been all the time."

"What do you want from me, a merit badge?"

"No. I just want you to know I've got my head together."

244

"That's fine, but what are you going to do when Linda tells you that some wino you once knew dropped dead on the Bowery?"

"I'll handle it."

"Sure you will; like you have everything else she's thrown at you."

"I ripped the phones out of the wall."

"Big deal. We're still going to have to pay the phone bill."

"May I have a scotch and milk, please?" I said to the bartender, and then, turning to Ace, "I'm sorry about throwing that punch."

"You call that a punch?"

"How did I know you would turn out to be a Speedy Gonzales with your hands. Anyway, whatever it was, I'm sorry."

Ace lowered his head to his drink. "I had it coming," he said softly, and then raised up and said, "But don't ever try it again."

"I won't."

The bartender handed me the scotch and milk. I tasted it, and turning to Ace, I said, "You know something Ace, we've been on the defensive since this game began. What do you say we take to the offense?"

Ace perked up a bit with that idea.

"Why don't we play a little game with them for a change? You're good at things like that. I bet that old brain of yours is already ticking away with some ideas of what to do."

"It could be," said Ace.

"It could be, hell. It's doing it."

"Maybe."

"We've been taking a back seat to all their glamour and glitter. I think it's about time we let them know we're here, don't you?"

Ace sipped his drink, and nodded his head. Slowly, he slid off his stool and walked away.

"Where is he going?" Fast Eddy asked.

"To start the offensive."

Ace had gone over to the hotel manager and had given him a huge sum of money. The purpose was to have the lounge band go out onto the terrace and play "Auld Lang Syne" up toward the rooms of the hotel until they were forced to stop.

Up in the suite, and much to all our joy, Ace was back in command. The second part of our offensive was to have Manny, Fast Eddy, and Izzie pack in the morning and check out of the hotel in full view of everyone right after breakfast when most of the guests would be lounging in the lobby and on the terrace.

"What's goin' on, Horace?" George Palmer Deeds asked as Ace and I entered the dining room for a late breakfast.

"Oh, nothing much. What's happening with you, George?"

"Where are those boys goin'?"

"Which boys, George?"

"Your damn boys."

"Oh, those boys. They've decided to go back to New York. They figured there was no sense in hanging around here for the rest of the day."

"Your playah is still seventy thousand dollars in the hole. Are you about to concede defeat?"

"My 'playah' is no longer enamored with the game. As a matter of fact, he's completely bored with it."

"Now just what in the hell is that supposed to mean?"

"Figure it out yourself, Georgie baby," Ace said as we continued across the dining room and found a table.

C. K. Langershim walked over and asked if he could join us.

"Whose side are you on these days?" Ace asked him.

"Yours, of course. I know a winner when I see one."

"All right, then take a seat."

"How's Linda feeling?" I asked.

"The word is, she's not too shook up, after all she's still seventy thousand up."

"How's the betting going?"

"You'll be pleased to know that George Palmer Deeds has

just swung back to your side. With his switching around, he'll more than likely break out even."

"Did you see Linda this morning?" I asked.

"Yes, she's out on the terrace now, laughing and talking with her parents."

"Laughing and talking, huh?"

"She may be a lot of things, Lefty, but one thing she's not. She's definitely not afraid of you."

"I told you, Ace," I said, "they've got her completely brainwashed into thinking she can't lose. Please don't give me that saying you made up about a person who can't win can win, won't win, or some damn thing."

"You know, it's wild," said C.K., "but everyone gets the feeling that today will be the day. What do you think, Lefty?"

"It wouldn't surprise me at all."

"What do you think, Ace?"

"If that waiter doesn't get over here before I starve to death, I think I'm going to break his leg."

# 33

Everyone arrived on time as if they knew this was the final day, the last hands, the decisive deal.

Linda was dressed in a very elegant white ruffled blouse, and smiled that smile when she sat across from me.

"Good morning," she offered in that angelic voice of hers.

"Good morning."

"They say today is the last day."

I looked up at the sky. "It's a nice day."

"If it should prove to be the last day, I want you to know that I think you are without a doubt one of the nicest people I have ever met. And I would like to go on knowing you."

"Linda," I began, and took a deep breath, "you could tell me things I already know, such as the world is round, Ivory soap floats, and that ants have relatives . . . and I wouldn't believe it ever again. You are the most deceitful and disgusting liar I have ever had the misfortune to meet. And the one thing in my life I don't want to do—is to go on knowing you."

Linda was actually hurt and embarrassed.

"I'm very sorry you feel that way. After all, as I stated in the beginning, this is only a game."

"It's still only a game, Linda. And I think we should get on with it."

Sporados began to deal. The cards were falling about even, and only my determination and merciless betting were inching me more and more into Linda's big stack. By dinnertime, we were finally even.

Linda had a childlike sadness in her eyes.

"That's four and a half days shot to hell," sighed Ace White.

"You're wrong, Horace," said Sporados. "This is by far the best match I have ever seen, even with all the garbage talk, which I personally despise."

Linda and her entourage entered the hotel as Ace shrugged and said, "We didn't do it."

"Whose idea was it to have that band out there last night?"

"Maybe the hotel owner had a premonition about today."

After dinner, Linda returned to the table with that same warm smile of hers.

Sporados set the black Bee deck down in front of me and I cut it.

"Here we go again," he said and dealt me an ace up and Linda a jack.

"Your bet, ace."

"I pass."

Linda bet a thousand dollars and I called. Sporados dealt me a deuce and Linda a six. We now had our eyes locked in on each other.

"Ace-deuce bets," said Sporados.

"I pass."

Linda looked at my cards and bet twenty thousand. I called. Sporados dealt Linda a nine and I caught a ten.

"Ace still has the bet."

"I pass."

Linda stared coldly at me and bet fifty thousand and I called.

On the fifth and final card, I caught a seven of clubs and

249

had an ace-ten high. Linda was dealt a king and had a king-jack on board.

"Your bet, Lefty."

"I pass."

The only thing you could hear at that moment was a seagull fluttering overhead. Linda kept staring at my ace, debating now whether to bet into me or not. I'm certain she was thinking back to the other hand where she had failed to bet correctly. Smiling, she looked up into my eyes, which were glaring back into hers without a hint of anything.

"What was the last bet?" she asked Sporados, stalling for time.

"Fifty thousand."

Linda thought for a moment and said, "I'll bet another fifty thousand."

I decided to look at my hole card again, but knowing full well what it was. I looked over at Linda, smiled, and shook my head.

"I'll see your fifty thousand and go all in for the one hundred and twenty-nine thousand dollars we have left."

Suddenly, the Masters began to roar in whispers.

"He's been checking aces on her."

"No, he doesn't have it."

"She shouldn't call."

"She has to call."

"No, she doesn't."

"She's got kings. She has to call."

"He has to be bluffing."

"Only a fool would check aces four times."

"Only a *rat* would check aces four times."

"Checking is part of poker."

"A *man* doesn't check aces."

Linda touched her chips and looked up at me again and I merely sat there, expressionless. Smiling demurely, she pushed her stack into the pot and almost fainted when I turned over my pair of aces. She had been bluffing all the way until she

250

caught the king to go with the one she had in the hole. I had no idea she was bluffing. Linda also wanted this hand to be the game. And it was.

She sat frozen.

Ace said, "You see, Linda, that's what happens when you play against a hot dog with a sixty-year-old monkey on his back, and don't you ever forget it."

"That's the lowest, slimiest thing Ah have eva' seen pulled at a poka' game," George Palmer Deeds shouted at me.

Ace stepped up and leaned into Deeds' face and said, "George, do me a favor, will you? Go piss up a cactus!"

"I see you haven't altered your method of winning," Duxbury said.

"I think there should be a law that no player be allowed to check aces." Laureate sneered at me.

"What in the hell do you know about poker, Malcolm?" Ace snapped back at him.

"I happen to be a Master."

"Who have you beat lately?"

"I'm getting awfully fed up with your insults, Horace."

"Fed up, smed up, blow it out your ass, Malcolm."

"Gentlemen, there are ladies present," Hank Boswell announced.

"Ladies!" shouted Ace. "Are you kidding me? With all the filthy things Linda has been saying at this table?"

"Perhaps we should take a vote," Kenneth Martin Jacobs suggested.

"You vote on election day in November," said Ace. "Now the deal was these two kids would play and whoever won would go to the Biazarro. That's it. Lefty goes."

"Actually, the decision is yours, Andreas," said Boswell.

Deeds leaned over to Sporados and said, "Ah personally don't think this boy should be allowed, Andreas. No poka playah worth his salt would check a pair of aces fo' times in a stud game."

Sporados shrugged, and I could tell after watching him for five days that he was pleased I had won.

Patiently, he turned to Deeds and said, "Would you rather have Grosse Pointe in there, George, so they can expose your past?"

"Ah got nothin' to hide."

"Lucky you," Sporados said, rising at the table.

Linda and I rose and shook hands with the dealer.

"What's your decision, Andreas?" Boswell asked.

The tall, handsome, silver-haired Greek raised his hands signifying he wanted everyone to take their seats. When we were all seated, he began to speak.

"I personally don't approve of the way this match was conducted by either of the principals. To me, poker is still the best game ever invented by man. And I will not stand by and watch the Big Biazarro fall to the degradation of this match. It is my belief that Miss Grizzard and her people have used every conceivable and irrelevant issue to destroy Mr. Wilson's concentration. And in some lesser ways, Mr. Wilson also conducted himself in an unsportsmanlike manner. So be it. I am certain that I have the backing of the majority of the Masters, and I am making a rule right now that if anything is said at the Big Biazarro that does not pertain to the game at hand, the party of guilt will receive a warning. The second time he does it, he will have a choice of withdrawing from the game or wearing a gag. Gentlemen, I am appalled, embarrassed, and bitter about what has happened here. And I personally will never be a part of anything like it again.

"Mr. Wilson won the match, and Mr. Wilson *will* go to the Big Biazarro in January." Sporados looked at me, and then turned to leave.

Linda was frigid and visibly shaken. Mrs. Grizzard, a fabulous-looking woman of fifty, came forward and placed her arms around her daughter's shoulders.

"You play a great game of poker, Lefty Wilson," Linda said.

"So do you, pretty girl."

"I'll try to give you more competition next time."

"I don't think I could stand any more."

"See you," she said, and let her mother and dad lead her away.

The millionaires had booked the hotel for two solid weeks. We had been there five days, and it took them less than two hours to leave the place almost vacant.

I told Ace I wanted to hang around for a few days to recuperate. He hesitated a moment, and then asked if I would be all right.

"There's going to be no one here except me. I'll be okay."

"I'll call you every day."

"I'll be back by Wednesday night. I told Bessie to leave us two tickets for the amateur show."

"See you on Wednesday," said Ace.

Loneliness is a scary thing. But there are times when one should be alone. At least one moment of every day everyone should have a meditating moment all their very own.

Wearing only a pair of swimming trunks and a light V-neck sweater, both black, I walked on the deserted beach in front of the hotel.

Thinking about a lot of things, I wandered north on the sand until I heard a child call his mommy and I looked up to see a large concrete pier. Walking out to the end of the pier that towered high on its barnacled piles, which had withstood time, weight, and the constant whacking of the reckless waves, I saw several slow-moving, warmly dressed persons dropping their hooks, lines, and bait into the murky waters.

The sun, which had warmed their faces for hours, was now making a mad dash for the ocean. It was then and there I witnessed one of the most gorgeous sunsets ever created. Even the usually indifferent fishermen stopped for a moment to gaze in awe at the spectacle. The big sky was all blue except for a narrow, thick layer of dark gray cloud that stretched for miles slightly above the horizon. The sun disappeared slowly behind the layer, pinked the big sky, and flushed the area beneath the cloud with a blood-red stream that melted into violet as it touched the sea. The magnificent panorama continued to build and build and build until everything and everyone glowed in its graceful brilliance. And then, as if accompanied by a lullaby being played on a million violins, it all began to fade. To fade, to dim, to lose its graceful brilliance, to wither, to disappear gradually, and then finally it vanished. It vanished. Never, ever to be seen again.

I love sunsets. And I respect others who do—and I am extremely suspicious and cautious of those who don't. I remained on the pier until the sky turned black enough to reveal the beautiful stars, planets, and galaxies it had kept hidden all through the day.

The moon was hanging high that night. Hanging high, full, round, clear, bright, and, like me, alone. Together, the moon and I, we strolled along the deserted sands as a sudden, engaging wind began to lift and heave huge waves against the shore one after another, only to have them slip silently away . . . again, and again.

Not that I took the time to count, or could have even if I wanted to, but there were no less than a million stars dotting the sky. And different ones would sparkle, or twinkle, and some would wink and disappear and reincarnate in another area.

I wondered then if there was a heaven. And if there was a heaven, if the stars were windows as someone had told me when I was a child. And if all this was true, was Angel standing at one of those windows and looking at me now? I felt someone was looking at me, and I wanted to believe it was Angel.

As I entered the suite, I saw her standing out on the moonlit terrace. A sea breeze ventured through her long hair and tossed it sensually across her face. I didn't know what to think —why she was there, or what she wanted.

Walking out on the terrace, I looked at her without a word. When she stepped over to me, I turned my back and she placed her arms around my waist.

"Stop it, Linda."

She stepped around in front of me then and we gazed at each other and then kissed for the very first time. We kissed again—a lengthy, youthful kiss, and we both sighed in relief. Linda's tiny waist fit into the curve of my arms as if it was meant to be, and I held her. I caressed her and felt her soft frame.

"Lie with me. Love me," she said.

"You know I can't, Linda."

"Don't say you can't. What else is there for us to do? This moment, this chance, will pass and we'll regret it for the rest of our lives. Take me, Lefty. Carry me to the sofa and take me, please!"

"Linda . . . ?"

"I want it to be you. I've waited and waited for it to be you. Take me and make love to me so that I'll never forget it."

"Linda . . ."

"Oh, God, shut up, please, and kiss me. Love me. I want you. Please, please, love me."

Linda began to unfasten her floor-length skirt and it dropped. She then unfastened her blouse and soon it also dropped.

"Take me, Lefty," she said, standing before me completely nude. "I'm frightened. I'm cold. Hold me and make me safe."

She stepped close to me then and her fear and warmth forced my arms around her.

"Take me," she whispered, and I lifted her and carried her to the sofa and placed her gently down.

Standing over her, I fully realized that to just ram into her tender, sweet, and delicious body would be no less than a major crime and a horrible waste—so I kneeled next to the

255

sofa and bit her softly on her knee. Linda twitched slightly and moaned. That was enough to make me want to go further. After partaking of both knees, I took the time to test the fragrance of her body by smelling, sniffing her from one end to the other. Linda loved it and I loved her fragrance so much that I decided to travel the same lovely route once again, licking, licking, licking as I roamed. I began at her dainty toes and moved patiently and passionately all the way to her ears, stopping at four or five strategic spots along the way.

"I love it," she whispered.

I moved my lips to Linda's mouth, and as I teased her, by running my tongue lightly over her top lip and then the lower one, and then the top lip again without entering her mouth, I undressed.

I liked kissing. I've always loved kissing. And kissing Linda was a special delight because she had such delicate lips and her breath carried a faint trace of fresh milk—youth—so I lingered there kissing her softly, then firmly, and then softly again.

"Give it to me now," I said, and Linda sent her small, sweet, savory tongue into my mouth and my cock grew as hard as a Santa Fe rail and almost as long. Grabbing her to me, I wanted to eat her up. I buried my face in her breasts and munched on one of her swollen nipples, and then abruptly sucked the whole tit up into my mouth. I then moved to the other tit and did the same, and Linda screamed and held me to her.

Moving further down her body, I kissed, nibbled, and tasted the tiny mound that surrounded her navel and then plowed my tongue into it and swashed it around and around. Linda and I were both beginning to build and shake. And as I moved further down, she began to tremble all over. Soon I was there—there and I buried my face into her warm, clean, precious brown patch.

Slowly, cautiously, I let my tongue slip past my lips and through the young, fine pubic hairs, and as I touched her wetness, a jolting, sensational chain reaction rocketed through our bodies and Linda screamed and tried to squirm away from me. I held her as I laid my face tightly between her legs and her huge, mellow thighs clamped up and around my head, locking me there. Locking me there to love. Locking me there to lick. Locking me there to do what Linda wanted and needed.

Some men say that it is dirty and nasty and vulgar—but some men are very shallow.

Some men say that it is degrading—but some men are fools.

Some men say that they are too good in bed to do it—but some men don't know their asses from a hole in the ground.

Lola Maldonado said we should make all kinds of love before we die, and I agree.

Mounting Linda, I slowly and patiently began to enter her. She grimaced from the initial pain and dug her nails into my back, but she wanted it and soon it was completed with relative ease. And then we began to fuck! Not screw, or make love; we began to fuck. Teen-agers screw. Married couples make love. But when you put a horny jerkwater dude with a gorgeous international virgin—they FUCK!

After doing it thoroughly on the sofa, we rolled to the floor. And then when Linda said she would like to do it on the desk, I cleared it with one swipe of my hand and laid her there.

"The coffee table," she said, pointing, and I carried her there without interrupting the act.

"Against the wall," she whispered, and her wish was my command.

After doing it on the television set, in the closet with the door closed, and on a chair, we finally ended up back on the sofa, where we finished up.

Lying there so close to each other, feeling our exhausted and sweaty bodies pressed so tightly together, we both admitted it was like a dream coming true because we had so often dreamed of what it would be like with each other. But now

257

that it was over, that it had finally happened, an eerie, frustrating relief came over us. As if this one, fantastic sex act was all that could ever happen between us. As if we could never meet for lunch, take a walk together as friends, or even talk on the telephone.

Gazing at Linda, this thought frightened me, and when I attempted to kiss her she held me away, got up without a word, put on her skirt and blouse, took that last look at me, and went to the door. Stopping, she said, "Now we're even. I made a man out of you at the table, and you made me into a woman tonight. But the one thing I know you have failed to realize, Lefty, is *this* was the last hand . . . and you lost."

"You know something, Linda? Fast Eddy was right. You *are* a cunt!"

"It didn't seem to bother you ten minutes ago, and I guarantee you it won't the next time we meet. Good-bye, Lester."

# 34

I arrived back at the brownstone on Wednesday night and Ace, Manny, Fast Eddy, and I caught the midnight show at the Apollo Theatre in Harlem. For the remainder of the summer we spent most of the time waiting. Waiting to hear where the Biazarro would be played. Waiting to hear for certain who the other six players would be and, waiting, waiting, waiting for the months to pass so we could get it on.

In order to keep my mind active and my head locked into poker, Ace arranged to have a seven-man session every Thursday night at the brownstone. There was an immediate list of at least a hundred assorted players, hustlers, and sharks who wanted to be admitted to the game. Ace screened them carefully and the games turned out to be fun. Of course, whenever a Poker Master wanted to play, he was immediately given a seat. During the months of September and October, Boswell, Laureate, Duxbury, Peter Sampler, and Kenneth Martin Jacobs paid visits to the Thursday night brownstone games and I continued to defeat them all.

Fall, autumn, has always been my favorite time of year. It would be extremely difficult for me to spend much time in

Southern California, or any other warm climate area, because I would definitely miss the changing of the seasons. I simply cannot imagine my life without at least that much diversity.

It was during the second week of November that the first cool breezes of oncoming winter made their initial appearance. Manny and I were walking down Broadway near Forty-seventh Street, and standing on the corner was Gatsby Brown, talking with a pair of streetwalkers. He saw us coming and debated whether or not to run. He told the hookers to move on, and then took a stand and prepared himself just in case there was going to be a fight.

"What's happenin', Lefty? Manny?"

"How was your trip, Gats?"

"Not bad. I always wanted to see Philly."

"What do you say you cough up that bread?" Manny asked him.

Gats sized Manny up, took a deep breath, and said, "If I had it, I might give it to you. I might give it to you."

"Can I ask you a question, Gats?"

"Lefty, you can ask me anything."

"Why me? I thought we were friends. Why did you rip me off?"

"Why not? Who else can you screw but your friends? Your enemies won't give you a chance."

Manny made a move toward Gats and I stopped him.

Gats was wide-eyed, not knowing for certain what to expect next.

"It's all right, Gats," I said. "Just don't ever come around me again."

The next morning a messenger delivered a hundred dollar bill to the brownstone with a note that read, "Thanks. Gats." I haven't heard from him since.

Carrie Evans, thin, delicate, completely independent Carrie, drifted into and out of town about every three weeks. She would stay with me at the brownstone, and she told me one day that I wasn't capable of giving her or any other woman the love they needed on a day-to-day basis and that is why she accepted every out-of-town modeling job she was offered. But the more I saw of her, and the more I held her, the more I wanted her to stay.

"Thanksgiving is next week," I said as we spent a lazy afternoon lying in front of the fireplace.

"I know. I'm going to Pittsburgh to spend the day with my folks. Are you going upstate?"

"No."

"Would you like to go with me?"

"That's not what I would like," I said. "You know what I would like."

"Yes, I know. You would like to be able to break my heart the way you have all the others."

"Carrie, come on."

"Come on, yourself," she said bitterly. "Do you think I enjoy leaving you? I have to do it, or I'll end up like Angel, or Cricket. Lefty, you're a great cat, but you're some-timey. Like right now, any woman in the world would love to be with you because you're so responsive and loving. But a half hour from now your mind will be on that game, and you'll make me feel like I'm not even important to you. Like I don't even exist. You're easy to love, baby, but God, you're a bitch to get through to."

"Carrie, I'm really beginning to love you. I can't believe you don't know this."

"I know it. I feel it. But you're like a volcano, gentle and cool one minute, and hot and running the next. I'm beginning to love you, too, Lefty, and I have never been so scared in all my life."

"You don't want to stop seeing me, do you?"

"You know—I really wish I could. But I'm afraid it's too late."

"Then you'll spend Thanksgiving with me?"

"No, I won't. I'm going to Pittsburgh and then I'll come

261

back. I'll stay with you until someone offers me a job. Then I'll be gone again. I won't allow myself to depend on you for my love, or my life, because I know I'll always come second to the game. It has to happen that someday you'll care more about someone than you do the game. And that's the day you'll become a man. I hope I'm around to see it. But until that time comes, you and I will just go on seeing each other the way we are now."

"What makes you think I'll accept you on those terms?"

"I don't think you have a choice," she said. "You've killed off almost every other woman who has dared to love you, but I'm not going to let you kill me, and I don't intend to let you go either. So lay back, Lefty Wilson—poker player—and hold me until you hear the ruffle of the cards, or the door when I'm leaving."

I did as she told me, and when I heard the door close the next morning, I missed Carrie and wished that I was capable of playing poker and loving someone at the same time. Maybe someday, I said to myself. Maybe. But right now all that was important in my life was the Big Biazarro.

On the fifth of December 1976, twenty-six days before the game, Sporados sent word around the world to all the Masters that the game would be played in the tiny African country of Gambia. Within hours, Izzie Rodriguez and Manny Robertson were on a plane bound for the little country that nestled on the westernmost coast of the ancient continent.

The six players I would be facing one minute past midnight on January the first would be Sporados, Peter Sampler, George Palmer Deeds, Duxbury, Boswell, and Kenneth Martin Jacobs.

Every day and night, Fast Eddy and I would sit and run over their dossiers again and again.

On the seventeenth of December, Manny returned from Gambia and reported that the country was beautiful, the Gambians spoke English, and that Sporados had built a special hotel just for the game.

"Andreas has got to be one of the straightest cats on this earth," said Manny. "He's doing everything he can to see that this game is run on the level. Plus the fact that he's working to see that everybody is made comfortable."

"Was it hot there?" I asked.

"Hot, but nice," said Manny. "It's really a beautiful little country."

As the game grew closer, I don't mind telling you my nerves were a wreck.

On the twentieth of December, Linda Grizzard called and Ace answered the phone and immediately hung up on her.

Christmas morning, Ace sent John upstate to bring Jack and Della down for the day and, this time, everything worked out fine.

On the twenty-sixth of December, Izzie Rodriguez called from Gambia, stating everything was ready for us and that he had fallen madly in love with a beautiful Gambian woman. Ace told him to forget it, his parents would never approve.

On the twenty-seventh of December 1976 all arrangements were made for us to be leaving the following morning.

Hank Boswell would be flying his private jet to Gambia and asked us if we would like to join him. Ace agreed, and the four of us were to meet him at La Guardia airport at 10:00 A.M.

On our last night in New York, Ace, Fast Eddy, Manny, and I decided we would have dinner at Montanagiano's on East Sixty-sixth Street. John drove us there and waited outside. We entered the authentic Sicilian restaurant and I believe I was the first one to see Stan Kondor sitting in the back of the room with a pair of huge bodyguards, and his arms around two young girls who looked as if they had just gotten off the bus from Newark.

"I don't think I want Italian food tonight," I said, but it was too late; Ace had already seen him.

"Ace, please?"

He didn't hear me, or if he did, it didn't faze him. He stood there, staring across that room while his breathing got heavier and heavier with anger.

"Please, Ace, let it ride. We got things to do, remember? We've come a long way. Please, let it ride."

Without turning to me, Ace said, "You just sit there, kid, and watch how I let it ride."

I turned to Manny for help, but he had already started across the room, and, as one of Stan's 250-pound bodyguards started to get up from the table, Manny hit him so quick and so hard that the man crashed halfway into the wooden wall behind him. As the other bodyguard started up, Fast Eddy smashed a split of untapped rosé across his forehead.

Ace White walked slowly across the room, and as he approached Stan's table, the hustler held tight to the two girls, who were immediately aware they were suddenly in a great deal of danger.

"Let them go," Ace said with a soft, malicious tone.

"This is neither the time nor the place for something like this," said Stan.

"Would you rather walk down to Sutton Place?"

"We'll do it sometime," said Stan. "Just you and me in a fair fight."

"Why not now?" Ace asked patiently.

"It's just the wrong time."

"Was it the right time the night you and your rhinoceros hoods jumped that kid and put him in a hospital where he almost died?"

"I don't know what you're talking about."

"You don't, huh?"

One of the teen-age girls began to cry and Stan gripped them even tighter.

"You better let them go, Stan, and get up on your feet."

"Name another place and I'll be there!" Stan shouted.

"I'm not going to give you another chance to run out of town. Now, let them go!" Ace said, stepping closer to the table.

Both of the young girls began to cry now, while struggling to get away from Stan, but keeping one eye on Ace.

"Let them go," Ace yelled and cleared the table with one swipe of his hand. "Get up!" he screamed and snatched Stan's tie with such force that it ripped away like tissue paper. He then reached over the table again and began to snatch and tear away pieces of Stan's shirt and suit jacket as if grabbing rags out of a clothes hamper.

"GET UP!" Ace screamed as loud as he could, while pulling at Stan, who kept holding on to the frightened and crying teen-age girls.

"Get up, you scum sucking shit!" Ace shouted and busted Stan's nose with a straight right, splattering blood on all four of them.

"GET UP!" he cried and yanked the table away and slung it across the room. He then moved in on Stan and began to pound him in the face with ferocious lefts and rights, and when Stan loosened the grip on one of the girls, Ace pulled her by the hair and threw her across the room. And then did the same to the other one, and both girls ran crying out of the restaurant. Ace hit Stan seven more times, causing his head to bounce around like a punching bag.

Finally, he stepped back, and Stan, whose face looked like a mass of red and purple pulp, tried at last to get on his feet, and once he did, he passed out.

Thoroughly disgusted and having seen enough, I left the restaurant. John followed me as I walked along the East Side for an hour and then reported back to the brownstone that I was sitting over at the Hippopotamus, drinking scotches and milk.

At about 10:00 P.M., exactly twelve hours before we were supposed to board the plane for Gambia, Fast Eddy and Manny came into the bar.

"Well, if it isn't the Dead End Kids," I said.

Their heads were lowered and something was wrong, and it wasn't because they had busted up Stan's bodyguards.

"What is it?"

"Ace had a heart attack," said Manny.

"When?"

"After the fight. He started to run after you and he couldn't take a step. I caught him before he hit the floor, but he was in trouble."

"Where is he?"

"At St. Anne's."

"Let's go."

I stood outside of Ace's room for quite a while, trying to compose myself. It didn't make sense that we had come all this way, through all the hassles and the obstacles and the heartbreaks to get this close and not be able to go to the Big Biazarro together.

I was also afraid to walk into the room because I didn't know what to expect. I mean, what if he was already dead, or would die while I was in there—I would never get over it. Ace had become such a part of my life that to lose him would be like cutting me in half. He was that extra something that took me beyond the real world and into a fantasyland where I could romp, love, play poker, and say to hell with tomorrow. Lola Maldonado once told me while we were making love that she didn't particularly flip over climaxing because, as she put it, "Getting there is all the fun. Once you're there it's over, and who wants it to be over."

As I stood out there in the sterile, beige, quiet hallway, a heavyset nurse came along and asked if I was all right.

"Yes. Thank you."

"Are you a friend of Mr. Whiting's?" she asked softly.

"Yes. How is he?"

She took a moment to answer, and it gripped me. "He's had a bad time," she said and started away.

"What does that mean?"

She merely shook her head and started away again.

"He's not going to die," I called to her.

She turned and "shhhh'd" me.

"He's not going to die; I won't let him die!" I yelled at her and then rushed into the room.

Standing back by the door looking over at Ace, I thought of the last time I was in a hospital. I had gone into her room and seen her lying there. And now—Ace was also lying there, so still, so sad, so quiet. I walked over to him and his skin was chalky white and almost gray in areas around the mouth and eyes. When I placed my hand close to his mouth and nose to see if there was a breath, he opened his eyes and said, "Will you please get your goddamn hand out of my face?"

"Hi. How are you?"

"What in the hell do you care?" Ace asked, speaking slowly. "You ran away, remember? You're a hell of a man to have around in a fight. You got beat up on Sutton Place. You threw slow-motion punches at me in Laguna, and you ran like a gazelle tonight. What's your name, Chicken Little?"

"You just be glad you didn't die on me, because I had already ordered up a keg of beer, and you know what you said you were going to do to my grave."

Ace smiled then and I felt so good, tears came to my eyes.

"Look, if you're going to cry, you can just get the hell out of here."

"I'm not going to cry. Why would I cry? I mean, I know you're just lying here because you're afraid of the Big Biazarro."

"I always have been," he said seriously.

After a moment, I said, "Is that the reason you never went?"

"Oh, I've gone to them. Gone to them all. Had fun, too. But I never quite had the nerve to sit down."

"I don't believe it."

"You don't, huh? How many people do you know who can sit down at a table and start playing for a hundred thousand dollars? The average person would shit at the thought of it."

"Maybe, but not you."

"Lefty, there's something you told Roland Lamacco the night you played against him; do you remember what you said?"

"Let's see. I told him he was good and to keep practicing, I think."

"You told him to *think* poker. Forget the money and *think* poker. So far, I've only seen three people in this world who have been able to do it, and you're one of them."

"Who are the other two?"

"Sporados, and the other one you beat in June."

"Linda?"

"Right. That girl is going to be some kind of poker player once she gets away from her parents."

"I got news for you, she's already away from her parents."

"In the years to come, you two are going to have some great matches—with or without the bullshit."

"That bullshit isn't going to bother me anymore."

"Then she'll find something else, but she's going to be the thorn in your side, kid."

"What do you mean, my side? Are you breaking up the partnership?"

"Let's don't kid ourselves, Lefty, I'm 'eighty-sixed' and you know it."

"I don't believe that."

"It doesn't matter anymore. If you'll just keep your head on the Biazarro, I'll have everything I've ever wanted in my life."

"Why are you talking like this?"

"Because it's over, kid. I'm too goddamn old to come back from something like this."

"I'm not buying that."

"You'd better buy it and keep your mind on poker. We've come too goddamn far for you to think about anything but that game. Now, who are you taking with you?"

"You."

"Do I look like I'm going anywhere?"

"So, we'll go in '82."

"Don't piss me off, Lefty, or I'll die right here in front of you. You're going to that game, and you're going to win. Now, who are you taking with you, and who are you using for adviser?"

"I don't want to go without you."

"Don't you understand, if you don't go, there is no Big Biazarro, because this year, you're it. They're all waiting for you. Sporados is the best player, but you're the target. And you can beat them, kid. You can beat them all. Now, who are you going to take with you?"

"If I go . . . Manny and Fast Eddy. Izzie's already there."

"Palusso's not playing. Why don't you ask him to act as adviser?"

"All right, if I can find him."

"He's in town. I spoke to him a few days ago. What about Carrie?"

"She's supposed to meet me there."

"I like that girl," said Ace. "She's good for you. Doesn't take any shit, does she? That's my kind of woman."

"Ace . . ."

"I don't want to hear any more. So get the hell out of here before you piss me off and I have a fatal coronary. Go get 'um, kid."

"Ace, I'm twenty-five years old. Don't you think it's about time you stopped calling me kid?"

"Quit stalling and get home and pack."

"I don't feel right about this."

"You will once you're sitting down with six million dollars in front of you just waiting to be won."

"You said I didn't think money, Ace, and I don't."

"But when you get right down to it, that's what the game's all about, kid. Now, go win, will you? I need some sleep."

I got up reluctantly and started for the door.

"Are you sure you won't be able to travel by the next Friday?"

"If I am, I'll see you there. Now get the hell out of here."

The four of us, Manny, Fast Eddy, Jimmy Palusso, and I, boarded Boswell's private jet and landed in Gambia twelve hours later. We were met at the Banjul airport by a fleet of limousines and a colorful parade of Gambian dancers and musicians. The hotel Sporados had built was called the Jawara, named after the country's first president. Izzie had talked Sporados into giving us a top-floor suite and Izzie met us there. He was naturally concerned about Ace, as we all were. I told Izzie that I wanted an hour-by-hour report on Ace's condition.

On the twenty-ninth of December, Izzie took Fast Eddy and Jimmy Palusso out to show them the city of Banjul while I remained in the suite, catching up on some sleep. At three in the afternoon, Manny woke me to say that Carrie Evans was calling from Stockholm, Sweden.

"Hi, what are you doing way up there?"

"What are you doing there?" she asked coldly.

"The Big Biazarro starts on Friday night."

"Is Ace White with you?"

"No, he had a heart attack, but he insisted that I come anyway."

"Good-bye, Lefty," Carrie said and hung up the phone.

Manny and I had dinner sent up that night and while eating we received a phone call from the hospital reporting Ace's condition as the same—"fair."

When Izzie came back, I had him contact every hotel in Stockholm searching for Carrie, but she couldn't be found.

On Thursday, December 30, several of the Masters came to the suite, wanting to speak with me, but I wasn't in the mood to see any of them.

On the thirty-first, twelve hours before the Big Biazarro was to start, Sporados gave a special luncheon for the Masters only. During the ceremony, which I wasn't too thrilled to be at, Linda Grizzard, who wasn't present, and I were officially declared Poker Masters.

There was a five-minute silence for two of the Masters, Lord Lichfield and another Englishman, Donald Rutherford, who had passed away since the 1972 game.

They also had a minute of prayer for three ailing members, one of which was Ace.

"That's odd," I said to myself, "five minutes for the dead and only one for the living? They must have a warped sense of values."

After their measly minute for the living, Sporados raised his glass toward me and said, "A toast to our newest and worthy opponent, Mr. Lester 'Lefty' Wilson."

Everyone stood and raised their glasses to me.

"Speech. Speech," George Palmer Deeds began to yell—just for spite.

"Would you like to say a few words?" Sporados asked.

I nodded that I would like to say something, and then took a deep breath as I stood.

"I want to thank you all for putting me through all that crap with Linda Grizzard before you would allow me to sit at your table."

Jimmy Palusso and Hank Boswell were the only two who dared to chuckle.

"And I want to thank Mr. Deeds, Mr. Laureate, and Mr. Duxbury, who tried their damndest to keep me out of the Biazarro even after I went through all that crap with Linda Grizzard."

"Why you ungrateful—"

"Let him speak!" Sporados shouted at Laureate.

"Before I make a complete fool of myself and ruin this fantastic luncheon, let me say that I greatly admire the vast majority of the men in this room. I honestly believe that there has never been a greater champion than our present Head Master, Telemachus Andreas Sporados."

The Masters agreed and applauded loudly.

"And finally," I said, "I have waited all my life for this week and I want the six men who will be playing against me to

271

know that they have got a *game* on their hands starting to-night."

"We wouldn't have it any other way," Kenneth Martin Jacobs said.

"In that case," I said, "I would like to be excused to prepare myself for the onslaught."

I looked at Sporados, and after a moment, he nodded for me to go.

# 35

The banquet room of the Jawara Hotel was constructed in a circle, almost as if they had poker in mind. The room was decorated in the colors of gambling: red and black for roulette, white for cards and dice, green to match the tables, and the color of gold representing money.

The game was to be played inside, out of the heat, and only the other Masters were allowed seats close to the table. The spectators were placed in comfortable chairs behind a circular aisle.

As I walked into the arena, it appeared as if every seat was taken and there were people standing way in the back of the room. People from all over the world.

There wasn't any cheering as each of the seven players approached the table. Sporados wouldn't allow it. Jimmy Palusso and I walked down the aisle, and sitting in the front row of spectators were Manny, Fast Eddy, and Izzie. I winked at them and they smiled back.

When I arrived at the table, which was regulation size, but had forest-green suede on its top instead of the regular green felt, Sporados and Boswell were waiting. Kenneth Martin

Jacobs came in right after me, and in succession came Peter Sampler, Deeds, and Duxbury.

The chips were of three denominations and colors, and were encrested with the letters "BB," made up in an elaborate monogram with 1977 under it.

We each received seventeen blue chips worth fifty thousand each; twenty red chips priced at five thousand, and fifty white chips worth one thousand a piece.

All moneys won and lost would be settled through Sporados after the game. No one ever welched, of course.

The decks to be used were made especially for the game by the Bicycle Company in America, the seals were broken, every card was carefully inspected by Sporados and six other Masters, and then the decks were resealed.

Each player would deal a hand of five-card stud, and then pass the deck to his left.

Sporados, as champion, would have the honor of dealing the first hand. I was seated on his right, so I would be the first "cutter."

As Andreas began to deal, I closed my eyes, raised my head, and whispered, "Thank you, God. Thanks, Ace. Thanks, Jack and Della."

I looked down at my cards, and there was a jack of hearts facing me.

Suddenly, the betting started and there I was, sitting at the Big Biazarro with six million dollars in front of me. More money than I could ever spend in a lifetime. All I had to do was win it, and I could retire anywhere in the world and live like a king for the rest of my days. I could have it all: cars, boats, planes, houses, a castle in the islands.

"Wow, if the people of Ferno could see me now."

"Your bet, jacks," Sporados said to me.

I didn't even realize I had jacks, or that I had already bet one hundred and fifty-one thousand dollars. Looking around the board, I soon learned that I was left in the first hand alone with Deeds.

274

"The man said it's your bet, jacks."

I glanced at Deeds' hand and he had a king, two nines, and a four up.

I had a pair of jacks, a ten, and a deuce.

Believe it or not, I hadn't even looked at my hole card.

"Are you gonna bet or not?" Deeds asked.

"No, I pass."

"You just hit a pair of jacks," Deeds snapped at me. "You ain't checkin' agin like you did with Linda, are you?"

"I don't know," I said honestly. "I haven't even bothered to look at my hole card."

"Well, look at it!"

I was in a daze. Probably because I was there. All the glamour and the glitter, the wealthy men and gorgeous women were there, too. I looked around the room again, shook my head, and pinched myself.

"Do you guys know something?" I said. "I'm here. Little Lefty Wilson from the jerkwater town of Ferno, New York, is here at the Big Biazarro. That's something for me, do you know that?"

"We're glad you're here," said Sporados.

"Are you gonna bet, or dream?" Deeds barked.

"I told you I pass."

"Well, I ain't passin'. I bet four blue chips. Two hundred thousand dollars at you."

I turned then and waved back to my friends as they sat there smiling.

"It'll cost you four blues," said Sporados patiently.

Looking at my hole card, I saw the third jack and smiled and shook my head. The best Deeds could possibly have was three nines. I had won the first hand of the 1977 Big Biazarro.

"I'll call your two hundred thousand and raise you all in," I said.

"What in the hell are you talkin' about, boy? You gonna raise me a million dollars on the very first hand?"

"Yes."

Deeds glared at me, and then, turning to Sporados, he said, "I told you he was gonna make a shambles of this game, and you wanted him in here."

Deeds threw in his three nines, and I buried my hand into the deck.

"He's not a poker player," said Duxbury.

"You damn right he ain't," said Deeds. "He's a phony. And Ah don't give a damn how much money he wins tonight, he's still gonna end up on the shitty end of the stick."

"I've heard that before," I said and tried to remember where. I looked back at Fast Eddy and Manny and recalled instantly that Angel DuPont had said it to me the night I had left her at the pimp's apartment. Looking around the lavishly furnished hall and the dozens of people wearing a billion dollars worth of clothes and jewelry, I turned to Sporados and said softly, "What am I doing here?"

"Calm down, Lester, and play cards."

"What am I doing here?" I yelled. "My very best friend may be dying back in a hospital in New York City and I'm sitting over here playing a game of cards with you people. You assholes, who have nothing better to do with your time and your millions but pass it back and forth between you . . . while two Puerto Rican kids stand on a Harlem street corner dying of heroin. You wouldn't even buy them a goddamn ticket to Kentucky if your life depended on it."

I stood up then and looked into each of their faces and said calmly, "My friend Ace White said he never had the nerve to sit down at this table, and now I think I understand why. I turned my back on Angel, Cricket, Carrie, and Ace. And now, I'm going to turn my back on you. One of these times, I'm going to be right, and it just might be now."

There was dead silence as Manny, Fast Eddy, Izzie, and I hurried out of the hall.

On January 2, 1977, at 5:00 P.M., New York City time, I entered Ace White's hospital room. He was sitting up and being fed by Carrie Evans.

"What happened?"

"I won the first hand and quit."

"You what?"

"I quit."

Ace was speechless. Completely dumfounded. Carrie, seeing his mouth hung open, stuck a spoonful of peas in it, and Ace swallowed them without a bite. He tried again to say something, but found it impossible.

Finally, he uttered, "You want me to die, that's why you did this to me. You're trying to kill me, aren't you?"

"No, I'm not trying to kill you; besides, I think you'd be too embarrassed to die with me standing here."

"We're through," he shouted. "I mean it this time. I'm fed up with you. It's over!"

"Sure it is, Ace. And the world is flat, there are no steers in Texas, and Willie Mays won't make the Hall of Fame," I said and walked up to Carrie and kissed her.

"You can't be trusted," said Ace. "All this time I thought you could be trusted. What do you think of this idiot?" he asked Carrie.

"I think he's wonderful," Carrie said, hugging me while kissing me on the cheek.

"There's always 1982," I said.

"You think I'm going to live another five years?"

"More like another fifty-five, knowing you. You're too damn stubborn to die, Ace."

"You think so, huh? Would you like to take a look at my cardiogram?"

"No. I can tell by looking into your ornery eyes, you've got years to go."

"Shows you how much you know. Doctor said I wouldn't make it until today."

"Shows you how much *he* knows."

"If you think you came back to make me well, you wasted your time and a hell of a lot of money. And with me gone, you'll starve. Now what are you going to do?"

"What else?" I said. "We're going to do what we've been doing . . . meet 'um, greet 'um, jam 'um, and beat 'um."

Ace stared at me, trying desperately to remain angry, but he couldn't. He just couldn't. He turned away, frowned and cursed, slapped at the bed with his fist, and then finally, rested back, looked at me again, broke into a smile and said, "Okay, partner, okay. What do you say you go get my clothes and let's get the hell out of here and get started."

Printed in Canada